SONGS

IN THE

NIGHT

THE WYLDHAVEN SERIES
by Lynnette Bonner

OTHER HISTORICAL BOOKS
by Lynnette Bonner

THE SHEPHERD'S HEART SERIES

Rocky Mountain Oasis – BOOK ONE
High Desert Haven – BOOK TWO
Fair Valley Refuge – BOOK THREE
Spring Meadow Sanctuary – BOOK FOUR

SONNETS OF THE SPICE ISLE SERIES

On the Wings of a Whisper – BOOK ONE

Find all other books by Lynnette Bonner at:
www.lynnettebonner.com

SONGS
IN THE
NIGHT

Book Six
WYLDHAVEN

Lynnette BONNER
USA Today Bestselling Author

Pacific Lights

Songs in the Night
WYLDHAVEN, Book 6

Published by Pacific Lights Publishing

Cover design by Lynnette Bonner of Indie Cover Design, images ©
    Depositphotos_232384046 - Flare
    Depositphotos_21219423_DS – Texture
    AdobeStock_606424995 – Décor and Dividers

Other images generated by Lynnette Bonner using Midjourney and Adobe
Photoshop.
Book interior design by Jon Stewart of Stewart Design
Editing by Lesley Ann McDaniel of Lesley Ann McDaniel Editing
Proofreading by Sheri Mast of Faithful Editing

ISBN: 978-1-942982-18-0

To my friend Sheri:

I'm thankful that God brought you into my life! Your kindness, humor, and thoughtfulness are a blessing, and it's a joy to call you friend. Here's to many more "I'm-busy-that-days" when the boys go on some crazy-long mountain hike. May God continue to be your strength and embellish your night seasons with song. Love you!

Psalm 77: 1-6a

I cried out to God for help;
I cried out to God to hear me.
When I was in distress, I sought the Lord;
at night I stretched out untiring hands,
and I would not be comforted.
I remembered you, God, and I groaned;
I meditated, and my spirit grew faint.
You kept my eyes from closing;
I was too troubled to speak.
I thought about the former days,
the years of long ago;
I remembered my songs in the night.

Chapter One

Aurora McClure wished she had the courage to march to Parson Preston Clay's house, throw her arms around him, and give him a kiss that would knock his indifference right into the next county!

Instead, she sat here in the barn with her forehead pressed against the warm flank of the Holstein, mind wandering as the milk rang into the bucket. She had a good life here, living on the Rodantes' farm, but a restlessness had plagued her for the past several weeks. Okay, months.

But especially since Liora had given birth to little Lawrence Robert. One look into that little fellow's scrunched-up, wrinkly face, and a maternal longing had exploded inside Aurora.

Would she ever have a little one of her own? Certainly not at her current rate of progress!

There was only one man she was interested in, and for a few moments last Christmas, she'd thought maybe there might be some hope of gaining his interest. But ever since then, any time she'd been around, Parson Clay had buttoned up tighter than a logjam. He'd made it more than clear that there could be no future between them.

And that left her despairing of ever having a child of her own, because could she give her heart to someone else? Certainly not while she remained here in Wyldhaven. For some reason, no matter the lectures she gave herself about moving on and giving quarter to another, her heart just didn't seem to get the message.

This was what had her mind traipsing this morning. She'd finally decided that she needed to move on, and now she had to find the strength to break the news to everyone.

She hated to leave Joe and Liora after all they'd done for her, and especially now that they had the new little one. But Eliza and Ada—women that Liora had coaxed from local brothels and was ministering to—were helpful and hardworking, so it wouldn't be as if she were leaving Liora to do all the work around here on her own. And if she gave up her room, there would be one more bed for Liora to fill with a rescued girl who would also pick up some of the slack. So the decision to leave the Rodantes hadn't really been all that difficult.

It was leaving her position as the pianist for the church that would fill her with the biggest disappointment, and yet was also the main reason she needed to leave. Her weekly afternoon of music practice with Parson Clay had become like a torture session. He'd grown distant in the past several months, and she knew it was all her fault.

If only she'd listened to Kin Davis that day when he'd told her that Parson Clay wouldn't want a puppy. A puppy that was now a well-trained dog that traveled with the parson everywhere he went. Yet when Aurora considered the tension that had sprung into their relationship, it all went back to the day she'd given him the dog. Or perhaps it would be more accurate to say it stemmed from the day after. Because on the actual day she'd presented him with the puppy named Allegra, the parson had seemed surprised, yes, but pleased. Grateful, even. He'd gone so far as to cover her hand and ask her to call him Preston. Yet from that moment to this, his attitude had shifted. The next time she'd seen him, he'd been stiff and formal. She'd never again dared to call him by his given name, and he'd never again invited her to.

She'd tried on numerous occasions to resign herself to only thinking of him as a friend, but her heart didn't get the message her mind tried to instill. So now there was nothing for it but to make her escape.

She blew out a breath, pushed back from Garnet, the cow, and carefully extracted the bucket of milk. Taking Garnet's lead, she guided her out of the barn into the streaming sunshine and paused to lift her face to the rays. It was one of those late-summer days that made one grateful to be alive.

Thank You, Lord, that I have You with me always, no matter where I go. I'm still uncertain of Your will for me right now. Please, if this is right, give me peace about this decision? And be with those I leave behind.

After returning Garnet to pasture, she took the milk inside and set it on the shelf in the icebox. By tomorrow morning there would be a thick layer of cream for Ada to churn into butter.

The scent of apples and cinnamon filled the air. Aurora's stomach rumbled. "Mmm, that smells good!"

Liora stood at the stove, jouncing Lawrence on one arm and stirring apple butter with her free hand. She looked up and smiled. "Morning."

Aurora folded her hands and returned her smile, glad to see that neither of the other women had made an appearance yet. "Morning."

"I'm making this for the tarts I plan to bring to Washington's send-off."

"Oh yes. That's tomorrow after church, isn't it? I'd almost forgotten. Tonight I need to finish knitting the socks I'm making for him."

"Oh, I saw those on your nightstand when I took your laundry in the other day. The fine wool yarn you chose will make a nice warm pair."

"Thank you. I hope he'll like them." Aurora cleared her throat and pressed ahead before she lost her nerve. "I'm glad it's just you and me. Do you have a minute to talk?"

The arch of Liora's brow revealed her curiosity. "Of course. This apple butter is mostly done anyhow. Do you mind?" She pointed to the jars that already sat waiting on the sideboard.

"Sure." Aurora quickly washed her hands, then took up the pot of steaming sauce and moved to fill the jars. She spoke in a rush. "I've come to a decision and need to let you know. I've applied to the Territorial University of Washington, and, happily, have been accepted into their music conservatory." If only the thought of going to study music gave her a measure of peace. Nothing seemed to be the right direction for her these days.

Liora gasped. "You what?" The sparkle in her eyes revealed a pleasure. And that at least filled Aurora with relief.

She scooped the last of the sauce into the final jar. "I'll first study violin and piano." She set the pot into the sink.

Lawrence fussed, and Liora started across the room in the bouncing minced step that seemed to have become her regular gait the past few months. "You're so good at both of those that I can't imagine anyone being able to teach you anything!"

Aurora blushed at the compliment as she wiped the lips of the jars clean and clamped the seals into place. "I hardly believe that can be true. But at any rate I'll be able to learn so much about writing music, instruments I don't currently play, and maybe even conducting an orchestra." She ought to be thrilled with the prospect, but really, though she loved music with all her heart, none of the opportunities excited her like they should.

She tried not to be envious of Liora, she truly did, yet the woman had everything Aurora wanted—a man who adored her, a healthy child, and a loving home. Aurora's problem was she wanted all those things with a man who most certainly didn't want them with her in return.

Liora assessed her. "You don't seem terribly excited."

With all the jars sealed, Aurora pumped water into the pan and set to scrubbing it. She lifted one shoulder. "A bit overwhelmed at all I need to consider, I suppose. The term starts in just two weeks."

"Two weeks! Oh my! Have you told Parson Clay yet? I'm not sure who he'll get to play the piano come Sundays."

Aurora swallowed. "I wanted to tell you first. I plan to head into town in just a few minutes to talk things over with him." She paused and studied Liora. "You're sure it's okay that I leave? I mean I know with the baby my timing might not be the best."

Liora blew a sound of dismissal. "Don't you worry about a thing. We'll be just fine. I mean, I'll miss you like crazy, but I'm so pleased that you are following your heart!"

Aurora pressed her lips together and turned the pot upside down on the drain board. Following her heart?

More like running from the crack in her heart that was gaping wider and wider, before it got so large it consumed her.

Kane Carver paused at the base of the church steps and took a calming breath. He gripped his Stetson in both hands and tapped the brim against the staccato beat of his heart as he stared at the double doors above. "Just get your sorry hide up there and ask him." He gave himself a nod and took the stairs two at a time.

The parson's dog, Allegra, lay in the shade on the church's covered porch. She lurched to her feet and wriggled over to him for a scratch.

After ruffling the dog's ears, he gave the doors a quick knock that was more a warning that he was coming in than a request for entry, and then stepped into the church foyer. A wall filled with cubbies and coat hooks—used mostly by the Wyldhaven students that utilized this building during the week for school—blocked his view of the sanctuary. On Saturdays, the parson used the building to study for his Sunday sermons.

"Parson?" He poked his head around the wall. The church aisle stretched toward the front, and just as he'd suspected, the parson sat at the desk on the platform with his Bible and papers spread before him.

Parson Clay offered him a smile. "Kane. Morning." The man glanced at his pocket watch. "I guess it's closer to noon now, isn't it? What can I do for you today?"

Kane swallowed as he stepped more fully into the room. "I'd like to, ah . . ." His throat closed off, and he studied the wood grain on one of the pews, silently chastising himself for every kind of a weak fool.

The parson rose and stepped from behind his desk. "You okay?"

Kane forced his gaze to meet the parson's. "Yes, sir. Yes. It's just . . . I spoke to Joseph Rodante, but he told me I should likely ask you since you were more like Aurora's pa than he was."

A frown immediately slumped the parson's brow. "Aurora? What's this got to do with Aurora?"

Kane swallowed. Great. He'd already upset the man, and he hadn't even got to the heart of his request yet.

"Is Aurora injured? Sick?" The parson strode a couple steps toward him. "Does she need Doc?"

Kane raised one hand. "No. No. Not at all. It's just . . . I'd like your permission to . . ."

"My permission to what?"

Had he ever noticed before how stony the parson's expression could turn when he was upset? Kane slid his hat brim through his fingers. Swallowed. "I'd like your permission to call on Aurora."

Chapter Two

$\mathcal{P}$reston Clay clamped his teeth together so his mouth wouldn't gape. This incomer wanted permission to call on Aurora? Over his dead body! Why he'd—

Wait.

"Joe said I was like Aurora's pa?"

Kane's feet shuffled. "Yes, sir."

Preston blinked and took a breath.

Joe thought of him as Aurora's father? He was older than her, but not by *that* many years. Barely seven years, if he recalled correctly. And the simple fact that she'd arrived in town under the guise of a lad and had lived in his home for several weeks before anyone had figured it out didn't relegate him to the role of her pa, did it?

Still, why was that upsetting? He'd been trying to convince himself that he should think of her in platonic terms ever since last Christmas, when she'd given him Allegra.

He was now a man of the cloth, after all. A profession that, especially in this area, demanded many a long hour and late night. Certainly not one that was amenable to a family man. It would be better for all involved—himself, his parishioners, and any woman he declined to pursue—if he remembered that fact.

He could remember it just fine, he supposed. It was ingesting the truth of it that had been a struggle. One of monstrous proportions. He'd been desperately trying to hammer home the truth of it for the past several months. Ever since that fateful Christmas day when he'd made the mistake of thinking of Aurora as a desirable woman, if only for a few moments.

His jaw was clenched so tight that it ached. How many times had he tried to banish the memory of her soft hand beneath his? The feel of his thumb caressing over her knuckles? The pleasure that had rippled through him when she'd called him Preston?

And banish them he must, because his calling was to his parishioners. Not to his own happiness.

So this was a good thing, right? Let Kane call on her, turn her head, make her his wife—

Whoa.

Wife? If he agreed to let Kane call on her, would it lead to matrimony? His heart shattered. And that right there was the very reason he ought to exuberantly offer his blessing to the young couple. Because no matter how he felt about Aurora, his chosen profession made time and space for a relationship impossible.

And apparently his parishioners thought of him as her pa. It would be some awkward for them if he started courting Aurora. And he didn't want that. A minister's job was to make things as easy for his people as possible.

But then there were Aurora's feelings to consider. She'd made it plain several times that she'd welcome his attentions. At least, that was what he'd thought she was doing. Or maybe that was only his traitorous, hopeful heart. At any rate, even if she thought she wanted to be a minister's wife, she simply didn't know what she'd be getting into. Her heart was too kind. Her experience too limited.

Poppy, on the other hand . . . she had understood immediately. Weren't her actions proof enough of that? She'd dropped him like a hot poker only moments after he'd told her that he felt the Lord calling him to be a minister.

Kane cleared his throat. "Parson?"

Preston snapped back to the present.

Kane peered at him intently. "I'll do my best to honor her and provide for her, and I swear she'll never lack for anything that I can rightfully gain for her. I'm a hard worker."

All Preston's thoughts brought him full circle. He wanted to send Kane packing, yet he knew it was only selfishness making him withhold his permission. "I . . . uh—"

The sound of footsteps crossing the entry snapped his mouth shut.

"Parson?"

Preston's heart stuttered, and his gaze flew to Kane's. The very lady of their conversation had just walked in on them.

Both men turned to face the entry.

Aurora stepped into sight. "Oh!" Her gaze sparkled as it settled on Kane. "Hello."

Sparkled? Preston forked his fingers through his hair. Perhaps he'd already lost what he knew he shouldn't want.

"Aurora." Kane gave a courtly little bow in her direction, hat pressed to his chest. "Afternoon to you."

Preston shoved his hands into his pockets and gripped the lining in tight fists so he wouldn't be tempted to whap Kane across the back of his head. The Wyldhaven parson probably ought not act like that.

"Aurora." Preston gave her a nod of acknowledgment. "What brings you by?" Too late, he realized the words sounded curt and irritated.

A little furrow settled on her brow. Her gaze darted between the two of them and finally rested on him.

He softened his tone. "You're early for our normal practice time."

"Yes. I know. I . . . I . . . was hoping to have a moment to speak to you."

"Sure." Preston tossed Kane a glance, realizing he'd never given the man an answer. But was it really his place to grant someone permission to call on Aurora? And yet, if not him, then who? Aurora had no other family. Family? He worked the dryness from his mouth. She wasn't really his family either.

Realizing they were both still staring at him, he lifted Kane a shrug of one shoulder. "I don't think I have the authority you are looking for. Yet no one else in town does either, so there's no one standing in your way."

Kane grinned like he'd just been handed the moon. "Thank you, Parson." He transferred his gaze to Aurora, hat pressed over his heart. "Aurora, I'll let you talk to the parson, but I wonder if you'd have a few minutes to speak to me when you are done?"

Her curiosity quirked one of her brows. "Sure."

"Thank you." Kane bowed several times as he made his way down the aisle. "I'll just wait for you outside. Just meet me outside when you are done. Outside by the oak tree." He pointed toward the tree visible through the window. "Right outside, there."

Preston couldn't help a chuckle as the man disappeared and they heard the church doors clank shut. Despite the humor he found in the man's nervousness, he couldn't deny that his heart was pinching more than a little.

Aurora searched his face. "What was that all about?"

He grinned at her. "He'll be waiting just *outside* to tell you."

She scrunched her mouth into a twist. "I hope he hasn't gotten it into his head to ask about calling. But . . . I suppose it won't matter much in a couple weeks anyhow."

Attention arrested, Preston scrutinized her. "Why won't it matter in a couple weeks?" For some unaccountable reason, he held his breath.

She fiddled with her reticule and didn't seem to want to meet his gaze.

"Aurora?"

Her focus did lift to his then, and he felt the impact of her green eyes like an unexpected punch.

He retraced his steps to stand by his desk, wishing she'd get on with whatever errand had brought her here. As fresh and pretty as she looked today, she was making it blamed hard to hang on to his decision to step aside for Kane.

She took a little breath, opened her mouth, closed it, and then finally blurted, "I've been accepted to the music conservatory at the territorial university."

A breath seeped out of him. So . . . she would be leaving. "I see. When do you go?" He picked up the fountain pen on the desk and tapped it end over end on the surface. He didn't like the thought of her living in Seattle alone. Not even a little bit. Yet he didn't have any right to stop her.

She pressed her lips into a thin tight line and looked at the piano in the corner. "I realize I might be putting you in a difficult spot for Sunday services. I'm sorry about that. I received notice of acceptance in last week's mail but spent a few days trying to decide whether to go." Her throat worked. "The term starts in two weeks."

"Two weeks." The strength drained from his legs, and he sank into his chair. "We'll definitely miss you." He didn't look at her. Had she heard the catch in his voice? He hoped not. He didn't want her to have any emotional ties that might keep her from chasing her dreams. And yet this was such an unexpected transition. "I didn't realize you wanted to go to university?"

She was fiddling with her bag again. "In all honesty, I've been trying to decide what I should do. I applied, praying the Lord would lead me to know if it was the right decision. And since I was approved, I suppose that's His blessing on it."

He swallowed. He supposed that was true enough. *Lord, give me the strength not to stand in Your way.* He'd been praying some form or another of that same prayer since last Christmas.

"Zoe is quite proficient on the piano. She could likely help out with Sundays."

Preston waved a hand. He didn't want her to worry about that. "Cora Harrison plays excellently as well. I'm sure we'll be fine."

"Yes, I suppose there are any number of women who could take my place." Her words were spoken so softly that he barely made them out.

Before he realized it, he'd risen and strode to stand before her in the aisle. She was wearing the rusty-red walking dress he liked so much, though he'd never told her so. It brought out the color in her cheeks and, unaccountably, the green of her eyes. Eyes that were at this very moment studying him with a softness that tugged at every fiber of his worldly flesh. Thrusting his hands behind his back, he clasped the wrist of his opposite hand into one palm. Firmly. "Neither of them have your proficiency, to be sure. I only meant to release you from the burden of concern over how we'll get along without you."

"Thank you." She melded her lips together, lowering her lashes.

He needed to hurry her on her way before he grabbed her by the shoulders and begged her not to leave. He blinked away the thought. "Better not keep poor Kane waiting." He forced a smile. "And I'm sure you have plenty to do before you leave, so don't worry about practice today. I didn't choose any songs that you don't already know."

Her gaze lifted to his once more, soft and hurt. "Oh, I see."

The muscles along the back of his neck felt like tightened violin strings. He looked down.

Long hours.

Called out at all times of the night.

Low pay.

Always someone challenging good biblical teaching.

He recited to himself all the reasons why it was best not to start a family, then forced himself to meet her gaze. "I've appreciated all that you've done to help me with services over the last few years. It's really been an encouragement. To me, and I'm sure to all the parishioners as well. Will we . . . have a chance to say goodbye before you leave?"

"Yes. I'm—I'll be in services this Sunday and next but will catch the stage that next Saturday." A strand of hair slipped from her chignon to tease her cheek.

He tightened his grip on his tempted hands. "I'll see you on Sunday, then."

"Yes. Goodbye. Thanks for understanding."

"I truly do wish you all the best, Aurora."

She nodded. "I know. Thank you." She turned then, and left.

Left him standing in the church aisle with his heart in scattered pieces around his boots.

urora stepped onto the church porch and paused at the top of the stairs. She bent to give Allegra a little love. Well, that had been awkward and stilted. And Preston hadn't even seemed like it bothered him to have her leaving.

Shooing Allegra back to her spot in the shade, she blew out a breath and glanced down the hill toward town.

Zoe Kastain was crossing the Wyldhaven Creek bridge, skirts lifted like she was on a mission. By the looks of things, she was headed to meet the Saturday stage that was just pulling to a stop in front of McGinty's Alehouse. Smoke drifted from the kitchen chimney of Dixie's Boardinghouse, cutting a gray swath against the mountains in the distance as Sheriff Callahan stepped from the front door of the jailhouse. He did so each time the stage arrived, simply to reveal his presence to any visitors. And there was Ben King crossing the street from the post office, likely to grab today's mailbag.

Aurora's heart ached. This was home. These people and so many more, the only family that remained to her. Could she really bring herself to leave?

Old Don hopped from the driver's seat of the stage and flipped down the steps as he opened the coach door and reached up to help someone descend.

A woman in a bright-red dress slid into view like a vibrant butterfly emerging from a cocoon.

Someone cleared their throat, and Aurora glanced to the church lawn.

Kane stood there clutching his gray Stetson in both hands. "Did you conclude your business with the parson?"

"Yes." She'd forgotten he wanted to speak to her. She returned her attention to the woman who now stood next to the sheriff on the jailhouse steps. Aurora raised a hand to shade her eyes. Something about the woman piqued her curiosity.

A man emerged from the stage and, to Aurora's surprise, enfolded Zoe in a fatherly embrace. Interesting.

But not as interesting as the woman who was still talking to the sheriff.

"What can I do for you, Kane?"

"I . . . Uh . . ."

From the corner of her eye, she saw Kane follow her gaze down the hill.

"Do you know who she is?" Aurora asked.

"No. Never seen her before."

The woman had sleek black hair and copper-kissed skin. She carried herself in a manner that sang "poise" and "presence" in dulcet tones. With a little gesture of one hand, she cocked her head and said something to the sheriff.

He folded his arms and made a short reply.

Angling her head just so, mouth gaped in laughter, the woman rested one hand against the sheriff's arm. Even from this distance, Aurora could tell that her lips were painted ruby red. What business could a woman like that have in Wyldhaven?

"Uh, Aurora, could I have your attention for a moment?" Kane's voice hitched, and he cleared his throat.

Dragging her focus from the new arrival, Aurora descended the steps and paused next to Kane. Whoever the woman was, she was none of Aurora's concern. She adjusted her gloves. "Sorry about that. What can I do for you?"

Hat pressed to his chest, Kane looked earnestly into her face. "As you may have surmised from what you overheard, I was asking the parson for permission to call on you. He seemed to think you ought to make your own decision in that regard. So I'm asking if you'd give me permission to take you to dinner at Dixie's one of these evenings?"

Despite that she'd suspected as much, Aurora felt everything inside her still. She had been praying for the Lord to guide her. Could this be an answer to that? Could she learn to love Kane Carver?

From everything she knew about the man, he was a gentleman, a hard worker, a good caretaker of his younger siblings. The Carvers hadn't lived in town for long. And his younger siblings had made some poor choices upon arrival in an attempt to save Kane because he'd been at death's door with pneumonia. Despite all that, she'd been impressed with the family, and had seen true repentance in Maude, Kane's younger sister, for the choices her fear had caused her to make. So in truth, if ever there was a man besides the parson who could turn her head, it might be Kane. And yet with her plan to leave town, now was not the time to start a new relationship.

Kane shuffled his feet. "I can see that I've taken you aback."

"No, no." Aurora gave herself a mental shake. "Well, maybe yes, a little. But not in a bad way."

A smile the size of a crescent moon broke out on Kane's face. "You do know how to make a man's heart go all hooves over horns, Miss Aurora McClure."

Aurora couldn't withhold a smile. "While I may be flattered, Mr. Carver, I'm just not certain you've caught me at the best time."

"Well now, Miss McClure, I didn't mean that I'd come calling right this moment." Charm dripped from the words, and he tossed her a wink that let her know he was purposely misinterpreting her put-off. "Would this Friday night be a better time?" His expression warm and hopeful, he searched her face.

The man's proposal was tempting. Mighty tempting. "It's not you, Mr. Carver. It's just that I've been accepted to the music conservatory at the Territorial University of Washington, and I start in just a couple weeks."

Kane's smile faded for only a moment before returning to full bloom. "Well now, that's a fine thing. A fine thing. I sure do enjoy the way you coax a tune from that old piano on Sundays, and your violin, too, when you do a special number. I imagine the good Lord has big plans for you and your music in the years to come."

Aurora felt the pleasure of his compliment zip through her. Still, she wished she felt as enthusiastic about going as he felt about it. "Thank you. I just wanted you to know in case . . . well, in case that might make you . . . change your mind."

"There's no fear of me changing my mind. No fear at all." The crinkles at the corners of his eyes appealed to her.

Perhaps declining his request wasn't going to be as easy as she'd hoped. With a blush, she looked toward town.

She couldn't have been more surprised when she noted the woman in the red dress walking toward them. There wasn't anything in this direction except the church and parsonage.

The woman lifted a brilliant smile that revealed pure white teeth and pink cheeks. "Good evening to you both. I understand Preston Clay may be around?"

Aurora's heart guttered and stilled before flickering into a staccato beat. She took the woman in from her head to her pert little black boots that peeked from beneath the raised hem of her scarlet skirts. She was petite but well-endowed in all the places a man would care about.

Aurora gritted her teeth and mentally chastised herself. She ought not allow such jealous, petty thoughts. She forced her scrutiny to other attributes.

Despite the woman's painted lips, she didn't seem to be a soiled dove.

Having lived for so many years in the company of her mother and her friends, Aurora ought to know.

The woman's smile was starting to look strained around the edges.

"Yes, ma'am." Kane nudged Aurora's elbow as he spoke, and she realized she stood in the way. "Right up the stairs there. He's inside."

"Sorry." Aurora stepped out of the woman's path.

"Thank you."

Aurora couldn't quite place the accent that ran like a stream beneath the bridge of the woman's words.

"I'm so excited to see dear Preston. It's been much too long." The woman's lashes lowered demurely, as though she hadn't meant to disclose that last bit.

Before she could talk herself out of it, Aurora stretched forth her hand. "I'm Aurora McClure. And this here is Kane Carver."

Loosing one handful of her skirts, the woman settled her slim hand into Aurora's broader one. "It's a pleasure to make your acquaintance. And yours." She transferred her handshake to Kane. "My name is—"

"Poppy, what are you doing here?"

Startled by the sound of Preston's voice, they all looked up to the church porch. Aurora sucked in a breath as his words crashed over her in a humiliating wave.

Poppy?

Allegra padded to a stop next to the parson, tail wagging so hard that her backside wiggled.

Aurora's mind flashed back to last Christmas, when the parson had been out of his mind with fever and she'd been so certain he was mumbling about wanting a puppy.

Puppy . . . Poppy.

Dear Lord in heaven, have mercy! She had given him a puppy, when it was a woman he was longing for.

A woman named Poppy.

Zoe gave a little squeal of greeting and stretched out her arms to envelope Mr. Harrow in a hug as he stepped from the coach. He looked just as kind and gentle as ever, and when he enfolded her in an embrace, Zoe unaccountably felt tears prick the backs of her eyes. For a brief moment, she was transported back to one of Pa's hugs. Firm but gentle. Protective. Sheltering.

He was only here for a short week's visit, but oh, what a thrill it gave her to see that sparkle of life returning to Ma's eyes with each letter she exchanged with this man. Why, this morning Ma had almost been her old self! And Mr. Harrow was just the sweetest. He and Ma had been corresponding ever since Ma met him in Seattle when she'd accompanied Zoe to take her teaching exam, but this was the first time either had visited the other.

Zoe pushed back and looked up at him. "It's so good to see you again. Do we need to get any other bags?" He held a brown carpetbag in one hand with his coat draped over that arm.

He glanced around at the other townsfolk who were there to greet passengers, and a look of disappointment crossed his face, but then he smiled. "Good to see you too, missy. I think you're even prettier than the last time I saw you. Hope your ma is keeping a shotgun handy?"

Zoe chuckled and linked her arm with his, starting toward the boardinghouse. The fatherly comment filled her with painful nostalgia and joy at the same time. But she chose not to give it a reply. If only Washington Nolan thought she was pretty, maybe that would be enough to keep him in town. Her stomach crimped at the thought of saying goodbye to him— maybe forever—at tomorrow's gathering. He was leaving for his post at Fort Vancouver on Monday morning. *Oh Lord, will You please keep him safe? I don't know if I can live in a world that doesn't contain Wash.*

"Something amiss?"

She gave herself a little shake. Here Mr. Harrow had just arrived, and she was turning melancholy. "Sorry about that. I was lost in thought for a moment. It's so good to see you. Your room is just there at the boardinghouse."

The look Mr. Harrow angled her way told her he realized she was dodging his question. But like a true gentleman, he didn't press.

She looked up at him. "How was your trip?"

"Good. I can't say that I'm sorry to be able to walk for a ways, however." He grinned at her.

She laughed. "Those long rides can be awfully cramped. I presume you took the train and then the coach from the station?"

"Yes. And my seat on the train was next to a mother with twin toddlers." He shuddered with exaggeration.

Zoe laughed. "I'm sure you'll have some stories to tell us about that! But here's the boardinghouse. Let's get you settled in your room, and then we can head out to the house. Oh! I almost forgot. Ma sends her regrets for not being able to meet you herself. But she's in the middle of helping our neighbor, Liora Rodante, who has a young baby, put up a large batch of raspberry preserves."

"Ah! I see." A great deal of relief filled his words.

Releasing his arm, Zoe led him into the entry, feeling a prick of guilt for not remembering to tell him about Ma first thing. He would see when he got to the house that, if anything, Ma's feelings for him had grown in the past months.

Cora Harrison stood at the desk. For several months now she had worked for Mrs. Griffin, the boardinghouse owner and also the wife of Wyldhaven's only doctor. Cora beamed a smile. "Hello. You must be Mr. Harrow? I have to tell you, the whole town has been buzzing about your arrival." She gave Zoe a quick wink.

Red crept up Mr. Harrow's neck.

Zoe leaned closer to him. "Small town. Aidan blabbed to a few of his friends that you were coming, and that was all it took."

"I see." Mr. Harrow chuckled and fiddled with a button on his coat.

Cora gave Zoe an apologetic wince, then unhooked a key from the board behind the desk. "If you'll follow me, I'll show you to your room. Do you have more bags on the coach?"

"No, no." He lifted the valise in his hand. "Just this."

"Right this way, then."

Zoe folded her hands. "I'll wait for you here, Mr. Harrow. But please don't rush on my account. I can chat with Cora while you get settled into your room."

He gave her a little nod. "It won't take me but a moment."

Cora showed him upstairs, then trotted back down only moments later. She paused, clasping her hands beneath her chin. "I didn't mean to embarrass the poor man. Everyone knows how fond your ma has grown of him, and I just assumed—well, never mind. How are you doing with Wash's impending departure?"

Zoe blew out a shaky sound of uncertainty. "I'm trying not to think about it."

"Oh, sweetie." Cora pulled her into a quick embrace. "I'm sure he's going to be just fine. He's going to come back in a few years all in one piece, and you two will get married and have ten children!"

Zoe laughed and pushed her friend away. "Do go on with you! Ten?! Lord, have mercy! How are things here at the boardinghouse?"

Cora straightened the register. "Oh, you know. Not much new. There is a woman who's supposed to check in, however. Did you see anyone else on the coach?"

"You know, come to think of it, a woman did get off before Mr. Harrow, but I didn't pay much attention to her. I'm sure she'll be here in a few minutes."

"Ready?" Mr. Harrow spoke from behind Cora.

Zoe peered around her friend. "That was fast."

He shrugged one shoulder. "Not much to unpack."

Zoe wasn't fooled. The man simply couldn't wait to see her mother, and for some reason, that fact filled her with reassurance. She wouldn't have wished Pa gone for anything in the world, but this was their reality now. And if it was one they had to live in, then Mr. Harrow was a pretty wonderful addition to it.

She waggled her fingers at Cora, who retreated behind the boardinghouse desk with another little wink that said she, too, understood Mr. Harrow simply wanted to see Ma.

With a smile, Zoe looped her arm with Mr. Harrow's and started them toward home.

Preston stood on the church porch, hardly able to believe his eyes. The very last person he'd ever expected to see in Wyldhaven was Poppy Scarlatti.

"Preston! Darling!" She gave a little squeal and darted up the stairs. Before he realized what she was about, she'd thrown her arms around his neck, and he had to take a bracing step to keep them from toppling. His hands settled on reflex at Poppy's waist, and over her shoulder he noted that Kane and Aurora were both staring.

Aurora tipped up her chin and spun on one heel to face the man next to her. "Kane, you did say Friday evening, correct?"

Kane blinked. "Y-yes, miss."

Aurora gave him a little nod. "Fine, then. I'll be looking forward to it. For now, I must be off to the mercantile to fetch a few things for Liora. Will you be at church in the morning as usual?"

"Yes."

"Fine. I'll see you then."

"Till tomorrow," Kane called after her.

Preston absentmindedly set Poppy from him and propped his hands on his hips as he watched Aurora take the path to town with smart, sharp steps. He scrubbed one hand over his jaw. So she'd agreed to allow Kane to come calling, then? His gaze slammed to Kane.

The man swallowed and stretched his hat in Aurora's wake. "I'll just . . ." He cleared his throat. "Evening to you, Parson." He settled his hat, gave Poppy a tug of the brim, and headed off.

Preston willed himself to remember everything he needed to from the Good Book about kindness and charity. It wouldn't do for Kane to feel any animosity the next time they met.

Poppy's hand fell to rest on Preston's arm. "I can't tell you how good it is to see you, dearest Preston."

He scrutinized her even as his walls of caution rose to full height. Whatever Poppy was doing here did not bode well for him. She was from another lifetime, an entirely *different* lifetime, before he'd come to a relationship with the Lord. Wyldhaven certainly wasn't up to her standards. She was a woman who expected—no, demanded—elegance and luxury on every hand. So whatever had brought her here had to be about business. She certainly wouldn't have ventured here without a plan. And whatever her plan was, he doubted he would like it.

"What are you doing here, Poppy?" He stalked back into the sanctuary.

Her soft tread kept pace behind him. "Now, Pres, don't be like that."

He froze and spun toward her, folding his arms. "Be like what?"

Stepping into his personal space, she stroked her palms down his arms. "You do get all stiff and distant when things don't go as you like. But don't forget, I know you almost better than you know yourself." She tapped the end of his nose with one finger.

He jerked away.

She blew out a soft sigh. "You're just upset because you don't want me messing up whatever con you have going, but don't worry. My lips are sealed." She batted her lashes at him.

Preston's heart slammed against his rib cage. Town founder, Zebulon Heath, knew of his past, but Preston had never revealed to any of his parishioners that he used to be muscle for a mob boss in Boston—a mob boss who happened to be Poppy's father. Not because he wanted to keep it a secret, necessarily, but simply because it hadn't ever come up. Okay, maybe that was a lie. He'd thought about bringing it up plenty of times but had just never followed through and done so.

But Poppy's words were a threat if ever he'd heard one, and having his church find out from a total stranger was not ideal.

"I tried to tell you before I left that it's not a con, Pop." He willed away the nostalgia her nickname raised. There could never again be anything between him and Poppy. At least not unless she repented of her ways. But if the Lord hadn't given him peace to move ahead with Aurora, he certainly didn't foresee Him offering peace for a relationship with Poppy.

She discarded his words with the flap of one hand. "I'll admit that I didn't expect you to carry it on for this long. Short cons were generally more your game. You may have this town fooled, but not me. I just have to figure out what your end game is." She tapped one fingernail against her lips, eyes sparkling. "Couldn't have anything to do with that pretty little gal that was just outside, because she didn't look like she had more than a few pennies to rub together."

Preston opened his mouth to tell her to leave Aurora out of this, but then snapped it shut again. If he came to Aurora's defense, it would only further Poppy's interest in her. "Whatever you think is going on, you're wrong."

"Am I?"

"Yes." He folded his arms and stared her down, hoping she would finally believe him.

"I hear there's a bank set to open in town. One that has been supposed to open for several months but has had delays."

Preston's pulse hammered with concern. Poppy never traveled far from her father. And if Antonio Scarlatti was in town, that could mean nothing good. The law needed to know right away.

Poppy advanced on him, but he retreated behind his desk.

She stilled and tilted him a pout. "I've missed you, caro. You can trust me. Just tell me what the plan is."

Preston set to gathering his sermon notes. He tucked them into his Bible and closed the cover. "You betrayed me once, Pop. But I don't hold it against you. Spending those years in jail was actually the best thing that ever happened to me, because it's where I met Jesus."

Her lips thinned. "Was he a fellow convict?" Sarcasm hung thick and heavy in her tone.

He lifted his Bible so she could see the gold lettering on the cover. "I've told you. The truth is all right here. I can get you your own copy, if you want."

Her laughter tinkled like bells. "Oh, you are good. You even almost have me convinced."

Preston sighed, despairing of convincing her. He gathered up the commentary he'd been using and tucked both it and his Bible into one arm, then started down the aisle. "You're welcome to stay. I'm going home." He needed to check on Tommy.

"Do they know? Your parishioners? About your past?"

Preston stilled. Threats again. Here were his sins come back as nightmares. He ought to have confessed on his first day in town that he had a criminal history, but the day he'd arrived, in fact, even before he reached town, he'd been knocked unconscious by the coach accident and by the time things had settled down, a few days had passed, and by then it had seemed too late. After that he'd never found the right time. He would amend that tomorrow. He *could* amend that tomorrow . . . Just the thought made him break out in a cold sweat.

"Services start at ten in the morning. You're welcome to come if you like. If you need a place to stay, Dixie's Boardinghouse just down the hill has the best beds and food in town."

"I can think of a better bed to sleep in."

He slammed through the doors and left her there. She'd been pushing to get into his bed ever since they were teenagers. Thankfully, though he'd been plenty attracted to her and had made more than his fair share of stupid mistakes, allowing her into his bed wasn't one of them.

Jail had likely saved him from that particular fate.

Chapter Four

oppy Scarlatti stood in the middle of the church aisle and squeezed her fists so tight that her nails bit into her palms. She knew it had been a few years, and after the way she'd testified against him in court, she hadn't expected the warmest of welcomes, but usually her charm garnered her whatever she wanted.

Babbo wasn't going to be happy with her.

With an unladylike growl, she banged through the church doors. Preston was nowhere in sight. That must mean he lived in the little hovel of a log cabin that sat just up the hill a ways. She turned in the other direction.

As she marched down the hill toward town, she considered Preston's words. Surely he couldn't be serious about his conversion? She shook her head. He had to be maintaining his role for a con. A bull didn't shed its horns. She would be patient and bide her time.

All a man needed was the right motivation, and it wouldn't take her long to figure out what might motivate him to work with them once more.

They needed the influx of cash. After the new mayor had taken over in Boston, he'd assigned new law officers that hadn't been as . . . susceptible to Scarlatti money. After losing half his crew, the heat had gotten to be too much for Babbo, and he was currently looking for a new place to settle. When she'd reminded him that Preston had left town for a place near Seattle, he'd consented that she could come check it out and sent her on ahead with just a few men while he explored options in Chicago. In truth, that city might offer more opportunities, because she hadn't realized just how remote this place was, nor how far of a distance it stood from the larger city of Seattle. Larger populations offered more subjects for their type of work.

She smirked.

Most likely they would settle in Chicago, but Babbo would bless her for bringing a man like Preston Clay back into the fold. She'd never seen a man better at safecracking, and that was the truth of it.

Her smile grew as she stepped into the entry of the boardinghouse. Yes. She could convince him. He would just need proper motivation.

And if they made off with the contents of the new bank's safe while they were at it?

So much the better.

Preston pushed through the front door of the parsonage and bumped it shut with his boot.

Tommy bounded over from where he'd been painting at the table. He was taller than Preston, and broader in the shoulders too. And looking at him now, Preston realized he needed to get him a haircut and shave.

"'Leggra!" Tommy stooped to enthusiastically pet the dog. In his excitement to see them home, Tommy wriggled almost as much as Allegra did. He lifted his gaze to Preston's. "I painteded at the t-table. And when I g-got scared, I s-said my verses. Just like you t-tol' me."

"Good lad." Preston felt a brief swell of pride. He'd been working with Tommy so that he could leave him alone for short periods at the house. But Tommy struggled with fear, so Preston had shown him Psalm 77, where the psalmist was also overwhelmed and crying out to God. It did his heart good to hear that Tommy had remembered to call on the comfort of God's Word. "Want to show me your pictures?"

With the weight of the world pressing down on him, Preston set his Bible and sermon notes on one end of the table. He planted his fists against the wood and stared at a knot.

Tommy didn't seem to notice his melancholy. He tossed watercolor picture after picture into the space between Preston's fists. "I maket-ed a horse. And a dog like A-ll-llegra. And a c-cat."

Preston filtered through the pictures, wishing he could summon more enthusiasm. "Nice job, Tom-Tom. Pin them to the board, okay? I'm going to get dinner started."

"I'm hungry!" Tommy proclaimed the words as he moved to the pinboard that Aurora had made for him to display his art.

"Good. Grant Nolan came around selling fish earlier, so I have two nice trout to fry up."

"Tommy want oatmeal!"

Preston dropped some lard into the cast-iron skillet on the wood stove. "You can't eat oatmeal for every meal."

"I l-like it."

"I know you do." Preston removed the fish from their paper wrappings and set them in the sink. He pumped the handle to fetch some water to rinse them. "Tonight, I just need you to try the fish and rice, okay? Rice is kind of like oatmeal. You liked it the last time you tried it."

Tommy's lower lip protruded. "Not as g-good as oatmeal."

Preston couldn't withhold a smile. "You stick that lip out any farther and it will make a good perch for old Peck, the rooster."

Tommy maintained his pout.

Preston hooked his thumbs together and made a flapping motion like a rooster swooping toward Tommy's mouth while at the same time cuckooing loudly.

Tommy laughed heartily. "Okay. Tommy t-try the t-tr . . . fish and r-rice."

Relieved to have that battle out of the way, Preston cracked an egg into a bowl. "Good lad. Wash your hands in the basin and then set the table for me, okay?"

While Tommy did that, Preston put on the water for the rice and whisked the egg. Throughout the task of battering the fish and cooking the rest of the meal, he let his mind wander.

He'd barely been out of short pants the first time he'd met Poppy Scarlatti . . .

"Ma! I finished my chores. Going out to play ball with the boys." Eleven-year-old Preston bent to gather his ball and glove from the bottom of the closet. Any time he could escape the cramped quarters of the tiny apartment he shared with his gaggle of siblings and his parents, he took the opportunity.

"Don't go fa' now, hear?" Ma called from where she was at the task of changing the baby. "The new neighbuhs ah comin' to dinnuh."

"Yes'm!"

Preston stepped out the door and paused to adjust his glove. The metal landing of the rickety stairs that led down to the street wasn't much more than a rusty grate. Movement below caught his eye.

A girl stood looking up at him with large brown eyes. She wore a red dress that, even from this distance, Preston could tell was finer than anything his sisters had ever owned, and her silken black hair draped down her back in two braids that almost reached her waist.

Preston studied her for a good thirty seconds before he realized that she was also looking up at him. He trotted down the stairs, well practiced at the balance needed to navigate the jouncing descent. He paused at the bottom, tossing his ball into his glove a few times as he watched her. She never broke eye contact.

"You with the new family?" Preston asked, then immediately realized it was a stupid question, since she was standing in the doorway of the apartment that had been empty until this morning.

"Just moved in, if that's what you're asking." She swayed a little, causing her skirts to swing.

"How old are you?"

"Nine."

Preston scratched his jaw on one shoulder, still tossing the ball in and out of his glove. An unsettled feeling squirmed around in his middle. He'd never paused to talk to any girl that he could ever remember. But there was something about this one with her chocolate-brown eyes and caramel-and-cream skin that made him want to stand and stare for a while.

"Where you goin'?" she asked.

"Just down the block to play catch with some of the boys. Wanna come?" The minute the words popped out of his mouth, Preston wished he could snatch them back. He'd invited a girl? The fellas were never gonna let him live this one down. But before he could figure out a polite way to retract his invitation, she accepted.

"Sure! Just let me tell my pa."

He thought about running off and leaving her, but then the largest man he'd ever seen filled the doorway. The man's shoulders were almost as broad as the door was wide. And the hands that he wrapped around the sides of the doorframe as he leaned forward to glower at Preston above his daughter's head could have engulfed Preston's throat with ease.

Preston swallowed. But his good training didn't abandon him. Taking off his glove, he stepped forward and stretched out one hand. "Evening to you, sir. My name's Preston Clay. I live with my family in the apartment just above you. I believe my ma has already met you because she said you were coming to dinner tonight."

He'd been wrong about Mr. Scarlatti's hands. When the man's grip enveloped his, Preston felt his knees go a little weak. Not only could the man's hand have engulfed his throat, his fingers could have met at the back of his neck. And while their clasp had started out as a handshake, Mr. Scarlatti was now using it to hold Preston in place.

The man's gaze drilled Preston. "Anything happens to my girl while she is-ah with you and I hold you responsible. Aye?" The thick remnants of his Italian accent lingered in Preston's mind, adding emphasis to his threat.

Preston worked the dryness out of his mouth. He withdrew his hand on the pretense of fetching his glove from under his opposite arm. "Yes, sir. I understand, sir. I'll keep an eye on her."

"See-ah that you do."

"You g-gonna turn them fish, PC?"

Preston came back to the present and snatched for a fork to flip the trout. Thankfully, they were only a little more brown than usual. "Thank you, Tom-Tom. You get the table set?"

"Yep."

"Why don't you get us some milk from the ice box? Then maybe we'll go down to Dixie's after dinner and get ourselves a piece of pie. How does that sound?"

"Tommy likes pie!"

"I know you do. Now set yourself down there at the table and drink some milk until I bring your plate."

Preston only hoped that Dr. Griffin might be home and have time to speak with him.

He was a man in need of advice.

Belle Kastain fled the house as soon as Zoe headed to town to meet Mr. Elijah Harrow. As much as Belle loved her mother and wanted her happiness, she wasn't certain she was ready to see her happy with another man. She carried her artist's case and easel to the wildflower field on the hill above town and set it up beneath the large oak where the bushes sheltered her from the view of any passersby.

Her grief over the loss of dear Pa came in unpredictable waves. At first it had nearly crippled her. Then it had tapered off to a dull ache that pestered her and caused sadness throughout each week. Then had come last Christmas where, watching the twins and Aidan open their gifts, she had experienced true joy for the first time since the tragedy. Her joy had been enhanced by Ma's own, when she'd opened the painting that Belle had made of their family riding in the wagon to Wyldhaven before Pa's injury. She had framed it with wood from Pa's scraps in the barn. The tears of sheer joy that Ma had shed over the painting had filled Belle with such a sense of satisfaction that for a few hours her ache had disappeared. And then on the heels of that time, insurmountable guilt had rushed in.

Day by day, month by month, and then over the course of a year, and then another, the grief had gradually become a distant memory. Something that, when she paused to think about it, filled her with guilt, because dear Pa did not deserve to ever be forgotten.

So today as she set up the easel in the shelter of the oak tree—the same easel Pa had built for her several Christmases ago—she was determined to paint dear Pa's face. She wanted to capture it before she caught her first glimpse of Mr. Harrow. For if Mama loved the man—as she surely did based on the glow that had been in her eyes this morning—Belle knew she would eventually learn to love him too. And before that next step along the path that separated their family from Pa, she wanted this one last moment in time to simply remember him, to honor him, before her emotions were muddied with love for another.

She stroked the outline of his face and the sketch of his crooked little smile that always revealed two teeth on one side of his mouth, the special way he squinted his eyes when he found humor in something, and the too-pointed-for-convention tip of his nose. The tracing of his ever-present Stetson came next, followed by the faint outline of the overalls he always wore.

And then as if the heavens opened and doused her with grief, the floodgates of her tears burst, and she collapsed to her knees right there in the grass before her easel. With no one near to hear her pain, she didn't bother muffling her cries as she had so many times lying on her bed in the dark at home.

"Oh, Pa. I should have been there. I should've been by your side that last day. Can you see how sorry I am? Can you see how hard I've tried to be everything Mama wants me to be since?"

She had been putting the final touches of shadow and light into the painting of their family on the night Pa had passed. But that was just an excuse. The truth was, she'd known the end was near. She ought to have stayed home. She could have finished the painting in the corner of Pa's sickroom. Then he could have seen it, even if it wasn't quite finished yet. But she'd come with a lantern here to this very spot and spent the night finishing it. She'd been finishing a painting of happiness and joy, while her dear pa had called for her—Zoe had made sure to inform her of that—and drawn his last breaths.

She bent forward and pressed her face against her knees, succumbing to a grief she wasn't sure she would ever be able to escape.

Chapter Five

K ane Carver walked the path through the woods toward home, surprised that he didn't feel as elated as he had expected to. Aurora agreeing to dinner had been the only thing that had occupied his mind for at least a week—ever since he'd decided she was the most eligible woman in town.

Recalling his bumbling words, he shook his head at himself. Had his mother and father ever been so ill at ease around each other? Was it even normal that he be so nervous around a woman that he'd pondered spending the rest of his life with? And what did cause him to be so discomfited around her anyhow?

Aurora was a beauty to be sure, but she had kindness as deep as her bones. She would never hurt him or even speak ill of him behind his back. So it seemed incomprehensible that he found himself so knock kneed and tongue tied in her presence.

He was just taking the path through the wildflower field now flush with wild rose blooms, when he heard a sound that brought him to a stop.

What was that? Where was it coming from? He angled his head. The fragrant perfume of the roses swirled around him in a dance that vied to drown the scent of the pine tree to his left.

From the back of the field. Beneath that old oak. Was it a fox caught in a trap? He pushed through the bushes and found a worn trail leading in the direction of the tree.

He approached cautiously, not wanting to frighten the creature any more than it sounded like it already was.

But he realized that the guttural wails were not the sound of some wild animal but of a woman in distress.

He paused outside the protective hedge of pink roses and spent lilac bushes that hid her from his sight. He snatched his hat from his head, sliding his fingers around the brim, as he pondered what he should do.

On the one hand, someone in such distress most likely didn't want to be disturbed. On the other hand, it sounded like she was alone, and he couldn't just go off in all good conscience and leave a woman in the woods by herself. Especially not one in such a state as this.

The woman cried out a prayer then. "God, forgive me for my selfishness! For too long I've held You at arm's length. I was prideful. Angry because of Pa. Help me to be better. Kinder. More thoughtful of others."

In the pause that followed, he recognized the voice as that of Belle Kastain. Her grieved humility pierced straight to his heart and took the strength from his legs. He squatted to the balls of his feet, hat dangling between his knees, unsure what he should do.

She went on praying. "Whether or not Mr. Harrow is going to be part of our lives, help me to make him feel welcome. And please don't let feelings of resentment grow. I know we all have to move on." Her voice broke. "But I'm going to need extra strength to see another man filling Ma's eyes with a light of love."

Kane felt uncomfortable with his eavesdropping. But now was certainly not the moment to step into her secluded little hiding place and reveal himself. And yet what a difference it might have made in his life during those days of grief after his mother and father had passed to have another adult to share the unfathomable sorrow with. Sure, Maude and Seth had grieved too, but they'd been naught more than children. His charges, not his confidants.

Decision made, he rose and stepped through the gap in the green lilac bushes.

It was indeed Belle Kastain. She was on her knees before an easel, forehead pressed to her thighs with her hands covering her face. Her form was slight. He could see the angle of her thin shoulder blades through the soft material of her blouse. Had he ever realized how petite she was?

A scant, yet totally decipherable, sketch on canvas was clipped to the easel. Amazing how she had captured the man's expression with so few strokes. Kane almost felt as though the sketch were grinning at him.

He was loathe to intrude on her solitude, but he couldn't just stand here without her knowing. He shuffled his feet and cleared his throat softly.

Belle gave a little screech and lurched to her feet, scrambling away from him.

Hat in one hand, he stretched out his arms. "It's just me, Belle. Kane Carver. I don't mean you any harm."

Belle rapidly scrubbed at her cheeks with the cuff of one sleeve. Then set to furiously returning her art tools to a little wooden case that lay open on the grass a few feet away. "Can't a body get any peace around here?"

Kane gestured to the picture. "Is that your pa?"

Belle hesitated for the briefest of moments. She glanced over at the picture, and new tears burgeoned in her eyes. She gave a tiny nod.

He had intruded. Now that he had seen she was safe, he ought to step back and offer to escort her home. But there was something about her vulnerability that drew him. "I've never seen anyone as talented. I didn't know you were an artist?"

Her shrug was barely discernible. "I've not had any formal training."

He looked at the picture again. "With talent like that, you don't *need* formal training."

Twin grooves settled between her brows. "It's just a sketch."

"That may be, but I can almost see him looking at me. If you can do that with just a few strokes of a pencil, I'd love to see what it looks like when you are done." He almost didn't proceed, but decided to throw caution to the wind. "Will you show it to me when it's finished?"

"I'm not certain I will finish it."

"That would be a shame. I can tell how much he meant to you. It would give you something to remember him by."

Her focus flashed to him, and she assessed his features.

He held his breath, feeling like he was being scrutinized by a fawn that might flee at his first flinch. Her eyes were as blue as a soft horizon just before dusk. And her blond curls framed a face with high cheekbones and pert lips.

Why had he never noticed her before? Well, he'd *noticed* her, but she'd always seemed . . . aloof. Above his station. Now he wondered if she simply carried her feelings so deep inside that it was difficult for her to bring them to the surface.

Her fingers twined together. "Pa passed just over two years ago now. My ma has been corresponding with a new man— Mr. Elijah Harrow—for about a year."

Kane remembered Zoe greeting the man in town. "I think I saw him getting off the stage."

Belle nodded. "Yes. He's coming to visit for a week. Only Zoe and Ma have met him. I just—"

He waited quietly, giving her time to formulate her thoughts as she studied her twisting fingers.

"Ma loves him—Mr. Harrow. I can tell by the way her face lights up just at the mention of his name. And if she loves him, I know we will all learn to love him too. But I don't want to forget Pa. And before I laid eyes on Mr. Harrow, I wanted—" She broke off and gave a little gesture of defeat. "It's silly."

"I don't think it's silly."

"You don't?" She raised her gaze to his again, and he wished he could keep this conversation going for an eternity, simply to keep her looking at him.

"Not in the least. Did you ever hear what brought my siblings and me to Wyldhaven?"

"I heard there was a fire. I'm very sorry for your loss."

"Thank you." He broke a leaf from the lilac bush next to him and spun it between his fingers. "The thing is, I'd give anything to have them captured on canvas or a photograph. We don't have any of that. So they remain a simple memory. But their faces are hazy. Like a beautiful mountain on a misty day. You know the image is there. You just can't quite pull it up clearly."

She tilted her head. "I've heard people say that. But I've never had that problem. Once I see something"—she tapped her temple—"it's here to stay."

"That's quite a gift."

She twisted her lips to one side in thought. "I suppose it is. But . . . It can be a curse too."

"We wouldn't truly understand light without the contrast of darkness."

Belle's features softened as a look of amazement swept over her. "That's very true. In painting, it's the shadows that help bring out the reflections and highlights. Even just the slightest shadow can add contour and definition."

Kane dipped his head toward the easel. "How long will it take you to finish?"

Her laugh was like a bubbling brook. "Oh weeks and weeks probably. But today I only wanted to get the broad strokes down before I meet Mr. Harrow."

He gestured her toward the picture with his hat. "Please don't let me stop you. If you don't mind, I'll wait and escort you home?"

She rolled her lips inward and pressed them together, studying him for a long moment. Finally, she moved toward the painting. Over her shoulder she said, "I don't want to keep you."

Kane settled into a comfortable position with his back to the base of the oak and watched her squeeze various colors of paint onto a thin flat board that she balanced on one hand. "You aren't keeping me from anything."

He couldn't wait to watch her at work. With a jolt, he realized that he hadn't thought of Aurora McClure even once during this whole conversation.

Crickets serenaded like a Fifth Avenue orchestra as Preston escorted Tommy down the hill to the diner. Tommy carefully carried a piece of paper and his wooden box of watercolor paints balanced on both hands before him like a servant presenting royalty with a crown jewel.

Preston always loved this walk into town. From this height he could see over the rooftops of the main part of town and the rowhouses of the logging workers that had been popping up like spring dandelions for the past couple of years. The purple mountains beyond nestled in a golden glow typical of this time of evening, and peach streaks broke up the blue of the sky, making a man wish he had time to simply stand and stare for a while.

But if he hoped to connect with Doc, he'd better get on down to the diner before some emergency called Doc out of town.

"T-Tommy l-like that s-sky."

"Sure is pretty, isn't it? God takes time to paint the world a new picture every morning and evening."

"T-Tommy l-love G-God."

Preston smiled. "I'm glad. I do too."

It did his heart good to consider that God had loved Tommy enough to bring him into Preston's life so that he could tell him about how Jesus loved Tommy just the way he was.

If only his wayward ward, Kin Davis, would have believed as easily. As he nudged Tommy to keep going down the path, he wondered about Kin. He'd left for Seattle months ago. At first he'd sent a few wires to let Preston know he was all right, but lately the wires had stopped. He worried about what might have happened to him. His ever-present prayer was ready to his mind. *Lord, don't give up on that kid. Hound him to the very gates of death if You must, but bring him to repentance and belief.*

With a sigh, he let the prayer go to do its work before the throne. He'd long ago concluded that he couldn't keep the burden over Kin's soul to himself. Nor could he carry it. He'd tried that. Spent too many sleepless nights in distraught beseechment. Finally he'd learned to say his heartfelt prayers and then leave them in the very capable hands of the Almighty.

As they arrived at the steps leading up to the boardinghouse, he reached past to open the door for Tommy and then nudged him through the entry and into the dining room.

He had timed his visit so that hopefully Dixie wouldn't have too many patrons, and as he stepped into the room behind

Tommy, he was gratified to see that his timing seemed to be just about right. Only one other table in the room was currently occupied.

He settled Tommy into a chair at one of the tables, with his watercolor paper and paints. "Be real careful now. We don't want to get a mess all over Dixie's table, understand?"

Tommy nodded vigorously as he popped open the lid on his wooden box of paints. "Tommy understand. N-need water."

"Yeah. I know. I'll get you some." Preston sank into his own chair. He looked up to see Dixie, a huge smile on her face, making her way toward them from the kitchen.

She held the steaming coffeepot in one hand and two empty mugs in the other. "Parson! And Tommy! What a pleasure to see you both here this evening. I know I don't have to ask if you both would like a cup of coffee." With a chuckle, she plunked the two mugs onto the table and filled Preston's nearly to the lip and Tommy's halfway.

Resting one hand on her hip, she asked, "Are you two here for dinner tonight? Or just dessert?

"Just dessert," Preston said. Then with a gesture to Tommy's paints, he added, "And a glass of water please."

"T-Tommy don't l-like f-fish." The lad's lower lip was once more in danger of having a rooster land on it.

Preston chuckled. He leaned back and looked at Dixie. "And, I guess, if it's not too much trouble, a bowl of oatmeal for my friend Tommy here." Tommy *had* given a valiant effort to trying the fish on his dinner plate, but Preston had finally given up urging him to take another bite.

Dixie chuckled. "Not a problem at all. I have fresh huckleberry pie with sweet cream. One slice of cherry pie left. And I think half of the Dutch apple. What will it be?"

Tommy rocked in his chair, as was his habit. He rubbed the side of his head. "Tommy w-want apple p-pie."

"Make that two." Preston smiled his thanks, and Dixie bustled toward the kitchen.

When she returned a few moments later to bring Tommy his glass of water, Preston cleared his throat and worked up his courage. "Flynn wouldn't happen to be home, would he?"

She nodded. "You're in luck. He just happens to be between patients. Would you like me to get him?"

"Only if I won't be interrupting the first few moments of rest that he's gotten for several days?"

"No, no. He's actually had a pretty good week. I will get him just as soon as I get Tommy's oatmeal cooking."

Preston couldn't deny his relief. He wasn't sure what he would have done if Doc hadn't been available. "Much obliged."

It was only a few minutes before Dr. Flynn Griffin appeared in the dining room and sank onto the seat across from Preston. "You asked for me?"

The tension churning through Preston's chest eased with just the prospect of sharing his burden with another. "I did. Do you have a few minutes to talk?"

"I'm all yours."

Where to begin? Preston suddenly felt like a child called before a school headmaster. He squirmed in his chair and laced his fingers together on the table before him. He was thankful to see the occupants of the last table leaving. Momentarily, the dining room lay empty except for them.

Preston finally lifted his gaze to Doc's. "I am often asked by people to maintain their confidence. But it's not often that I have to request the same from others. However, I find myself in need of some advice. And would appreciate your discretion."

"I'll not break your confidence." Doc's expression reflected a sincerity that set Preston's mind at ease.

He cleared his throat. "I appreciate that. I'm just not certain exactly where to start."

"I find that the beginning is always a good place to begin." Doc gave him a smile.

With a nervous chuckle, Preston took a fortifying breath and plunged ahead. "I used to be muscle for a mob boss in Boston." The words emerged so rapidly that they were all strung together like popcorn on a string.

Flynn settled against the slats of his chair and blinked. "I can honestly say that's the very last thing I expected you to tell me."

Preston spread his hands and gave a little shrug. "You said to 'start at the beginning.'"

"That I did."

 Chapter Six

The tabletop was smooth beneath the stroke of Preston's fingers, until he recognized the nervous gesture for what it was and folded his hands once more. "There was this girl . . . woman. She was . . . still is . . . my boss's daughter. I mean, the man who used to be my boss."

"Okay?" Flynn's quizzical frown made it plain that he didn't understand why Preston was bringing up a woman.

"She arrived in town on today's stage."

"Oh!" The good doctor's brows jumped nearly to his hairline.

Willing himself to finish what he started, Preston pushed on. "I'm afraid she's up to no good. She made a subtle threat about revealing my past to people in town."

"So tell your side of things first and take her legs out from under her." Flynn's inflection made it sound as though it were the simplest of solutions.

Preston's cold sweat was back in full force. The thought of standing before his congregation and making such a confession sent his stomach into a slow turn. And yet . . . there was wisdom in that advice. It was actually something he should have done long ago, if he was honest with himself. He sighed. It seemed he wasn't going to be able to shrug off this conviction. "That's a good idea. I'll rework tomorrow's sermon."

Flynn nodded. "Do you think she might cause trouble around town?"

Giving himself a moment to ponder, Preston took a swallow of coffee. "Maybe. I'll need to inform Reagan, Joe, and Zane, but . . . she's only partially why I wanted to talk to you."

Flynn remained silent, but his expression was open and expectant.

"It's about . . . Aurora."

"A-Aurora's n-nice," Tommy piped up, proving that he had at least one ear tuned in to their conversation, even though, by the evidence of his tongue tucked carefully between his front teeth, he was intent on painting small strokes.

The doctor folded his arms with a broad grin. "I wondered when you were going to get around to acknowledging your feelings for her."

Preston frowned "You did?"

"I did."

Preston despaired. If Doc had taken note of his feelings, how many other people in town had as well? "See? That's just the thing. I thought I was doing good at *suppressing* my inclination toward her. And yet here, without me ever having said anything on the subject, you already knew why I brought her up." He blew out a miserable groan. "A minister should not be experiencing these types of . . . longings for a woman."

Doc swept a gesture of dismissal. "Why shouldn't a minister have a family?"

Dixie arrived just then with their pie and Tommy's oatmeal. She also slid a slice of cherry pie in front of Doc. The gleam in her eyes said she'd overheard at least part of their discussion, but like the kind woman she was, she said nothing. Even though he would have liked to have kept this discussion just between him and Doc for now, Preston didn't worry about her gossiping the news around town. Dixie wasn't one of those types.

Preston pondered his response to Flynn's question as he waited for her to settle their plates, refill his coffee mug, and pour one for Doc.

"Oatmeal!" Tommy exclaimed in glee, and Preston couldn't withhold a smile as the lad pushed his pie to one side and dove into the bowl of his favorite food first.

"Anything else?" she asked.

He gave her a smile. "This all looks good. Thanks."

"Thank you, darling." Flynn caught her hand and gave it a quick kiss. "A good woman is a blessing to have in one's life."

With a tug to free her hand, Dixie laughed. "If you are angling for another piece of pie, it's not going to do you any good. That's the last slice."

"In that case, I take it all back," Flynn teased.

Dixie arched a brow and reached for his plate. "Oh, you want me to take it back?"

Flynn scrambled to retrieve his dessert before it was out of reach. "Now don't go getting your feathers all in a twist. I was just joshing!"

Dixie left his pie, but her laughter trailed after her as she returned to the kitchen. "I have a few dishes left to do, then I'll be up," she called as she disappeared.

Flynn lifted a pointed gaze to Preston and tapped his plate with his fork. "A good woman is a blessing from the Almighty."

Dallying his own fork through his pie, Preston sighed. "I don't dispute that. It's just . . . I simply don't have time to give a woman a proper place in my life, if that makes sense. Unless I'm preparing for a sermon or preaching at the church, I'm usually out to the camps, or fetching groceries for families in need, or dealing with . . . other people." He tilted a subtle nod in Tommy's direction, not wanting him to feel like a burden, even though he was somewhat one.

"I'll wager your current salary is another thing on your mind." Flynn swigged from his cup to down a bite of cherries.

Preston's discomfort rose. He never wanted the people of Wyldhaven to think he was dissatisfied with what they paid him, but it certainly wasn't enough to support a family. "I can't deny that has crossed my mind."

"Have you prayed on it? Your feelings for Aurora?"

Blowing out a breath, Preston downed a scalding gulp of coffee. "Only multiple times a day, every day, for months now."

"And what has your prayer been, specifically, if I can press that far?"

Preston didn't have any trouble answering that question. "That the Lord would take these feelings away! For all the reasons we just mentioned. Plus the fact that I'm older than she is. Why just this morning it came to my attention that Deputy Joe thinks of me as her pa!"

Flynn offered a smirk that was half grin, half dismissal. "You're not *that* much older than her. Besides"—Flynn set down his fork and met Preston's gaze head-on—"seems the Lord has offered His answer to your prayer."

The full realization of that hit Preston like the tepid bucket of wash water his mother used to douse over him on bath days. He shook his head in denial. "No. That can't be the answer."

Flynn chuckled. "And why not? She's of age. You're eligible."

"It's just my weak flesh trying to pin me to the strictures of this world."

"Hate to break it to you, but we *are* pinned to the strictures of this world. At least until the good Lord sees fit to bring us home. And even the Word says it's better for a man to marry than to burn with passion."

Preston felt his face flame, even as his reasoning faltered. "I want to be clear that I've never touched her in any inappropriate way. I mean, in any way really. Well, I did touch her hand one time, but—" He stumbled to a lame stop and narrowed his eyes at the grin Flynn angled his way.

Doc was undaunted by his glower. "Couldn't it be that the Lord directed your steps to her all those years ago just when she needed a protector because He had good plans for your future?"

"Well, yes, I suppose, but I always simply felt like the Lord had sent me there to help her escape from John Hunt. Not to—" He gripped the back of his neck, unable to even bring himself to say the rest of that sentence.

Flynn smirked. "Fall in love with her?" He forked his last bite of pie into his mouth.

It was as though Flynn's words had cleared Preston's mind of storm clouds. He blew out a breath. "Dear Lord Almighty, I *am* in love with her."

Flynn spread his hands as though to say, "See, wasn't that easy?" He nudged his empty plate aside. "So it sounds like the constraints on your time and your salary are really the only two things holding you back from her?"

Preston wasn't sure. He shook his head. "I just don't know. I've got other considerations." He angled a look to Tommy, who had emptied both his plate and his bowl and was once again contentedly applying splotches of color to his paper.

Flynn nodded. "And don't you think that Aurora has proven her feelings in that regard? When you were sick last Christmas, she stepped up and took care of everything like a champion."

Preston closed his eyes, willing away the reminder of how exhilarating it had been to watch Aurora cooking at the stove in his small cabin. The feel of her skin beneath his when she'd brought him Allegra and he'd covered her hand in thanks. The way her green eyes had invited him closer.

Doc cleared his throat.

Preston came back to the present with a chagrinned glance at Doc.

Flynn was beaming broadly. "God hasn't answered your prayer to take away these feelings, and the Word says not to burn. I think you have your answer." He rose and lifted his empty plate and cup. "The rest will fall into place. Just take it one step at a time."

Preston's stomach swirled with a heady mixture of nerves, despair, and excitement. "She's leaving town."

Flynn stilled. "What? When?"

"She applied and was accepted to the territorial university's music conservatory. She leaves for Seattle in two weeks."

"Well, I guess that means you better hurry and let her know how you feel." Flynn gave him a double pump of his brows and then retreated toward the diner's kitchen, calling "Goodnight" over his shoulder.

Preston stared dumbfoundedly at the crumb top on the apple pie that he'd hardly touched. *Lord, is this really the path You want me to take? Don't let me blunder ahead and walk only where my feelings lead me.*

He didn't hear an audible reply. Or even sense a word in his spirit, as he sometimes did. Yet in that moment, a wave of such peace washed over him. An emotion that had eluded him ever since last Christmas when he'd first started fighting these feelings for Aurora. It was as though he'd been harnessed to a wagon full of rocks and someone had just cut the ties.

He broke into a broad grin and tugged his pie plate closer.

Tommy looked up from his painting. "Y-you l-look h-happy."

Preston nodded. "I am, Tom-Tom. I am." For the first time in an awfully long time. "Please rinse your brush and put it away. As soon as I finish this pie, we can go. You can paint some more back at the house."

He reached over and closed the lid on Tommy's paints, but his mind was already spinning with possibilities of how to make a relationship with Aurora work.

Poppy stood outside the dining room door with her fists clenched so tight that her fingernails painfully gouged her palms. She'd planned to get some dinner but had paused outside the door when she'd recognized Preston's voice coming from inside.

Thankfully, with no other diners and thus no other discussions taking place, there had been nothing blocking her from overhearing the conversation he'd just concluded with the doctor. From the sound of things, she'd missed a good deal of the beginning of the conversation, which was a pity, but she'd arrived in time to hear the doctor convincing him not to fight his feelings for the woman Aurora.

From inside the dining room, the laughter of a man and woman floated out.

"Parson, if there won't be anything else, I'll just head upstairs with Flynn." The voice was that of the woman who'd checked her in earlier, if the soft southern drawl could be trusted.

"No. Nothing else. Thanks. This is delicious, as usual." A fork clinked against a plate.

"Thank you. Just leave the dishes on the table when you're done, and I'll clear them in a little while." Footsteps headed Poppy's way.

She retreated, dashing up the stairs to her room before she was caught. Not only had her eavesdropping filled her with angst, it had also cost her the opportunity to get an evening meal. Irritation swept through her.

Her stomach growled as she flopped onto her bed and stared at the ceiling.

Maybe she was wrong about Preston? Just now he'd certainly seemed sincere about this God thing, because what man would deny himself a woman he wanted? Unless he was totally deluded by religion.

She scoffed.

It couldn't be! Preston had always been thoughtful and levelheaded. There was no way he would be duped into believing that a few stupid rules, meant only to keep people from happiness, were the way to an eternity in heaven. He was much too practical for that.

Besides, if it were all about rule keeping, Preston would have been counted out a long time ago. How many times had they stolen apples or penny candy from the corner store in their neighborhood? Or played hooky from school to kick around the streets of Boston, simply to enjoy breaking the rules?

No, Preston was a born rule-breaker and much too smart to fall for such tripe. There had to be more to his story.

He was on a con. A very long one, from what she could determine. But she aimed to find out what it was. Maybe then she could get back into Babbo's good graces.

She'd had that little incident with the handsome Mr. Fortier. Babbo had not been happy with her for consorting with a married man. Especially not one as wealthy as Mr. Fortier. After all, they couldn't give the man any bargaining power when it came time to conduct a "business deal." When it turned out that the man was only wooing her for the advantage it gave him over Babbo, Poppy had felt such a humiliation, especially when Babbo had made it clear that he no longer thought of her as a good businesswoman. She needed to prove him wrong!

So yes, she needed something—something good—to help her get back on Babbo's good side. And she had a strong feeling Preston was her key.

The problem was, now she also needed to figure out what this nuisance Aurora meant to Preston. Because, unfortunately, while Poppy couldn't see Preston falling for religion, she could see him falling for a beautiful woman. And the woman Aurora was beautiful enough to make Poppy's eye twitch.

Had Preston been serious about his feelings for her? Or was that conversation with the doctor all part of his long-range plan? What could a woman like Aurora have to do with it though? She'd seemed simple. Innocent. Certainly not wealthy, nor the type of woman who would help Preston pull off a con.

With another growl of frustration, Poppy surged off the bed and reached into her bag for her nightdress. An earlier inquiry had informed her that church services started at ten in the morning. If she was going to be awake at such an ungodly hour of the day, it was best she get an early start on her night.

There would be time enough tomorrow to sort out how to handle this new set of problems.

Chapter Seven

Aurora stood in the middle of her room in the little bunkhouse at the edge of the Rodantes' ranch. Hands propped on her hips, she surveyed this space that had been her own since she was a late teen, brought here by Parson Clay.

This had been her refuge, her sure foundation when her world had been rocked by the death of her mother, and the place where she had come to truly know her Savior. How many hours had she spent reading her Bible in the little rocking chair in the corner? How many mornings had she risen before dawn to go fetch the eggs and milk the cows? For a while, she'd shared the room with Ruby, another woman Liora had taken in. But then Ruby had stolen an expensive saddle and run away, only to befall an accident that had killed her. After Ruby had left them in such a tragic way, Joe and Liora had not assigned Aurora another roommate. So this room had been hers and hers alone. She would miss it.

Was she ready to leave all this security and stability for the unknown of a Seattle education? Her heart thumped.

Throwing up her hands, she reached for her shawl and reticule where they lay on the end of the bed. *Lord, I thought that getting the acceptance to the conservatory would be the answer that brought me peace about this decision. If it is not meant to be, please make it clear before I do anything permanent.*

She knew the exact moment that had compounded the questions that had already been in her heart. It was the moment she'd seen that woman Poppy walking up the pathway from town.

Aurora felt like she was a pressure cooker with the lid sealed. She'd been doing her best to keep all her scattered emotions under the lid. But with each new decision she'd made, the pressure grew.

Walking by faith was never easy, it seemed.

But the way Preston had greeted Poppy had blown the lid off Aurora's pot. And now, the niggling hesitation that had lingered at the back of her mind when she pondered leaving for the territorial university was a potful of jam exploded all over the kitchen of her life.

With a huff of frustration, she tucked a hanky into her sleeve, just in case she might need one. Then she swung her shawl around her shoulders and stepped into the yard where Joe and Liora waited to give her a ride to church. Liora sat, pretty as a picture, on the wagon seat with little Law in her arms, and Joe was settling a basket into the back of the bed—likely Liora's fixings for Washington Nolan's goodbye gathering today.

Which reminded her . . . She held up one finger. "I just need to grab the pies I made."

"That's them. I just put them in the back of the wagon," Joe said.

"Oh. Thank you. Sorry if I've made us late."

"Not at all." Joe shook his head. "I happened to be in the kitchen and remembered they were there. Thought I'd help out. I was bringing Liora's basket out anyhow." He reached a hand to help her into the wagon.

"Thank you." She settled onto the seat and clasped her hands in a tight knot.

And as she turned her mind to the morning ahead, her stomach crimped.

In just a few moments she would play the piano in the Wyldhaven church for nearly the last time. Another jitter of trepidation swept through her, and she smoothed a hand over her middle.

This transition certainly wasn't going as smoothly as she had imagined it would all those months past when she'd applied to the conservatory.

An exploded pot of jam indeed!

But the decision to leave had already been made and announced. Liora had even spoken to her the evening before about organizing a farewell party for her in a couple weeks.

It was too late to go back now.

As Belle dressed and braided her hair on Sunday morning, she pondered the events of the evening before.

She wasn't sure how to feel about Kane Carver stumbling upon her in her grief, and yet he'd seemed like a man who understood just exactly where she'd been emotionally. He hadn't belittled her or made her feel inadequate for showing such emotions. And the praise he'd lavished on her sketch had trickled inside and filled empty places that she didn't even know were empty.

Pa had always been the one to compliment her on her work. Well, he and Zoe, but Zoe had been so busy teaching at the school for the past few months that Belle hadn't bothered her with any of her pieces.

Kane seemed a good man. And perhaps, if circumstances were different, she might even be interested in getting to know him better, but a couple things stood in the way.

The first was family. Without Pa here to run the farm, Ma and the kids needed every scrap of income they each could muster. Mr. Hines, the Wyldhaven Mercantile owner, also owned their property. Pa had sold it to him when he'd become so sick and couldn't work, because they'd needed the money. Because of that, they now had rent to pay, and since Mr. Hines had sublet the fields, they didn't have the option of making an income from them. Each month they made it, but only because they lived hand to mouth. So she simply couldn't allow herself the freedom to think about anything other than work and family at the moment. They'd all been working hard to contribute to the family coffers, even Aidan. And her hours at the diner in town, plus her chores around the house, didn't leave her much time for lollygagging—or courting.

Despite being alone in her room, she felt her face heat. The man had only been a gentleman, not offering his hand in marriage!

The other reason that stood in her way was born from her own silliness in years past. At sixteen she'd gotten a fancy in her head that she could make Sheriff Reagan Callahan take note of her. She smirked and rolled her eyes at herself in the mirror as she coiled and pinned her braid at the back of her head. She'd succeeded in gaining his attention, though not in the way she'd hoped. And now, when she thought back to the way she'd acted, her cheeks burned with shame. Why, when Mrs. Callahan had come to town—at the time, still Miss Brindle, the new Wyldhaven schoolteacher—Belle had made quite a fool of herself trying to usurp the woman in the sheriff's eyes.

After Pa's accident, subsequent decline, and eventual death, she'd seen her immature actions for what they were, but the damage to her reputation had already been done.

Small towns had long memories, and Wyldhaven was no exception.

She wouldn't want to subject Mr. Carver to any ill will for associating with her.

She blew out a sigh. It wasn't as though the man had asked to come calling. He'd heard her crying and come to check on her like any gentleman would have, and that was all. Yet, she'd felt lighter of spirit as she'd walked home last night, and that was certain. Perhaps it could have stemmed from the good cry she'd had under the oak, but she felt a stirring in her spirit that said it was more than that.

And so this morning she reminded herself to proceed with caution.

As she fetched her Sunday gloves from her dresser, she heard Zoe stirring out in the kitchen, and that turned her mind to yesterday's evening meal. When she'd returned to the house, Zoe and Mr. Harrow had already arrived from town.

Belle had liked the look of the man from the very first. Not because he was handsome in an older-man sort of way, which he was, but because he had a soft expression whenever he looked at Ma, and a lively twinkle in his eyes the rest of the time. Though the meal could have been awkward and stilted, the man had smoothed the pauses with tales from his clock shop in Seattle. He'd had them all in stitches when he told about the time a woman arrived at his door first thing in the morning with her hair tangled in the hands of a rather large table clock. She'd fallen asleep on her settee, as he'd told it, and woken with her hair twined in the hands of the clock, which had been on her end table. The way he'd described how he'd tried to detangle the mess, with her yowling like an alley cat, had brought them to gales of laughter.

Even now Belle chuckled at the memory.

The meal had done her a world of good, and she dared to think it likely had helped the rest of the family as well.

The man had left with the promise that he would return in the morning for breakfast. And the lingering look that he and Ma had shared before he departed had filled Belle with a warmth she hadn't expected.

She'd thought she might be resentful, even though she'd prayed for the Lord to keep her from that. But instead, she'd found herself more than overjoyed for Ma to have come to know such a good man and for the fact that he'd recognized the amazing woman Ma was.

Belle felt as though she were a daisy that had languished for years beneath the dark, dank soil and had just now pushed through to feel the sunlight on her face.

Her tranquility wouldn't last for long, however, if she didn't get out of her room and go help Zoe prepare breakfast. Besides, she had a feeling that Zoe was going to need a little more love and compassion today to make it through Washington Nolan's farewell gathering. In fact, just the thought of Wash's departure had darkened Belle's own mood, and she'd never carried a torch for the man.

Belle snapped her teeth together as she stepped down the hall and set her hat and gloves on the table by the door.

The man was a lunkhead if he thought running off to join the cavalry would make him happy. Why, everyone in town knew that Zoe and Wash had been moon-eyed for each other for years. Belle was miffed on her sister's behalf that Wash was leaving without even giving Zoe a choice over whether she wanted to go with him.

Knowing Zoe, she would weather his departure with her signature sunny smile, but that didn't mean Belle had to like him for what he was putting her sister through.

If the man had any sense, he would take the safety of hearth and home over the dangers of war and wandering.

With a sigh, she headed for the kitchen.

Chapter Eight

When Preston nudged Tommy out of their cabin on Sunday morning, he noted that smoke already drifted from the church chimney and several horses were tied in the yard. He shouldn't have been surprised because that was the normal practice of the church women on days when there was to be a gathering after the services.

But he did wish that he could have eked out just a few more moments of quiet in order to think through his sermon one last time. After all, today's sermon could be the one that got him fired. He wanted to make sure he had all the wording exactly right.

And his sermon wasn't the only thing on his mind, nor was it the consideration that was making him the most nervous today. Not even close.

He'd decided as he'd tossed and turned late into the night that he'd never be able to live with himself if he didn't at least have a frank discussion with Aurora about his feelings. He hoped to be able to find a few minutes alone with her at the gathering later today, but the chances of that were slim to none with so many planning to attend Wash's send-off, so he'd likely have to ride out to the Rodantes' place tomorrow. And that meant either taking Tommy with him or finding someone to watch him, because while he could be trusted to entertain himself for a few minutes on his own at the house, he certainly couldn't be left for the couple hours Preston would need to ride out, have the conversation, and then get back home.

Perhaps he could prevail on Kane Carver to allow Tommy to help with one of his current horses. Kane and his siblings were renting Kin's old homestead from him while he was out of town, and Kane had taken on the reputation of the best horse trainer around. From what Preston had heard, he must be doing well for himself.

A fluke of an incident last Christmas had revealed that Tommy had a way with the big animals, which had surprised everyone, Preston most of all. So Preston had been taking him to Kane's place once a week on Fridays. Of course, tomorrow was only Monday, but perhaps Kane wouldn't mind having Tommy for a few extra hours.

As he stepped through the doors of the church and past the cubicled divider, he called a greeting and smiled to Mrs. King and Mrs. Hines. "Morning, ladies. Tommy, go to your spot on the front bench and sit down, all right?"

Tommy nodded and complied.

Both Dixie Griffin and Charlotte Callahan hustled in behind him, arms laden with greenery.

He greeted them also, then offered, "I'll just leave you ladies to your decorating." He strode to the podium and laid out his Bible and notes. Just stepping behind the pulpit returned his nerves to full roil. *Dear Lord, help me to be honest no matter the consequences. I've certainly put this off long enough.*

He read through his notes and the verses he planned to use one more time, and soon the church filled with parishioners. Right. This was it. He lifted his gaze.

The Nolan family stepped to the far end of the aisle. Washington appeared to be wearing a brand-new suit. He fiddled with his necktie in a nervous manner. Preston remembered what it had felt like when he'd decided to leave Boston. He imagined Wash was feeling some of those same emotions. Excited to be headed off to search out his dreams. But also a bit nostalgic over leaving his childhood home behind.

Preston strode down the aisle and stretched a hand to Butch Nolan and then to Wash as well. "Wash, I'm sure it's a day full of excitement for you, son."

Wash shook his hand. "Yes, sir. Thank you, sir."

"What time do you take off in the morning?" Preston shook the hands of each of Wash's brothers in turn.

"I catch the train first thing. Should arrive at Fort Vancouver by Tuesday evening."

"Well, I'm sure today will be a little hectic. So if I don't get to speak to you again, I just wanted to wish you all the best. Keep on serving the Lord. It's the only way to true happiness, no matter what lies this world might try to tell you."

"Yes, sir. Thank you, sir."

"Butch." Preston met Mr. Nolan's gaze and hoped he'd believe his next words. "You come on by to chat anytime you need to. I know sending a child off to join the cavalry can't be an easy thing."

Butch Nolan wagged his head in a gesture that indicated how right Preston was. "Thank you, Parson. You sure got that right. But I'm real proud of Wash here. He's a good man."

Washington's feet shuffled at the compliment. He looked down and poked the tip of one boot at a pine knot in the floorboard.

The church was filling even more now, and as several people squeezed around them, Preston wanted to free the aisle. "I should let you sit and get myself to the pulpit. Wash, best you start praying we get out of here before your train leaves in the morning." He gave a friendly wink, and the Nolans all chuckled, if a little nervously.

Preston turned from the Nolans and crashed into a warm body. A woman gave a squeak. He'd about bowled Aurora over. He gripped her arms and then quickly released her. "Sorry about that. You all right?"

She swallowed and gave the barest of nods.

Had there ever been a pair of such wide, inviting eyes? Jade with flecks of gold. Lined with lashes so long they caressed her brow bone as she looked up at him.

"'Scuse me." Ewan McGinty passed them in the aisle, bumping Preston so hard he had to take a balancing step to keep from knocking into Aurora again.

Preston frowned at the man over his shoulder.

"Sorry, Preach." Ewan gave him a smirk and a wink, then slid into the nearest pew.

Preston did have the presence of mind to be thankful that Ewan had shown up for services today. That was not his usual pattern, for certain. Wash's farewell seemed to be good for more in the town than just himself.

By the time Preston returned his focus to Aurora, she was moving forward. "I best get to the piano."

"Aurora?"

She turned back. "Yes?"

He lowered his voice, knowing that the hum of the multiple conversations in the room would give them a little privacy. "I wondered if . . . we might . . . find time to have a short conversation? Today after services? Or maybe I could come by the Rodantes' tomorrow?" That was, if she even wanted to speak with him anymore after she heard today's sermon.

A tiny frown crimped her brow. "Yes. I think that would be fine. Maybe tomorrow? Today is likely to be hectic."

He nodded, releasing her to the piano. "Thank you. I appreciate it."

He made his way to the podium and gripped both sides in a tight clench. It was time to focus on the task at hand. *Lord, give me strength.*

He lifted a smile to the congregation and called a greeting to silence them. "Good morning, everyone."

A chorus of "good mornings" filled the room, followed by the rustling of everyone finding their seats. Aurora played the opening notes of the first hymn. Preston led the congregation in singing without really paying attention to any of the words. Tommy, late with each word and severely off key, sang with a gusto that put everyone in the room to shame, just as he did every Sunday.

Preston saw Mrs. Hines's lips press together, puckered in disapproval. She'd spoken to him many times about telling Tommy not to sing so that the rest of them could enjoy Sunday morning worship. She hadn't been happy when Preston refused her request. After today's sermon, she would be one of the first to call for his dismissal, he felt certain.

He noted with interest that there was a man sitting next to Mrs. Kastain. He was about her age with a full head of brown hair and gentle brown eyes. Preston gave him a nod of greeting, which the man returned. This morning Belle looked more peaceful than usual, and her sister, Zoe, less so. But Preston figured her melancholy had much to do with Washington Nolan's impending departure.

The Rodantes looked proud and strong. Joe stood with his arm around Liora's shoulders while Liora cradled their baby in her arms. Seated on the bench next to them were Dixie and Doc, and Sheriff Reagan and Charlotte.

As they started into the notes of the last hymn, Preston felt his nerves rise once more. He repeated his cry for strength from the heavens, and then Aurora stroked the last note of the song, and the room fell silent.

Every eye in the room was on him, and his notes and the pages of his Bible were nothing but a blur. He stood, leaning heavily against the podium for a long moment, and then finally raised his gaze to the congregation. "My sermon this morning—"

The back doors of the church burst open, and Poppy scrambled into view. Everyone turned to see who was arriving late. Poppy stood in the aisle searching for a place to sit. She gave the room a sheepish smile. "So sorry to be late."

Jackson Nolan, who was seated in the back row next to his brothers Grant and Lincoln, scooted his brothers as close to the wall as they would go and spoke up. "You can sit here, ma'am, if you'd like." He offered Poppy a charming smile.

Preston suppressed the desire to call out a warning that the young man better watch himself where Poppy was concerned.

Instead, he returned to his sermon. "As I said, my sermon this morning is likely going to be a surprise to many of you." He met Doc's gaze for the briefest of moments. Doc gave him a nod of encouragement.

"I've titled today's sermon 'The Chiefest of Sinners.' This, of course, was what the apostle Paul labeled himself. But today I am standing before you to put myself in the same category."

A ripple of gasps, Mrs. Hines's the loudest of all, swept across the room.

There was no going back now even if he wanted to. "I've not spoken much of my history since coming to serve here in Wyldhaven. Today I would like to amend that. Tell you about my past. A past lived before I came to know our Lord and Savior." Of its own volition, his gaze settled on Poppy.

Her eyes were narrowed, her lips pursed.

He could tell she was trying to figure out how his words fit into the con he was pulling on his congregation. If only she would believe that his relationship with the Lord really had changed him.

A few in the congregation squirmed restlessly on the pews, and Preston realized he'd left everyone hanging. "You see, before I got saved, I lived in Boston. I grew up poor. Lived with my father and mother and all of my siblings in a one-bedroom apartment. We were often without food. And rarely had enough money for new clothes and school supplies. When I was eleven, a new family moved into the apartment below us."

Poppy folded her arms and daggered him a look.

"That family did not stay there long. They had just arrived from Italy. And were only living in the apartment until they could find a home to buy. But through the years I remained in contact with the man's daughter, as we had struck up a friendship during the time they lived in the apartment below us."

Several eyes in the room turned to look at Poppy speculatively.

But Preston did not plan to toss her to the wolves. "That girl's father eventually became a mob boss."

This time the audible gasp emanated from nearly every throat in the room.

"And yes, as you might have guessed, I went to work for him when I was just fifteen." Preston swallowed and forced himself to tell the rest of the story. "I tracked down people that owed him money and . . . did whatever it took to make them pay." Preston studied his notes, not willing to see the expression on any face. "During those years, I practiced safecracking. And I became good at it. Eventually, my boss had me helping out with bank jobs." This time Preston's gaze settled on Aurora. He immediately wished that he hadn't looked at her.

Her expression was slack with shock and disappointment.

He felt his shoulders slump. "I was on my second job, when things went south. But how many of you know that when the devil intends something to go south, the Lord can turn it into north?"

A series of "amens" and "preach its" filled the room. "I was arrested. Sent to jail."

Mrs. Hines's fan snapped back and forth before her face like the tail of an aggravated cat.

"That, my friends, is where I met the Lord. There was this little pastor. Mr. Baker was his name. He came to the jail faithfully every Friday. I went to his meetings simply to escape my cell. For six months I listened to that man share the gospel with me and my fellow inmates.

"Then came the day when I knelt in one of his meetings and gave my heart to the Lord. I dedicated myself from that moment forward to living for the One who died to save me."

"Amen, Parson," Doc called from his seat.

Preston appreciated the supportive comment. With Poppy still glowering at him, and Aurora looking as though he had slapped her, he needed all the support he could get. "I have not looked back. While I finished out my sentence, I devoted myself to studying the Word. And it was in those years that I felt strongly that the Lord was calling me to become a pastor. And so I stand before you today, imperfect by the world's definition, and even more so by God's definition. Just like the apostle Paul, I can confidently declare that I was the chiefest of sinners, mired neck deep in the bog of my sin. But by the grace of God, He reached down, snatched me up by the scruff of my neck, and set my feet on solid ground."

"Praise the Lord," someone said.

"If there is anyone here today who has not committed their life to the Lord, He can do the same for you. If you would like to experience freedom, in the truest sense of the word, I invite you to come down to the altar in just a moment, and I will pray with you."

Preston released a breath. It was done. He had completed what he set out to do. He concluded his sermon by reading a few verses and then closing in prayer.

When he opened his eyes, it was to see Poppy disappearing at the back of the sanctuary.

Disappointment surged through him. Had he really thought that something he said might break through to her? If he hadn't believed it, he had at least hoped it. But it appeared those hopes were futile.

Several of the congregants were already clearing pews to one side of the room and preparing the space for the social.

His gaze drifted to Ewan.

The man stood in his pew, staring toward the front of the room like he might truly be considering on coming to the altar.

Hope fluttered like the wings of a bird.

But then Ewan turned away. He made a comment to Jerry Hines that had both men laughing.

Preston felt the weight of his failure settle deep in his heart. Another week with no repentant sinners at the altar. Was being a parson truly what the Lord had called him to? Most Sundays he figured the Lord could have found a better man to do this job.

Mrs. Hines was already whispering to several of the ladies in the back corner of the sanctuary.

Aurora remained exactly where she'd sat throughout his sermon, staring at a spot on the wall.

Preston took a step toward her, but, at his elbow, someone cleared their throat. He turned to see who it was.

Kane Carver stretched out a hand. "Good word, Parson. All of us have sinned and fallen short of what God wanted for us. I, for one, appreciate being led by a man humble enough to admit his imperfections."

While Preston appreciated the words of affirmation, he couldn't help but wonder if the young man was simply trying to improve his opinion of him.

He thrust the cynical thought aside and accepted Kane's handshake. "I appreciate that. Thank you." He noted how the man's grip wrapped around his, firm and steady. No evidence of guile. "It wasn't easy."

"I'm sure it wasn't. But I'm also certain your parishioners will think even more highly of you now than they did before."

Preston darted a glance to Mrs. Hines, still gossiping in the back corner. He wasn't so sure. Besides, he needed to connect with Aurora. Try to explain. "Thanks, Kane. If you'll excuse me?" He turned.

But Aurora seemed to have shaken off her ponderings, because she was now helping to clear a pew. And before he could navigate his way to her side, the flurry of women laying out food on the tables at the back of the sanctuary engulfed her. After a moment, she looked up, saw him watching her, then darted out of sight into the entryway.

And with her departure, she took most of Preston's heart.

He tucked his notes into his Bible and set it on the shelf in the podium. So much for baring his heart to her later.

She likely didn't want to hear it now.

Chapter Nine

urora was so shocked by what she'd heard from Preston this morning that she could feel her pulse beating faster than usual. It wasn't so much the fact that he had a sinful past, as it was that she had served with him weekly for years now, and he'd never said anything to her about his history.

Her emotions had run the gamut from realizing that it probably wasn't something he was proud of, and therefore would not speak of often, all the way to anger that he had not trusted her enough to share his past, and then back to somewhere in between.

Mechanically, she retrieved her basket from the wagon and returned to the sanctuary to set out the pies that she had baked the evening before. This morning's melancholy had kept her from breakfast, and all the food smelled delicious. Right about now, she could have been tempted to give up an eyetooth for a slice of Dixie's chicken pot pie. Her stomach rumbled loudly at the mere thought, and she laid one hand over it. Hopefully, the social would get going quickly. She would just return her basket to the wagon and then get in line for some food.

The main doors of the sanctuary were clogged with people, however, so after a surreptitious search to make sure she wouldn't bump into Preston, she headed for the side door just off the platform.

The minute she stepped outside, she heard sniffling. She paused, head tilted to listen. Someone behind the church was crying! Aurora stepped to the corner and peered beyond.

Zoe Kastain, back against the wall of the church, stared up at the sky as tears streamed down her cheeks.

Aurora's heart went out to her. "Zoe?" She set her basket on the ground and stepped to her friend's side.

Face crumpling further, Zoe mopped at her cheeks with a limp handkerchief. She opened her mouth as though to speak but then snapped it shut again and pressed her lips together with a little shake of her head.

Gently, cautiously, Aurora wrapped an arm around her shoulders. "I'm so sorry. I know this is hard for you."

Zoe tilted her head against Aurora's with a sniff. "I promised myself I was going to hold it together."

Aurora didn't know what to say to that, so she maintained her silence.

"Now here I am blubbering worse than a baby denied its milk."

Tugging free the hanky she'd tucked into her sleeve this morning, Aurora traded it for Zoe's wet one. "There's nothing wrong with a few tears. They just show how much the one who is departing means to us." With a grimace that she hoped Zoe didn't see, Aurora noted, based on the dampness of Zoe's hanky, that she had shed many more than just a few tears.

To Aurora's surprise, Zoe clenched her teeth and emitted a ferocious growl. "That's just it. I don't want to care about stupid Washington Nolan. He can go off and get himself shot to smithereens, for all I care!"

Aurora blinked and felt her brows rise.

Zoe growled again. "And of course that's all lies. I'm just so mad at him for . . . For . . . oh!" She tossed one hand in the air, hanky fluttering like a white flag of surrender. "I don't even know why I'm so mad at him. I just *am*."

Aurora tucked the inside of her lip between her teeth to prevent a smirk from breaking free. Zoe and Wash had been soft footing around each other for years. She knew exactly why Zoe was mad at Washington Nolan, even if Zoe couldn't put her finger on the reason. She was mad at the man for putting himself in a dangerous situation. Frustrated because fear made her wonder if she would ever see Wash again.

Aurora stepped back and gave her friend's hand a squeeze. "I know it's hard to watch him leave. Just don't miss your opportunity to say goodbye, all right?"

Zoe snuffled and dashed at her tears. "I won't."

"Can I bring you a slice of pie or something?"

Zoe shook her head. "No thank you. I'm feeling better now. Thanks for checking on me. I'll come inside in a few minutes."

Aurora accepted the dismissal for what it was. "All right then, I'll see you in there." She took her basket to the wagon and then returned to the gathering.

She was thankful to hear Preston calling everyone to silence for the prayer and was only slightly ashamed for navigating close to where she knew the line would form for the food. Dixie's chicken pot pie was always quick to go. When the prayer concluded, she looked up to see Belle standing next to her.

"Have you seen Zoe?" Belle asked.

Aurora nodded. "Yes actually, and you might go check on her. She's at the back of the church." She gave Belle a meaningful look that she hoped could be interpreted without her having to say anything more.

Belle's eyes rounded softly, and she dipped her chin in understanding.

As Belle left to check on her sister, Aurora searched the room for Wash, and to her surprise, found him watching her intently. She tipped her head for him to follow Belle and was thankful to see that he'd understood her meaning. He extracted himself from the group gathered around him and trailed in Belle's wake.

Aurora returned her attention to the food, hoping her meddling wouldn't cause more angst. Maybe it would be good for Wash and Zoe to have a few moments of privacy to say their goodbyes.

Belle hurried around the side of the church. Zoe was leaning against the building, arms folded. The dappled shade from the big oak at the back corner of the property, obscured her features until Belle stopped before her.

Zoe met her gaze, and then her face scrunched in misery.

"Oh, Zoe." Belle pulled her sister into an embrace. "I'm right sorry for what you're going through. I know he doesn't mean to hurt you." What she wanted to say was that Washington Nolan didn't deserve even a scrap of Zoe's consideration, but she knew her kind sister would jump to that scoundrel's defense.

Zoe clung to her tightly, and Belle relished the moment of sisterly bonding. "What am I going to do if I never see him again?"

Belle set Zoe at arm's length. She wanted to reassure her Wash would be fine, but they both knew better than most that death could reach out its ugly fingers to find anyone. "One day at a time, hmmm?"

Zoe slid her fingers beneath her eyes. "This is one day that I could gladly skip."

Belle couldn't believe she was coming to Wash's aid. "But you will be upset with yourself if you miss saying goodbye."

Zoe emitted a groan that seemed to come from the very heart of her. "I know. I just need a few minutes. And don't go sending Ma out here. I'll be fine. I promise."

"All right. I'll leave you be, and when I hug Wash goodbye today, I'll be sure to 'accidentally' step on his toe good and hard."

Just as she'd hoped, Zoe laughed. "Maybe I'll do that too. That will give him something to remember us by."

Belle smiled. "Don't think he's going to easily set you from his mind, Zoe."

"She's right."

With a gasp, Belle spun toward the voice, feeling Zoe do the same beside her.

Wash stood at the corner of the building, hat in hand, his soft gaze full of concern and fixed on Zoe.

Belle gave Zoe's arm a squeeze and questioned with a look if Zoe wanted her to stay.

Zoe shook her head.

With a squint of her eyes at Wash, Belle left them to their goodbyes. But she hoped he got the message that she would come for him, no matter how far, if he did anything else to hurt her sister.

As Belle walked away, Zoe's mortification soared. She'd come out here to the back of the church so that no one would see her emotions, and now the very man she'd been trying to avoid until she was more in control stood before her.

She used Aurora's hanky to dry her face. Folded her arms. Tipped up her chin. She didn't know what to say, so she kept her silence, letting her gaze blur against the bark of the oak.

Wash's feet shuffled. "I don't mean to hurt you, Zo, but joining the cavalry is something I've wanted to do since I was just a boy."

Despite her determination not to fight with him on his last day home, she flashed him a glower. The pity in his expression as he took in her countenance made her humiliation rise. Here she was, barely holding it together, and he didn't seem to care at all that he was riding off and leaving her with a broken heart. Certainly wasn't feeling any of those same emotions himself.

That kiss he'd given her all those months ago really must not have meant anything to him at all. If it had, wouldn't he have asked her to marry him? Join him at the fort? There was housing for married people. She knew because she'd researched it. But no! Not a peep from him on the matter.

Well, at least that left her knowing where she stood. It would take time, but she'd get past him. Maybe. Would she? She dropped her eyes closed in despair. "What time is your train?"

"First thing in the morning." A long beat of silence stretched. "I'll miss you like crazy, Zo. And I promise to write. That is, if you say it's okay?"

She nipped her lower lip. Should she let him write? Wouldn't that simply be prolonging her heartache? In a town as small as Wyldhaven, she would easily hear any news that might pertain to him, so for the sake of moving on, she really ought to decline. Yet she couldn't bring herself to do so. "That would be fine. I'll write you back. After all, you wouldn't want to miss out on any of Mrs. Hines's latest antics." She looked up to see if he'd caught her sarcasm.

He smiled, but there was a soft knowing in his gaze that made Zoe tear her focus from his.

"I'll pray for you every day, Washington Nolan. Come home safe, hear?"

"I will, Zo. Things are mostly peaceful now. I doubt I'll even see combat."

But Zoe wasn't fooled by the words. She could hear the note in his voice that said he hoped his statement wasn't true, and she knew that he'd be the first to volunteer for dangerous missions. It was just the kind of man he was.

She dismissed him with a nod. "Best you get back inside, or people are going to wonder where you got to."

Instead of leaving, he stepped closer. "I can't leave with this"—he swung his finger back and forth between them—"whatever this is, hanging between us."

She clenched her teeth. He was just going to have to, because as far as she was concerned, there was no fixing this. He'd kissed her. She'd taken it as a promise and had been waiting months now for something to come of it. And now he was riding off, content to leave her in his past. So obviously that kiss hadn't meant anything to him and she'd just have to deal with it and be more cautious with her heart in the future.

She forced a smile. "We're fine, Wash. I'm just having a hard time with losing one of my dearest friends from school days."

He took another step closer, his gaze capturing hers. His expression said he didn't believe a word of what she'd just said. "Is that so? You didn't act this way when Kin left town."

It was very ungentlemanly of him to point out her lie! She threw back her shoulders and lifted her chin. "How would you know?"

To her chagrin, he reached out and cupped the side of her face with one hand. His thumb stroked over her cheek. His fingers swept a strand of her hair behind her ear. "Because I know you, Zo. We share something. And you're mad at me because you think I don't care. But you're wrong. I just . . ." He shook his head. "Life in the cavalry is no place for a woman."

She jerked away from his touch. "But you didn't give me the choice to make that decision for myself, now did you?"

Wash tossed up his hands and spun on one heel, presenting her with his back. He propped his hands on his hips, his Stetson still gripped in one. "We're young, Zoe. How can we know what we want? Don't you think we both need some time to figure that out?"

The words were the final dagger to her heart. Because she knew exactly what she wanted, and if he didn't know, then it was obvious that he didn't care for her as much as she cared for him.

She blew out a breath. She must release him. He didn't need the burden of worrying about her while he was trying to serve his country. She reached deep inside herself and called upon every thespian element she could muster. "You know, you're right. We are both very young. It's just with Kin leaving, and now you, I'm seeing life changing. And I'm not quite ready for that, I guess. But I'll be fine. My students will keep me busy, and who knows, maybe I'll move to a larger city myself someday soon." She forced a smile. "Ma and Mr. Harrow are growing closer, and I expect they'll marry any day now. And then I'll be free to pursue my own dreams."

He spun to face her. "You might leave town?"

She gestured her uncertainty. "Who knows. Not for some time at least. I'm contracted through the next school year. Forgive me for getting all blubbery?"

He eyed her, and she could tell he was uncertain if her change in attitude was real. "So . . . you'll be fine?"

She pushed out a laugh. "Of course I'll be fine. I truly do wish you all the best, Wash. Now if you'll excuse me"—she spun and started toward the side door—"I'd best get inside and help the ladies with the food."

She left him there, standing alone, in the shade of the old oak tree.

But she did allow herself one peek over her shoulder. And like a camera, she shuttered away the image of him standing, hat clasped against his chest, legs wide in a firm stance, and gaze fixed on her.

Maybe it would be enough to get her through the next few years.

Chapter Ten

ashington stood still for the longest of moments after Zo disappeared around the corner. Finally he turned to look down over the town. Scanned the buildings from the livery on the south end all the way to the newly cleared plot of land on the north side of Wyldhaven Creek, where the new mill was slated to be built.

There had never been a day when he hadn't woken with the certainty of this home. These good people. Not a day when he hadn't ridden through this town and paused to have comfortable conversations with friends he'd known his whole life. Not a day when he couldn't walk a few miles to see Zoe Kastain.

He sighed and gripped the back of his neck. He'd hurt her, and he hadn't meant to. In fact, that was the absolute last thing he'd wanted to do.

Her change of attitude just now puzzled him. He'd been so certain that her angst was because she loved him. He loved her too, but he couldn't take her to Fort Vancouver with him! She would be far away from her family and anyone she knew and spending long, lonely hours by herself at the fort while he was away on sorties. It was no life for a woman, especially not a newlywed.

Even though he was standing here alone, his face burned at the thought.

He'd thought about asking her. My, how many times he'd come close to making the selfish decision to bring her with him. But in the end, he'd managed to quash his selfishness. He would put in his years. And then he'd come home. They'd both be a little older. Wiser. And he'd have money set aside to provide for her in the way he wanted to.

Right now he didn't have two pennies to rub together, but he planned to save most of his cavalry pay. It would be worth it when he returned and could build them a home.

It really was the best plan in the long run.

Yet somehow, in all his planning, he'd still managed to hurt the very woman he'd been trying to protect.

"Wash?! You out here, son?" Pa's bellow emanated from the front steps of the church.

"Yes, sir. Coming!" He dusted his pants with his hat, more out of habit than necessity, then settled it on his head and made his way back to the front of the church.

Maybe he'd try to find time to speak to Zoe again before he left.

At least she'd agreed to let him write to her. For a moment he'd been afraid she would decline.

"Here he is! Told you he wouldn't have gone far!" Pa's words were no less loud than they had been a moment ago.

With a smile, Wash reached past Pa to shake the hand of Mr. Olann, Wyldhaven's new banker, and then tip his hat to the man's wife.

"If you'll pardon us," the man said, "we need to be leaving. We're expecting a shipment later this week, and I still have a fair bit of work to do at the bank." He leaned close and spoke conspiratorially. "Just don't tell the Parson I'm working on a Sunday, aye?" He laughed heartily.

Wash smiled and offered his farewells, but his mind was only half on the conversation for his gaze had settled on Zoe

Kastain across the yard. She was having a quiet conversation with Taulby Eklund, the new man who'd come to town to build the mill. Wash swallowed.

The man was just a bit older than they were. He was a strapping blond giant with an easy smile and broad shoulders that stretched the fabric of his shirt. Wash had seen him pick up logs that would have taxed horses and move them around like they were nothing more than firewood. He'd never seen a stronger man.

And until this very moment, Wash had really liked him.

In her room down at the boardinghouse, Poppy seethed and paced and fumed as she marched a path from the door to the window, then stomped the other direction, only to repeat the process. She wanted to scream. Wanted to throw things. But she couldn't do either of those because she had to maintain her cover as a respectable woman. Besides, she didn't have the money to pay for any damages she might cause to the room.

Finally, when she tired of pacing and still had no answers, she paused before the window to stare down at the street.

What now? Her plan had been to slip the information about Preston's history to the right ears at the right moment, but he'd beat her to it. Taken her legs out from under her. Now if she tried to bring it up, she would simply look like she was trying to lower people's estimation of him, and no one ever took kindly to that.

She had to come up with a different plan. A con that would see her through until she could get more information about the bank and when the shipment of gold was set to arrive. She also needed to buy some food and supplies for her men who were camped in the foothills outside of town.

She had another problem too. The need for a safecracker. Because she was going to need one to get her hands on that money. The coach carrying the gold would no doubt be heavily guarded, and she and her few men wouldn't be any match. So that left out taking the money on its way to Wyldhaven.

Besides, an attack in open country could get people killed—maybe even her. And she wasn't about to risk that. No, her plan had been good—to break into the bank quietly at night, have Preston open the safe, and then escape town before anyone was even the wiser. But now . . .

She closed her eyes in despair as she remembered the sincerity that had rung in Preston's voice during his sermon. Because that was the moment she'd understood he truly had been deluded by this whole religious thing. She could hardly believe it! He'd always been so levelheaded and practical. Never one to fall for a con himself. And what was religion if not a—

Her eyes shot wide.

Yes! Yes indeed!

What was religion if not the biggest con of all?!

Her lips spread in a full smile, and she felt the first burst of joy she'd felt in weeks. She pinched some color into her cheeks, straightened her skirts, and assessed herself in the swivel mirror in the corner of the room.

She gave a little nod.

How Babbo would laugh at her were he here to see what she was about to do. But she didn't see any other way, and all that mattered was for her to get back into his good graces. And if this was what it took to restore Babbo's opinion of her? So be it.

She left her room and headed back up the hill to the social. She needed to find Preston.

Preston chatted with Doc Griffin and Sheriff Callahan on the lawn outside the church. He'd eaten his fill from the many delicious dishes, and now, between the tossing and turning he'd done the night before and the stress of this morning's sermon, he was looking forward to getting home and resting. He couldn't remember the last time he'd taken an afternoon nap, but today he sure was tempted. He'd have to figure out a way to occupy Tommy, though, to make it happen.

He was glad that he and Aurora had settled on having a conversation tomorrow. As tired as he was, if he tried to speak to her today, he was likely to bumble it badly. Maybe while he rested this afternoon, he could think through what he wanted to say to her and lay out a plan.

Of course, he couldn't leave until all the cleanup was done, and that would be at least a couple hours yet, since no one seemed ready to wind down.

Both Doc and Sheriff Reagan had made it clear they appreciated his confession in church this morning, something that filled him with gratefulness. If it came down to a few members wanting him to leave, having these two speak up for him would go a long way to calming the situation.

Yet if it was going to cause a division in the church? He would sooner step down than demand to be kept on.

If it came to that, what would he do? He certainly couldn't go back to his former profession. Which reminded him . . .

"Reagan, I've been meaning to mention . . . The woman who arrived on the stage yesterday?"

"Yeah?"

"There you are, Parson!"

Poppy stopped by his side.

He blinked down at her. He'd seen her run out of the church earlier in what he thought was a fit of anger, or at least frustration, yet now tears ran down her cheeks. Had she been hurt?

Every protective instinct rose to the fore, even though he knew from experience that Poppy was well able to take care of herself. "Are you okay? What's wrong?" Anytime they had played together as children, her father had enjoined Preston to guard her with his life. A task he'd always given himself to wholeheartedly. The instinct returned, like a bear ready to fight.

Both Reagan and Doc scanned the crowd for danger.

Poppy smiled through her tears. "Nothing is wrong. Everything is right!"

Releasing a breath, Preston narrowed his eyes. Despite the fact that his heart hammered with hope, his caution begged for circumspection.

"Your sermon . . ." Poppy laid one slender hand over her chest. "I'm not sure what to say exactly, but it was as though it reached deep inside me and opened my eyes to what a sinful woman I've been—am still."

Speechless, Preston felt his jaw go slack. Could it really be? His mind flashed back to the many times when they were children when Poppy had manufactured tears from thin air to extract herself from one sort of trouble or another.

He felt his doubt—and consequently guilt—mount as she tipped her face to the sky and closed her eyes.

Both hands now over her heart, she said, "I prayed. Confessed my sins, like you said. Like you told me to do so many times before you moved here." She straightened and beamed him a watery smile. "And I feel like . . . like . . . Oh, I don't even have words to describe it!" Her laughter tinkled through the afternoon gathering, drawing the gazes of several nearby.

Doc and the sheriff looked to Preston, waiting for him to respond. He couldn't seem to find his voice.

Doc was the first to react. "That's wonderful!" He reached out a hand and shook Poppy's with gusto. "Simply wonderful. God is good."

More tears sprang into Poppy's eyes. "I can hardly believe how magnificent I feel."

The sheriff shook her hand next. "Welcome to the family, Miss . . ."

Preston knew he should make introductions, but he still couldn't seem to find his tongue.

After a moment, Poppy supplied, "Scarlatti. Poppy Scarlatti." Her demure gaze settled on Preston. "Well? Don't you have anything to say?"

Had a more faithless man ever walked the face of the earth? He'd given a sermon. Hoped and prayed people would respond to the salvation call. Been disappointed when no one had.

Yet now, when Poppy stood before him saying she had indeed responded, he didn't believe a word she said.

The sheriff and the doctor studied him, brows furrowed.

"Parson?" Reagan asked. "Everything all right?"

Preston jolted into action. He could second-guess her true repentance later after he saw whether her life was bearing fruit. He reached a hand to Poppy. "Forgive me for my surprise. I'm real happy to hear you say so, Poppy. Real happy."

Her soft hand settled warmly into his. "Thank you for your sermon. I don't know what it was that you said, but it was as though a lantern suddenly ignited in my soul."

Preston looked up to see Aurora watching him. He searched her face, withdrawing his hand from Poppy's.

The side of one lip tucked between her teeth, Aurora glanced from him to Poppy and back again, and for some reason she seemed to be carrying the weight of the world on her shoulders. Maybe she wasn't as indifferent to him as he'd feared after this morning's sermon? That thought alone lifted his spirits. Aurora tore her gaze from his and, lifting her skirts, took the steps up to the church doors and disappeared inside.

Preston only realized that another awkward silence had descended when Doc cleared his throat.

Doc offered Poppy a smile. "That's the way it often happens. Let me introduce you to my wife. Dixie!" he called with a happy laugh. "Come meet this woman. She just gave her heart to the Lord!"

Retreating to the church steps, Preston watched as a cluster of women surrounded Poppy, all offering congratulations and rejoicing over her salvation.

Reagan stopped by his side. "What is it?"

Arms folded, Preston sighed. "Would you think me the most faithless parson in the world if I said I doubt her story?"

With an assessing squint, Reagan watched the cacophony for a moment. "My pa used to say, 'Never trust a rattler just because it's lost its rattle.'"

Preston blew out a sigh. "That about sums it up. It's not that I don't believe the Lord can change a heart like hers. I guess we'll just have to wait and see what fruit comes from this."

"You were about to tell me something about her before she interrupted."

Preston nodded. Met Reagan's gaze. "She's the daughter of the mob boss I worked for back in Boston."

"I wondered if she was the one you meant in your sermon." As if on instinct, he adjusted his gun belt. "What's she doing out here?"

"That's why I wanted to let you know. In my opinion, today's confession of faith notwithstanding, the law should be on high alert, at least until we discern whether her confession of faith is real. When is the bank slated to open?"

Reagan frowned, and though it lingered for only a split second, Preston felt the distrust and doubt that flashed through the sheriff's eyes like a dagger to his heart. After this morning's sermon, it was to be expected, he supposed.

He lifted his hands. "Right. You don't have to tell me. Just . . . I think it's highly likely the money arriving for the bank might be the reason she's in town."

"I told Zeb it was a bad idea to announce the opening of the bank." Reagan looked chagrinned. "And I'm sorry. I truly don't think you would ever be part of a bank robbery . . . again."

Preston couldn't withhold a wry smirk.

One hand going to the back of his neck, Reagan gave him a look of consternation. "It's just going to take us all some time to get used to this new information about your past."

"I understand. Truly I do."

Reagan scoured the crowd. "I'd better find Zane and Joe and talk to them about your concerns."

"I think that might be a good idea." His gaze darted to Poppy once more. She chatted animatedly with Dixie and Charlotte, who both laughed at something she said. Preston's lips pressed together. "I think that would be a very good idea."

Chapter Eleven

Aurora clenched her fists and marched into the sanctuary to start packing away food and carrying dishes down to the diner. The final prayer had been said. Washington Nolan and his family had already left, and many others were gathering their dishes and leftovers to do the same.

She was weary and ready to get back to her little room at the ranch, but she never left until the last dish was clean. Dixie donated her boardinghouse dishes to the church gatherings, and it wouldn't be fair to leave her with the bulk of the cleanup. With all the women working, it wouldn't take much longer.

She pulled in a deep inhale and forced her clenched fists to relax. Her tension was born from anger with herself. She felt like the lowest kind of creature.

What kind of woman was she to be jealous of another simply because she claimed to have given her heart to the Lord? Aurora ought to be rejoicing with Jesus over a sinner come home, yet all she could muster was a deep dread and a burning jealousy, because Preston had history with the woman, and how easy it would be for them to build on that foundation.

Poppy, with her thick black hair, generous curves, and infectious laugh, had done nothing to earn Aurora's dislike, yet earn it she had nonetheless. Peeved with her own pettiness, Aurora stacked dirty plates into a basket. All she could think was that she wished the woman had never come.

Cora Harrison already bustled around the sanctuary, clearing dishes and wiping tables. She looked up with a smile that faltered the moment her gaze settled on Aurora. "What is it? Are you all right?"

Aurora sighed and plunked onto one of the benches. "I'm a terrible person."

Cora set her rag down and eased onto the bench beside her. "I know for a fact that's not true."

"It is. And since the Lord looks on the heart, I know He sees it too."

"Ah." Cora smiled. "Is this about our dear parson and the red vixen? A touch envious perhaps?"

Aurora blinked, taken aback by Cora's bold statement. She searched the woman's face.

Cora shrugged one shoulder. "You thought your feelings for the man were a secret?" She winked. "I've a good nose for people, and you and the parson . . . there's something there. He has feelings for you too, you know."

Aurora scoffed and rolled her eyes at her friend, plucking at the hem of her sleeve. "You'll forgive me for doubting your self-proclaimed 'good nose' on that subject." Preston seemed to think of her as his charge and nothing more.

"We'll see." Cora's smile remained undaunted. "As for your feelings about the newcomer, I have to concur. There's something . . . off about that woman."

Aurora nodded. "That's how I felt too, but she just told everyone outside that she gave her heart to the Lord today."

Cora's brows lifted. "Well, I certainly hope it's true."

Feeling her guilt rise to the fore, Aurora brushed at a wrinkle on her skirt. "I ought to hope it true. But all I can feel is doubt."

"And jealousy." Cora said the words not as a question but as a statement.

And Aurora couldn't help but laugh. Cora's bluntness was partly what made her so likable. She never said anything unkind, but she had a way of stating truths that no one else wanted to face, and doing so in a manner that was all at once tactful and clarifying.

Shoulders slumping, she sighed. "Yes. I suppose some of that too, though I have been offered no hope to give me the right to such an emotion."

Cora patted her knee and rose to resume her task of stacking dishes. "Don't you worry on that count. Preston is going to come around now that he knows you're leaving town. I just have a feeling about that."

With a frown, Aurora pondered his request to stop by the ranch and speak to her tomorrow. He hadn't said what exactly he wanted to speak to her about, however. Could it be a proclamation of love?

Her pulse thundered in her ears. After all these years of pining for him, wouldn't that be a shock, if it were true? She dismissed the thought with a snort as she rose to follow Cora to the diner with a basketful of dirty dishes. She highly doubted he wanted to speak to her about anything so intimate.

The notion was reinforced by the memory of the way he'd jumped to Poppy's defense when he believed she'd been hurt.

If anything, the man probably wanted to tell her how thrilled he was to have his first love arrive in town. After all, since he still considered Aurora his charge, he'd likely want her to get on well with the woman.

Aurora rubbed at the region to the left of her breastbone, where it felt like a knife might be protruding from her chest.

Saints preserve her. She'd better prepare her heart for whatever eventuality might be bringing Preston to her door.

Zoe woke with the chatter of the birds outside her window on Monday morning and bolted upright in her bed. Jinx leapt to his feet from where he slept on the rug by her bedroom door. Patting the dog's head, she pondered. Her plan had been to let the goodbye she'd shared with Wash on Sunday be the last, but this morning she found that she couldn't tolerate the way they'd left things.

Decision made, she leapt off the bed and hurried into her dress. She yanked her brush through her hair and pinned it up as she rushed to the living room, Jinx on her heels.

Ma must have heard her, even though Zoe had tried to be quiet, because Ma stepped into the living room, tucking her night robe around herself. "Zoe?"

Tugging her boots on while Jinx waited patiently by the door, Zoe cinched the laces with quick movements. "I'm riding to the train station. I'll be back in a couple hours. Well in time for the school day."

Ma's lips pressed into a thin line. "You are going to wear yourself out, traipsing all over the country before the sun is even up."

"I can't let him leave without . . . Well, we simply didn't part on the best of terms yesterday, and I can't let him go with that hanging on my conscience."

Ma headed for the kitchen. "Saddle the horse. I'll make you some coffee."

Zoe darted to her, threw her arms around her shoulders, and pecked her on the cheek. "Thanks for understanding, Ma. I'm more than blessed to have you!"

Grabbing her coat from the peg, she dashed out the kitchen door and ran to the barn. Jinx yipped a couple times in excitement, as though he knew he was about to have the pleasure of a morning run.

Their mare wasn't as young as she used to be, but she was a good horse and would get Zoe to the station quicker than if she tried to go by foot. However, irritated to be pulled from her stall this early on a chilly morning, the mare swung her head around and nipped at Zoe's hip.

"Go on with you, Lilac." Zoe pushed her head away. "I promise to give you an extra scoop of oats for your trouble once we get back home."

Ma waited for her, steaming cup in hand, when Zoe stopped by the kitchen porch, leading the horse behind her. Jinx dipped his head and watched her, just waiting for the command to run.

Zoe gulped the contents of the cup so quickly that she nearly scalded the inside of her mouth.

"Slow down, child. You aren't going to miss the train. You've plenty of time."

Zoe handed her back the cup. "Thanks, Ma." She didn't add that she was concerned about having time to actually have a conversation with Wash, not just waving goodbye from the platform.

"Let's run, Jinx!" The dog didn't have to be asked twice, and Zoe pushed the mare harder than she normally would. She was relieved to see the station come into sight, with the long body of the train still stretching, unmoving, into the distance.

The Nolans' wagon and horses were tied up at one of the hitching rails, so she knew they had already arrived.

Patting her mare on the neck, she looped her reins around the crossbar. "I won't be long. Then we'll get you back to your warm stall." She motioned to Jinx. "Stay."

He gave a soft whimper but did sit by the mare's side.

Hoisting her skirts, she hurried up the short set of stairs to the train platform. As she searched the small crowd, she feared that Wash had already boarded the train, but then a porter with a pile of luggage on a trolly moved, and she saw Wash hugging his pa and shaking each of his brothers' hands.

Relieved, Zoe hurried their way.

Wash must have seen her coming from the corner of his eye, for before she even reached him, he turned to face her.

Her heart threatened to stop and then changed its mind and rushed ahead of itself into an all-out tumble. Her mouth was dry, and her throat felt like a fist had closed around it. "Morning," she managed.

Mr. Nolan clapped Wash on the shoulder one last time, then nudged his three younger sons down the platform. "We best get back to get our chores done before the boys need to get to school." He directed the last words at her with a lift of his brow, as though to question whether there actually would be school today.

Zoe smiled at the two younger boys, Grant and Lincoln. "I'll see you at the schoolhouse, right on time."

She heard the two boys groan as they followed their father down the platform. Jackson guffawed and gave his younger brothers a hard time. The sound of their scuffling faded into the background as Zoe met Washington's gaze.

He stepped toward her, searching her face. "Morning. I didn't expect to see you here today."

A tall man, lugging a large suitcase, stepped between them before hurrying to climb aboard the nearby passenger car.

Zoe took a step forward to minimize the distance separating them, seeing Wash do the same.

She moistened her lips. "In all honesty, I didn't plan to be here, but then . . ." She lifted one shoulder. "I couldn't live with the way we parted company yesterday. I'm sorry for the way I spoke to you."

Wash drew closer. "You've nothing to apologize for."

"No, I do. I was short tempered and cross, and—"

Wash took her hand.

Snatching a breath, Zoe darted her tongue over her lips.

He curled his fingers around hers and pressed their clasped hands to his chest. "This parting is going to be hard on both of us, Zo. But we'll make it through it. Before you know it, I'll be riding back into town." His gaze was soft and warm on her face. He searched her features, as though memorizing them.

Zoe swallowed. She highly doubted it was going to feel like "before she knew it." Maybe for him. He would be away, busy, working hard. She would simply be stuck here in limbo, waiting.

With his free hand, Wash reached near her cheek and fingered a strand of hair that had come loose from her bun. Zoe sighed. Her fine hair was forever slipping from the pins that tried to constrain it. She should have thought to fix her appearance before rushing onto the platform. She started to pull away to fix it.

But Wash tightened his grip. "You're as pretty as a picture, Zo." He slid his fingers down the strand of her hair. "This moment—this image of you—is going to linger with me and help me make it through."

Zoe felt her face warm, even as she blew a sound of dismissal. "Do you forgive me, Wash? I need to hear you say it."

He shook his head. "Not gonna say I forgive you when there is nothing to forgive." He paused for a beat. "Wait for me, Zo? I'm gonna come back for you. I promise."

She pressed her lips together and willed herself to remain rooted. It would do no good to throw her arms around him and beg to go with him. "You don't need to ask. I'll be right here."

"When all those men come calling, you beat them back with the business end of a broom. You tell them you're spoken for."

Zoe held her breath. Scrutinized his face. If she couldn't go with him, this was the next best thing. "Am I? Spoken for?"

She saw Wash's throat constrict. "You are, if you'll have me."

She closed her eyes. Leaned forward and pressed her forehead to his broad, strong chest. "Of course I'll have you, you numbskull. And of course I'll wait." She felt the warmth of Wash's arms sweep around her, settle gently into place like a favorite blanket. His breath caressed the side of her head, and his lips pressed ever so softly to the spot just above her ear.

"All aboard!" a conductor yelled.

Neither of them moved. Wash's heart beat a steady rhythm beneath her palm.

Travelers scrambled around them, calling final farewells and clambering aboard the passenger car. The engine chuffed as it came to life, and Zoe wanted to scream her protest.

Finally Wash set her from him. Hands still gripping her shoulders, he looked down at her. "You're strong, Zo. If something happens to me, just know that I . . ." He swallowed. "I love you. Will love you to my final breath."

Despite her resolve not to cry, she felt tears well up to sting her eyes. "You're not going to die, Washington Nolan. Do you hear me? If you die, I'm going to come find you and kill you myself."

He chuckled. "Understood." Still, he didn't release her. He continued to search her face. "Zoe?"

She took a breath.

"All aboard!" the conductor called again, louder this time.

"I love you too, Wash. Come back to me."

He blew out a puff of air, then nodded. "I will."

The train rolled forward, the chuffing louder now.

Wash released her, snatched up his bag, and leapt onto the step. He hung on to the brass support and looked back at her.

Lifting her skirts, she strode down the platform, keeping up with the train. She memorized him. The taut stretch of his sleeve over the bulge of his bicep. The way the dark stubble coated his jaw in proof that he hadn't shaved for a few days. The way his broad shoulders tapered to a narrow waist that swept down to the sturdy specially crafted boots that Kin Davis had given him as a parting gift when he'd left town at Christmas. The way he leaned out of the passenger car's door, studying her the same way she was studying him.

The platform ended, and she had to stop. She leaned against the rail and lifted her hand for one last farewell.

Wash waved, and then he disappeared inside the car.

Her heart fell, and she rubbed both palms over her face, sealing in the memory of him, the image of him, the scent of him.

God, please don't let this be the last time I see him. Go with him. Protect him. Bring him back to me.

She remained at the rail until the train was nothing more than a smoke-spewing speck in the distance.

Finally, with a heavy heart, she fetched her mare and started for home.

The moments between now and the first letter from him would be the longest moments of her entire life.

oppy greeted Monday morning with a twofold plan. First, she headed for the bank. The business wasn't open, of course. But she could see Mr. Olann behind the counter and tapped on the window to get his attention. When he looked up, she offered the friendliest smile she could muster.

The man hurried across the room and opened the door. "Good morning, ma'am."

"Good morning. I saw you at the services yesterday, but we didn't get a chance to meet. I'm Poppy Scarlatti." She held out her hand.

He accepted her shake. "Olann. Merle Olann. How can I help you?"

Poppy reached into the reticule dangling from her wrist and withdrew the wad of cash within. It was the last of her money, but the man didn't need to know that. She stretched the roll toward him. "I would like to deposit this, please." She infused naivety into her tone.

Mr. Olann blinked and stuttered. "Well . . . Uh . . . We . . . Well . . ."

Poppy drew the cash back toward herself. "Oh, do forgive me. Perhaps your bank does not work like the one back in Boston?" The role of *helpless woman* was one she played well.

It made a man feel like he had the upper hand when he thought he was helping a woman in distress.

Thankfully, Mr. Olann seemed to be the same as any other man. "Forgive me." He rushed to reassure her. "We do operate the same as any bank. That is . . . At least we will once we open."

"Oh!" Poppy inspected the interior of the bank, as though she were a little lost. "So I can deposit my money once you open?"

The man nodded. A look of relief crossed his face. "Yes. Just so."

Poppy returned the wad of cash to her reticule, feeling relieved to once again have it tucked safely away. "Well, I'll just have to return when you open. Forgive me for arriving so early. What time should I come back?"

Mr. Olann's look of discomfiture was back in full force. "Sorry. I'm afraid I'm not communicating well this morning." He offered a chagrined smile. "We will open next Tuesday."

"Tomorrow?"

"No, ma'am. A week from tomorrow."

Tuesday.

Satisfaction spread.

The money would likely arrive a few days before that. Not the day before, because they would need time to do the accounting to make sure everything was as it should be. Not on the Sabbath, for the guarded coach wouldn't run on that day. Maybe Saturday? Could be Friday.

Mr. Olann assessed her, as though to decipher whether she'd understood him.

Poppy rounded her eyes and her lips, then giggled. "Oh my! I guess I won't wait on the front step in that case."

Mr. Olann chuckled. "No, ma'am. That would be somewhat of a long wait."

"Indeed. But never fear, Mr. Olann. For I will be your first customer." Just not in the way he expected.

"That'll be fine. Fine. You planning on staying in town for a while?" He thrust out an arm to urge her back to the door.

Poppy followed his prompting. "It is a very beautiful town, isn't it? If I'm honest, I hadn't planned to stay for long. More of a stopover on my way to Seattle. But . . ." She stepped onto the front porch of the bank and searched the street, feeling Mr. Olann watching her. "I like it here so much that I may just be here a little longer than I expected."

"The place does grow on you, Miss Scarlatti. If you do decide to stay and need a small loan to build a place, you look me up. The bank will be happy to help a fine, upstanding woman such as yourself."

"Why, thank you. I will definitely keep that in mind." She dipped the man a little curtsy. "I won't keep you any longer. Good day to you."

"Ma'am." He gave her a sketch of a bow.

Poppy left him there and headed toward the livery. A thin smile tipped up her lips. Already she had accomplished her first goal for the day. She knew the approximate timing of the delivery of money for the Wyldhaven bank.

Now on to her next task.

Aurora was just finishing the milking in the barn on Monday morning when she heard a loud shout. "Help! Someone, help!"

Her head snapped up and she almost tipped the bucket of milk in her hurry to get to the door to see what might be happening. Outside the barn, she set the bucket on the rock ledge by the pump and searched the surrounding area.

There! A man stood in the field that lay in the direction of the Kastain place. He waved an arm above his head to get her attention. Then cupped his hands to his mouth and yelled, "Bring bandages!"

"Coming!" She ran with the milk bucket to the house.

Liora, who stood holding Law and searching the yard through the window above the sink, startled when she burst in. "What on earth?"

Aurora shook her head. "Not sure. A man is yelling for bandages. I should probably bring water too. I think it's the new mill owner."

"Land sakes! And Joe already gone on his rounds!" Liora flapped a hand toward the empty bucket by the door. "You get the water, I'll fetch bandages."

Aurora grabbed up the empty bucket and dashed back to the pump. By the time she had the bucket three quarters full, Liora was by her side, shoving bandages into her arms.

"Here, take these and run. I'm right behind you."

Aurora's heart hammered as she dashed up the hill as fast as she could while at the same time trying not to spill the water.

As she approached, she saw that it was indeed Mr. Eklund and he was kneeling on the ground beside—

"Zoe!" Aurora fell to her knees by her friend who was sprawled on the ground, staring up at the sky. "What happened?"

Jinx, Zoe's dog who paced nearby, growled low in his throat. His gaze roved from Mr. Eklund to Aurora and back again.

Zoe reached out a hand to the dog. "It's okay, Jinx. They're here to help." Tears streaked past Zoe's ears and into the flames of her curls that fanned against the grass of the field. She motioned to a caved-in gopher hole. "The ground gave way beneath us, and Lilac took a tumble. I hit my head." Her gaze transferred to Mr. Eklund. "Thankfully, Mr. Eklund was driving by on the road just as I fell." Her gaze skipped beyond

Mr. Eklund's shoulder. "Is she going to be alright? I'd never be able to forgive myself if something happened to Lilac!"

Lips pressed together, Aurora took note of the Kastains' old horse, limping nearby.

Mr. Eklund propped his weight against hands pressed to his thighs. "I have looked over her and she seems a back leg to have injured. She doesn't want pressure to put on it, but broken it seems not to be. Do you want I should put her down?"

"No!" Aurora and Zoe chimed the word together.

"Thank you, Mr Eklund." Zoe started to sit up but winced and reached for her head.

"Here. Let me help you. Take it slow." Aurora curled an arm behind Zoe. And when Mr. Eklund leaned close to help, Aurora noted he was much more muscular than she'd realized. He took Zoe's hand, which disappeared into his like a child's might into a baseball mitt, and together they helped Zoe sit up.

Even kneeling down, the man towered over them. He patted Zoe's small hand gently with broad blunt fingers, as he met Aurora's gaze. "What action to take beyond removing her boot, I was not sure." The man had a soothing tenor to his voice and with his pleasant Swedish accent, Aurora could have listened to him talk all day. "But, her ankle, I think, needs a look."

Zoe reached to inch up the hem of her skirt. "Yes, I'm afraid it does, at that. Hi, Liora."

Only then did Aurora realize Liora had arrived.

Liora settled Law more comfortably on her hip and assessed the scene. "Morning. What happened?"

While Mr. Eklund caught Liora up on the events, Aurora's hands moved to examine Zoe's ankle almost before her mind had comprehended the injury. The joint was swollen to nearly three times its normal size. Gently she pressed and probed. Before her mother had passed and she'd run from the logging camp to avoid being forced into service as a lady of the night, Aurora had often been the one to bandage and care for the injured or sick. Carefully, she watched Zoe's face as she angled her foot first one way and then the other. Zoe winced, but she didn't gasp or cry out. Those were good signs.

"I think your foot is badly sprained but not broken. Of course, Doc will have the final say on that. For now, I'll wrap it up good and tight. But first, let's soak it in this cold water. It will help to dull the pain and lessen the swelling."

Mr. Eklund gave Aurora a nod of satisfaction. "The cold . . . This is good. My da, he used to this do for the cows."

Aurora pinged a glance off of Zoe. They both resisted a smirk. She highly doubted the man realized he'd just compared Zoe to his father's cattle. She set the bucket into the area that had caved in, and lowered Zoe's ankle into it.

Zoe gasped and flailed her hands to distract herself from the pain.

"Sorry. It will feel better in just a few moments, I promise."

While Zoe's foot soaked, and Aurora wrapped her ankle, Mr. Eklund examined Lilac's back leg again. He took her reins and led her a few steps. The horse limped a little, but was willing to put weight on the foot this time. He gave a satisfactory nod and tied Lilac to the back of his wagon, which was on the road a few paces away. "We will go slow on the way to your house, Miss Zoe. And I think your Lilac will recover."

"I'm very relieved to hear that." Zoe reached her hands up so Aurora could haul her to her feet.

But Mr. Eklund beat her to it. "If you don't mind?" At Zoe's nod, he stooped and scooped her up as though she weighed no more than a puppy. As gently as a papa with a newborn babe, he settled her onto the back bench of his wagon with her legs stretched along the seat. "Let us get you home." He hauled himself up to the front bench.

Aurora lifted a hand of farewell and Zoe smiled. "Thank you for your help. The pain is considerably less. I'll have to remember your trick."

Aurora nodded. "Epsom salts dissolved in warm water will also help alleviate the pain. You can alternate between the cold and the warm every other time."

"Thank you. Ma has some, so I'll do that too."

"Get up." Mr. Eklund clucked to the horses.

And as they set off on the road toward Zoe's house with Jinx loping along beside, Aurora was struck by how satisfied she felt to have helped Zoe in her time of need.

Chapter Thirteen

elle woke early Monday morning to the sounds of clattering in the kitchen. She crawled out of bed, hastily dressed, and went out to help. With Mr. Harrow coming for breakfast and Zoe needing to leave first thing for her teaching job, Ma would need all the help in the kitchen that she could get.

Belle was surprised when she reached the kitchen to find Ma working alone. Zoe was usually the first of any of them out of bed.

"Morning, Ma. Zoe not up yet?"

Ma looked up from the sideboard, where she was chopping an onion. "She left hours ago for the train station but hasn't returned yet. I'm getting a little worried about her."

Belle frowned. "She went by herself?"

Ma blew a strand of hair out of her face and lifted one shoulder. "Jinx went with her, and he'd have come home if something happened to her, don't you think?"

"Probably."

"I couldn't deny her one last goodbye with Wash." Ma studied the yard outside the window with concern furrowing her brow. "But perhaps I should have."

Belle was already reaching for her jacket. "I'll go look for her."

"No!" Ma snapped. "Then there will be two of you that I'm worried about."

Belle studied Ma, despairing of what the best solution was. They couldn't just leave Zoe out there all on her own, potentially in trouble. But neither did she want to add to Ma's worry.

Mr. Harrow's soft brown eyes came to mind. "What if I go straight to town and ask Mr. Harrow to come with me to find her?"

Ma dropped the knife with a clatter next to the pile of chopped onions. She propped her wrists on both hips. "Do you think I'm being overly concerned? Perhaps she went straight to the schoolhouse?"

"The only way we'll know is if one of us goes looking for her. But I don't want to cause you more worry."

Ma blew out a breath as the twins and Aidan stepped into the kitchen. "Yes, you're correct. Mr. Harrow should be here at any moment. Then you and he can go searching for Zoe. Aidan and the girls will help me with morning chores and breakfast."

As if summoned by Ma's words, Mr. Harrow knocked on the front door at that very moment. Belle knew it had to be him. If it had been Zoe arriving home, she would have simply entered, and no one else would be knocking on their door this early in the morning.

But when she opened the door, she was shocked to see Taulby Eklund standing on the porch, holding Zoe. He had one arm beneath her knees and the other behind her shoulders.

"Zoe!" Belle stepped back and held the door wide.

Zoe, arms draped around Taulby's neck, gave Belle a teary, sheepish smile.

"Please come in," Belle said to Taulby.

Jinx bumped his head against Taulby's ankles, as though herding him into the room, then trotted in on his heels.

"What happened?" Belle directed the question to Zoe.

Zoe motioned for Taulby to set her on the couch. "Just set me there. That's fine, thank you. I'm so thankful you came along when you did, Mr. Eklund."

"As am I, Miss Kastain. As am I." The large man set her gently on the couch, as though she were the most delicate of porcelain in his big hands.

Belle waited to one side. Her concern mounted as she saw Zoe wince when she adjusted her position. And there were still her tears to account for. Ma bustled in from the kitchen, while Sharon and Shiloh and Aidan peered into the room from the kitchen doorway.

"Zoe! Land sakes, child. I've been right worried about you. What happened?"

Mr. Eklund shuffled his feet. "I'll leave you to do the explaining, Miss Zoe. I'll go and take care of your horse."

There was something about the way he said "take care" that raised Belle's awareness. She pinned Zoe with a searching gaze as Mr. Eklund left the house.

Large tears spilled down Zoe's cheeks. "Oh, Ma! I'm so sorry. This is all my fault."

Sympathy fueled Belle's consternation.

Ma rushed forward. "Hush, child. Whatever happened, you're alive, and that's all that matters to us."

Hurrying to the chest beneath the window to fetch a throw, Belle could no longer withhold her curiosity. "What did happen?"

Zoe's tear tracks glistened in the morning light from the window. "I'm so stupid. I just feel terrible. I was hurrying back from the train station and decided to cut across that old field. I knew Mr. Harrow would be here for breakfast and that you all would need my help. I didn't want to push Lilac too hard, and I thought the shortcut would save some time. But . . . I don't rightly know what happened. I didn't see a hole, but suddenly we were both on the ground." Zoe shuddered. "Thankfully, Mr. Eklund happened to be riding by on his way to the mill. He saw our distress and came to my aid. I think a gopher tunnel must have given way beneath Lilac's hoof. Mr. Eklund says he doesn't think her leg is broken, but he also offered to put her down." Zoe's gaze searched first Ma's and then Belle's as if to see if they had understood her words.

Belle raised one hand to her mouth, eyes dropping closed. Even before Zoe said her next words, Belle knew what they would be.

"He doesn't think she'll ever be able to be ridden again, Ma. I'm so sorry."

From the kitchen doorway, Sharon gasped. She fled through the living room and down the hall toward the bedroom she shared with Shiloh. Her door slammed. Belle's heart went out to her. Of all of them, Sharon was the most softhearted. The thought of Lilac in pain would torment her.

Ma looked torn between Zoe and Sharon.

Resting a hand on Ma's shoulder, Belle offered, "I'll go to her."

Ma reached out to stop her. "Shiloh, please see to your sister."

With a roll of her eyes, Shiloh tromped down the hall in Sharon's wake.

"Do you think she's the best one to send?" Belle asked.

With a hand pressed to her forehead, Ma looked frazzled. She stared at Zoe but didn't really seem to see her.

Belle took her arm. "Here, Ma. Sit down. Zoe's going to be fine, aren't you, Zoe?"

Reaching out, Zoe squeezed Ma's fingers. "Yes, I'm truly going to be fine. It's just a sprain, I think. Aurora McClure even soaked it and wrapped it already. It will be fine until we can get Doc to take a look at it."

Belle was thankful to see Ma sink into the chair she directed her to.

Another knock sounded on the front door just then.

"Aidan, get the door please," Belle instructed as she bent to assess Zoe's injury. When she lifted Zoe's hem and caught sight of her sister's ankle, she could tell it was bad from how fat the bandage was. She looked at Zoe. "Do you think it's broken?"

Her question was drowned out by Ma's exclamation. "Oh, Elijah. I'm so glad you are here!"

Belle turned to see Ma reaching for Mr. Harrow from where she remained seated in the chair. Mr. Harrow hurried to her side and took the hand she'd stretched toward him, but his gaze flitted from Zoe on the couch, to her ankle, to Belle.

The warmth and softness in his eyes somehow infused Belle with a strength she didn't know she possessed.

She snapped her fingers at Aidan. "I need you to run into town and fetch Doc."

"But I can't ride Lilac!"

Belle hurried toward the kitchen, squeezing his shoulder reassuringly on the way. "I know, monkey. You'll have to run. Zoe needs you to be strong."

Aidan blew out a breath. "Fine. At least I don't have to go to school."

Belle kept her back to him as he darted out the door so he wouldn't see her smile. She opened the ice chest and took up the hammer and ice pick. She chiseled a few pieces from the block, wrapped them in a towel, then returned to set the cold pack gently against Zoe's ankle. She looked up to assess Zoe as she did so.

Zoe's face scrunched in pain, but she made no sound.

Belle hoped she was making the right decision. "Sorry. I've heard Doc tell people plenty of times that putting ice on an injury right away can lessen the pain and swelling."

Zoe pinched the bridge of her nose and rocked a little. "Yes. When Aurora soaked it in cold water that did help—at least after the first shock of the cold."

Mr. Harrow squatted before Ma and said a few low words to her. Belle was thankful to have the man here to console her mother. She returned her focus to Zoe, who still rocked in agitation. Was the weight of the ice too much? "Is it causing you pain?"

Her sister shook her head. "No. I'm just an idiot, that's all. I simply"—she waved a hand—"feel terrible about poor Lilac!"

Realizing that Mr. Harrow still didn't know what had happened, Belle quickly filled him in.

"Ah!" He pointed down the hall. "Sharon is in this direction?" He took a step, and Belle was relieved at the thought of him going to Sharon.

Belle released a breath. "Yes. And it would be very helpful if you could see to her. Thank you. Shiloh isn't the most compassionate sometimes." She started toward the kitchen once more. "Ma, you sit. I'll bring you coffee and get breakfast going. Oh!" She spun back. "Mr. Harrow, could you please send Shiloh to the schoolhouse to let everyone know that school is cancelled for today?"

He gave her a nod, and there was more in it than just concession. Somehow his nod conveyed not only his agreement but also reassurance and pride for the way she was taking charge.

And as Belle started in on a pan of scrambled eggs and layered toast onto the grate in the oven, she felt for the very first time a complete thankfulness for the fact that Ma had met Mr. Harrow on that trip to Seattle with Zoe.

Monday morning Aurora surveyed her bedroom at the ranch. After this morning's incident with Zoe, while she'd been doing her chores, she had thought about Cora's words from the evening before. It hadn't taken her long to recognize that Cora was correct. Her irritation with Poppy was born directly out of jealousy. And that simply would not do.

Preston had made her no promises, nor given her any indication that he considered her anything more than a friend and fellow worker for the Lord—no matter what Cora might have implied.

Therefore, she had no right to have expected him to tell her about his past, nor to be jealous of Miss Scarlatti.

The jealousy, especially, was a sin she needed to repent of.

And she could tell Preston of her decision to leave early when he stopped by this evening.

She had been praying for the Lord's leading for months, now. And trying to walk by faith felt like standing blindfolded on a narrow bridge without any rails while tasked with crossing a raging river. Today however, it was as though the blindfold had been pulled away. The only thing keeping her here in town was her feelings for the parson. And since he did not return her estimation, Aurora couldn't help but feel the Lord was nudging her to spread her wings and take this chance on an education.

If only the realization had brought with it a measure of peace. Instead, she felt a restless churning that she couldn't banish. If leaving was the right thing, shouldn't she feel more at ease about it? Perhaps it wasn't the leaving that had her feeling discouraged, but the reason for her leaving? Maybe she was meant to leave but not to study music?

She loosed a sound that was part groan, part growl of frustration.

She simply wasn't sure.

Yet . . . she couldn't remain here waiting on a man who would never come around. It was definitely time to move on.

So this morning, as soon as she had finished her chores and concluded with helping Liora in the kitchen, she had returned to her room and set to packing with a gusto. It hadn't taken her long to fill her trunk with the few meager clothes she owned. After that she had swept nonexistent cobwebs from every corner of the room, polished the room's one window until not a spot could be seen, and in turn scrubbed the floor with such passion that when she had paused to arch her back, she'd been able to see a line delineating the clean side from the dirty. She would leave this room spotless for whoever might be the next inhabitant.

Because she'd made a decision today. And it had come easier than she had expected. She'd decided to leave for Seattle a full week early. She would speak to Cora this evening and ask her to fill in at the piano next Sunday. She felt certain Cora would readily agree, and Aurora was relieved to have the decision made.

Arriving in Seattle early would give her time to explore the city and learn the neighborhood near the home the school had assigned her to. It would also give her time to adjust to new night sounds that might keep her awake, since she was not used to city noises. Then if she had trouble sleeping at first, at least she wouldn't also have classes to face the next day.

Yes. It was a smart decision. She dipped her scrub brush into the bucket and set to work on the last corner of the room. Tomorrow she would call at the train station and pay the small fee to transfer her ticket to this Saturday's run. That meant, not counting today or Saturday, she had four days left in town. Instead of the melancholy she had expected, the thought filled her with anticipation and joy. She might never get to share life with the man of her dreams, but that didn't mean that the Lord had stripped her of all things that brought happiness.

She would choose to focus on the good in her life rather than her dashed hopes.

A knock sounded on her door, and she bolted to her feet and stared at the clock on her nightstand. How had so much time passed? That had to be Preston!

With dread, her focus slipped to the mirror. She curled one lip at her reflection. Hair bedraggled, blouse wrinkled, and skirt liberally sprinkled with both damp splotches and dirt, she looked like a fare-dodger fresh from an empty boxcar.

The knock sounded again.

Perfect.

Just perfect.

Chapter Fourteen

oppy reined the horse she had rented from the Wyldhaven livery to a stop in front of the Cle Elum Mercantile. For a city girl who had grown up surrounded by tall buildings and straight streets, she was quite proud of herself for navigating the winding roadways between Wyldhaven and Cle Elum without getting lost.

She could have purchased the supplies from the Wyldhaven Mercantile, but it wouldn't do for people in town to know she was buying large amounts of food and then riding off into the forest with them. In a small place like Wyldhaven, it would be too easy to put two and two together.

Cle Elum was set apart by enough distance that she hoped word of her purchases wouldn't spread.

The Cle Elum Mercantile was well stocked, and she found everything her men would need. She even threw in a side of bacon, though she grumbled at the dear price of it. But keeping her men happy was key, and by this time next week, her cash problems would be behind her.

If the mercantile owner wondered at a woman alone purchasing a man's shaving razor, he kept his curiosity to himself. Just the way she liked it.

As she rode from the mercantile with the supplies tied into gunnysacks draped over her horse, she contemplated her next steps.

If she were honest with herself, she'd really only come west to see Preston again. But now the memory of him that had held her enamored, had lost its captivation. He was stiffer and more solemn than she'd remembered. And then there was the sticky element of his faith. He definitely wasn't the same boy who had charmed her all those years ago. Nor did he seem inclined to trust her as she'd hoped he would.

She wasn't done trying to charm him. Not by a long shot. There was still hope that she could turn him to her way, but the hope grew dimmer the more she thought about it.

And the biggest problem remaining was still the bank's safe. If she couldn't convince Preston to help her pull off this job, all her time and effort would be wasted.

Yet, Babbo had always told her that anyone could be made to do anything so long as the right tools were utilized. So if Preston remained her only solution, she simply needed to figure out the right pressure to apply.

The problem was, she'd arrived thinking that she knew Preston. Would have laid down money on a bet that no one knew the man better than she. And yet this new version of him had shaken that foundation of belief. She was no longer certain she knew him at all. So she would watch. She would wait. And she would do her best to earn back her position as his best friend in the whole world.

That was going to be quite the mountain to climb after the way she had testified against him. But her charms had always worked on him in the past.

And as she worked at beguiling him, she would study him and figure out his weaknesses. Because if it came down to it, she might have to use one against him.

When she arrived at the location where she was to meet her men this morning, a fine mist had started to fall. It had the peculiar quality of barely being felt and yet seeming to birth ice deep in one's bones. She tucked her coat tighter about herself.

Her men huddled under the meager shelter of a scraggly pine, wet and glaring at her as she rode up.

Here was yet another problem to work through. If the money would not be arriving till the end of the week, she needed to do something different with her men. They would be miserable staying here all week without shelter, not to mention that if they didn't have a place to store their food, especially the flour, it would be ruined inside an hour in this weather. And she couldn't be renting a horse and riding off to Cle Elum every day to fetch them supplies. She could give them money so that they could ride in and buy their own supplies, but the truth was she didn't trust either man not to simply take the money and run, leaving her high and dry. Both were shortsighted enough to see only the few dollars in their hands and not the much larger amount they could soon have after the heist.

A memory surfaced of a conversation she'd overheard on Sunday after services. The owner of the new mill being built in town had explained to a redheaded woman, whom Poppy hadn't met, how he needed several more workers. Her men wouldn't like it, but that solution would do nicely.

She smiled, feeling quite proud of herself. Babbo would soon be proud of her again too.

He would see.

She could be the savvy businesswoman he wanted her to be.

Preston had trouble concentrating all morning. His usual pattern on Mondays was to travel to Camp Sixty-Five, where he repeated his sermon from the day before to the camp's occupants.

This week's sermon was greeted with a great deal of difference by those who lived in the camp than it had been the day before in Wyldhaven.

The loggers cheered and guffawed and seemed rather proud of the fact that the man who led their little flock hailed from a sinful past. One of the loggers—a man fairly new to attending services—had even clapped him on the shoulder afterward and proclaimed he was proud to be led by a man with "sand."

While thankful to be recognized as a man with grit, Preston despaired of getting them to realize the evil of his past choices. To his chagrin, though he had tried to explain to the man the error of his thinking, he didn't feel that he had gotten his point across.

Mostly because his thoughts kept flitting to the conversation he planned to have with Aurora. Even now as he rode toward the Carver place—Kane had agreed that he could keep Tommy for a few hours—he was disappointed over his failed teaching. But for now he must put the failure from his mind. Maybe he'd have another opportunity to speak to the man next week.

With Tommy by his side, he rode into the old homestead. Memory washed over him of the first time he'd seen this place. Kin had been a mere boy—one who had just lost his drunkard of a father. And the place had been in shambles. He and Kin had lived here for several months until the parsonage had been built.

Kane was in the corral, working with an Appaloosa.

As Preston and Tommy swung from their mounts, Kane stepped to the cedar-rail fence and leaned his arms on the top. "Howdy!"

Tommy plastered himself to Preston's side, crowding him up against his horse. "D-don't f-forget to c-come back for m-me."

Preston draped an arm around Tommy's shoulders and walked with him toward the corral. Several years ago, Tommy's brother Horace had been sent to jail and Tommy had fallen in with an abusive gang of outlaws. Preston didn't even want to consider all the torment the poor man had likely been through. "Who never leaves you, Tom-Tom?"

Without hesitation, Tommy answered. "God n-never leaves me."

"That's right." Preston turned to look Tommy right in the eyes. "And I promise I'm coming back. In the meantime, what are you going to remember to do?"

Tommy thought for a moment. "Help K-Kane with the h-horse and s-say my v-verses."

"Good, yes. Let me hear the first of it."

"I c-cried out to God for help; I c-cried out to God to hear me."

Preston squeezed Tommy's shoulders. "God always hears us, Tommy. Always. Now . . ." He nudged Tommy toward the corral. "I'll be back in just a few hours." He looked at Kane and touched the brim of his hat.

Kane nodded, then turned his focus on Tommy. "Hey, Tom. Come look at this beauty we're working with today. How have you been?"

Preston was amazed once again at the transformation that came over Tommy the moment he stepped into a corral with a horse. Tommy had a way with the animals that bordered on miraculous. And though his stuttering had minimized since he had come to town and moved in with Preston, it had never completely dissipated. But when Tommy was in a ring with a horse, Preston had never once heard Tommy stutter. He spoke to the animals as clear as day, sweet and smooth. And as though the horses sensed the miraculous, they responded to Tommy with calm obedience. Even Kane was left shaking his head. He said he'd never seen a man as good at taming a horse.

With a final wave of his hand, he mounted up and headed down the trail.

Now, as he crested the hill and the Rodante place came into sight below him, Preston felt a crimp return to his stomach. This would be the telling moment. The moment when he figured out whether Aurora really did have an interest in him that went beyond friendship. The moment when he laid his heart bare, put everything on the table, and left the rest in God's hands.

He rode into the yard and tied his horse to the hitching rail before the Rodantes' door, swiped his damp palms against his pants, and took the steps to the front porch.

Liora must have heard him coming, because she opened the door with Law on her hip. "Evening, Parson. I trust you had a good day?"

He snatched his hat off. "I did, thank you."

"Something amiss?"

"No, no. I was just . . . uh . . . is Aurora around?"

A sparkle of realization settled in Liora's gaze.

Preston felt heat prick across the back of his neck. He fiddled with the crown of his hat.

She jutted her chin toward the bunkhouse building across the yard. "She's in her room. Been packing and cleaning up a storm all day. Seems she's decided to leave for Seattle a week early." Her piercing gaze seemed to convey something to him.

What it was, though, he couldn't quite decipher, because he was too busy trying to pick his heart off the ground. Leaving early? He studied the building across the yard. What had made her decide to do that?

Realizing Liora still watched him from the porch, he offered, "Thank you. I'll just step over and see if she has time to talk for a few minutes."

Liora smiled. "Can you stay for dinner? It's really no trouble."

"I better not. Tommy is over at the Carvers', and he'll need something to eat when we get home anyhow."

Liora brushed away his dismissal. "Stay and eat. I'll wrap Tommy a bowl and send it with you when you go home."

"Well, when you put it like that, how's a man to resist?" He offered her a smile of thanks.

She chuckled. "I knew I could talk you into it. And honest, it truly is no trouble."

She disappeared into the house, and he worked on his breathing as he crossed the yard and knocked on the door to Aurora's room.

There was no answer. He tipped his head, listening, but no sound came from the room. Maybe she'd stepped out? He knocked again.

A moment later, she answered the door wearing a skirt with wet knees and a partially untucked blouse. The bun on her head was halfway undone and falling around her shoulders. She held a scrub brush in one hand and wore a stunned expression. He couldn't withhold a grin. It was the most beautiful he'd ever seen her. This image was so typical of her giving spirit. Her work ethic. Her lack of fixation with her own appearance.

"Forgive me! I must have lost track of the time." She tossed her scrub brush into the bucket of dirty water, sending another splash across her skirt. With a grimace, she set to putting her hair to rights. "I've been a scattered mess all day since Zoe's injury."

"Zoe? Injured?" Preston's concern rose. The last thing the Kastains needed was more tragedy in their lives.

Aurora waved a hand. "I think she'll be fine. She and her horse took a tumble. But I assessed Zoe's ankle, and I think it's just a sprain."

"You assessed her ankle?" Of course she had. It was simply part of her giving nature to jump in and help.

"I did, and it was actually very gratifying to help her."

"I'm glad she's okay."

"Me too." Aurora was still pinning up her wayward locks.

He could see a line of red creeping up her neck. Though the realization that she hadn't been worrying about this meeting all day as he had, gave him a bit of angst. He swung his hat toward the bench down the porch. "I'll just wait for you, unless . . . now is not a good time?"

"It's fine. I'm terribly sorry. I just got so engrossed in cleaning my room for its next occupant. I'll be right there."

He waited for her by the bench, planning to ease into the conversation. But the moment she stepped onto the porch, he blurted, "Liora tells me you're leaving for Seattle a week sooner than planned?"

Her brow furrowed.

Too late, he realized that the disappointment in his tone might be taken for disapproval.

But before he could rectify his words, she folded her arms and responded. "Yes. I decided it would be good to get to know the area before classes started."

"There's nothing for it then but to plunge in to the reason I've come." He paced to the edge of the porch and stared out across the yard. "Aurora, I have a confession."

"You do?"

He turned to look at her, taking her in from her now tidy hair to the small boots that peeked from beneath the hem of her work skirt. She was petite in a way that had deceived him when he'd first met her. He had thought her a scrawny boy, though now that he knew her, how he had ever thought her a lad made him shake his head at himself. How blind had he been? Her long lashes and high cheekbones alone spoke of her femininity.

He took a breath, reminding himself to slow down. "I do have a confession, but first I need to ask you something. Please answer honestly."

The flash in her eyes told him she was hurt that he would question whether she would answer honestly. "All right." Her hands trembled as she smoothed them over the front of her skirt.

"Have you ever thought about . . . marriage?"

Her brows shot up, and she plunked herself onto the bench next to the bunkhouse wall. She didn't meet his gaze. "I'm not sure there's any woman my age who has not thought of marriage a time or two."

Preston felt like his throat might close off, and he scrubbed a knuckle over the knot that had formed beneath his Adam's apple. "Have you ever thought about . . . the . . . kind of man you would want to marry?"

Aurora seemed to be in deep concentration on her fingernails. "I suppose first and foremost I would want a godly man. One I could trust. One who would partner with me to"—she cleared her throat—"raise a family."

He had to tread carefully here. In no way did he want her to feel like he was pressuring her. After all, he highly doubted that a man his age would be her first choice. And yet he did fit all her criteria. He spun to face her. Tapped his hat against his leg a couple times.

Her voice was barely audible when she looked up and asked, "How long are you going to make me wait for this confession of yours?" Her gaze, wide and searching, captured his.

"I think I'm in love with you." He blew out a slow breath, wishing his heart would quit hammering so loudly in his ears.

She stared at him without moving for a long moment. And then she leapt off the bench and paced several steps down the porch.

Of course she had retreated. What else had he expected her to do? He turned once more to scrutinize the ranch yard, hat still tapping his leg. "I realize that especially after what you learned of me yesterday, I might not be your first choice in a man. Maybe I've already lost out to Kane Carver. But I couldn't let you leave town without at least telling you how I feel."

Silence filled the space between them for so long that he finally pivoted to assess her. He wasn't sure what he had expected, but tears certainly hadn't made the list.

She stared down at the porch boards, seemingly focused on nothing. Rivulets tracked down her cheeks and dripped off her chin.

He strode to her side and gently tilted her face upward. The green of her eyes seemed magnified by her tears. He let his thumb sweep the drops from her chin. "The last thing I want is to cause you angst. You don't have to worry about hurting me. I understand that the life I have to offer is not the substance dreams are made of. Please know that if you tell me to walk away, this will be the last we ever talk of this. And I will still consider you a friend."

To his surprise, Aurora covered his hand with her own. "Preston Clay, you are the biggest dunderhead I have ever met in my entire life."

He blinked. Frowned. "I see."

Chapter Fifteen

onfusion swirled through Preston. Aurora had just called him a dunderhead and yet sat smiling at him with her hand pressed over his own, though tears continued to stream.

She laughed. "No. You don't see. Because I can read the confusion written all over your face."

"I do confess confusion is an emotion I am currently feeling." He allowed one side of his mouth to lift in a smile. Dare he hope?

"I think I've loved you since the first moment your horse almost tromped on my head."

A sense of wonder started somewhere in the region of his chest and spread through him, warming him to his very extremities. "You have?"

She nodded, dashing at her tears. "I have."

"Then, if you don't mind my asking, why is it you are leaving town?"

She angled him a look and cocked one eyebrow. "Do you really not know the answer to that?"

Consternation puckered his forehead. "I wouldn't have asked if I knew the answer."

"Because you . . . just seemed . . . so . . . indifferent to me, and I have felt like I was dying a little more each day that you ignored me."

Ignored her? That was all she'd seen? "Trust me when I say, I have been far from indifferent. And if I was ignoring you, it was because I was forcing myself to. For months I've been trying to convince myself that I should walk away and let you alone."

She frowned and pulled her hand from his. Stepped back far enough to break their contact.

He let his hand fall to his side.

Her gaze drilled into his. "This is what I don't understand. If you love me, why haven't you said anything?"

Needing a moment to formulate his words, Preston settled a hand at her back and nudged her to the bench. But once she was seated, he had too much angst to sit beside her. He dropped his hat onto the bench and paced the deck instead. How to make her understand? "Because, Aurora, the life of a minister is not an easy one. Certainly not one of leisure. I work long hours. And you know how small the town is. They can't afford to pay me much. If we should court and later decide to marry, I won't be able to afford to provide for you in the way that you deserve. I won't be home to spend as much time with you as I would like."

She smoothed a palm over the arm of the bench. "I should hope that by now you would realize money doesn't matter to me. And what is to prevent me from traveling with you to the camps? We could spend time together in ministry."

He shook his head. "The camps are rough places, Aurora."

She huffed a sound of agreement. "Have you forgotten that I grew up in the camps?"

Scooping a hand through his hair, he continued to pace. "I have not. But that does not mean that I want my wife constantly exposed to that type of life, whether she would be shocked by it or not." He turned to face her once more, needing to read her expression on his next question. "So you don't want to get your degree from the music conservatory?"

She suddenly seemed intently interested in the hands she'd clasped in her lap. It was several moments before she responded. "I'm honestly not sure. I must confess that I have questioned whether I need to further my music education. And I've not had much peace about the acceptance." She cleared her throat, as though reluctant to utter her next words. "My impetus for applying was more to escape my attraction for you when you didn't seem to notice that I existed as a woman."

Of its own volition, Preston's gaze swept over her. "Trust me when I tell you that I definitely knew—know—that you exist as a woman."

She fidgeted, cheeks pinking. After a beat, she asked, "And what of Poppy Scarlatti?"

Preston frowned. That wasn't a question he had expected. "What of her?"

"Did you ever love her? Could you learn to love her again? After all, with her confession of faith, there is now nothing that should prevent you from . . . courting her."

Preston scoffed. "I'm not sure I believe her profession of faith, if I'm honest." He held up one finger. "And I'll ask you not to repeat that. But . . . No. I may have thought that I loved her at one time. But our relationship remains firmly in the past. At least for my part."

Aurora's lips thinned. "I'm not so sure she knows that."

He shrugged away the comment. "Nothing I can do about that. What about my age?" He stared at the side of the barn, unsure he could handle the truth if it were revealed in her eyes.

"Your age?"

"I'm more than seven years your senior. It might not make such a difference now, but if we were to marry, it might leave you widowed down the line."

"No one is assured any number of years on this earth. I could marry Kane Carver, and he could be kicked by a horse and killed tomorrow."

He spun to face her. "And do you want to? Marry Kane Carver?"

She laughed. "Have you heard me say recently what a dunderhead you are?"

There was that dangerous hope again. He searched her face. "I'd still like to hear you say it."

"Parson Preston Clay is the man, and the only man, who I have ever considered marrying."

He couldn't stop a grin. "Well now, we do seem to be getting somewhere. But I need you to understand that I can't condone your accompanying me to a place I know to be dangerous day after day after day."

Aurora's face fell, and her jaw jutted to one side as it did whenever her irritation had reached a peak. "Then it seems we are at an impasse. Because I am not the kind of woman who will enjoy sitting around cleaning an already clean house while I wait for you to get back from your ministry each day."

He sighed. "Perhaps I shouldn't have come to you with this. But I felt it would be good for us to have a conversation."

Aurora felt like a spinning top. First, her decision to leave early for Seattle, then Preston's arrival at her door, and now his final words that seemed to in one fell swoop dismiss their confessions of love for each other.

She clenched her fists in her lap. "What do you mean by that?"

Preston scooped a hand through his hair and gripped the back of his neck. A gesture of frustration. "It means that I feel we still have a lot to work through. I certainly don't want to hold you back from your dreams."

"And if my biggest dream is to be your wife?" Heat slapped her face. She couldn't believe she had actually just blurted that.

He looked at her. Scrutinized her features. His gaze softened. "Do you really mean that?"

She pressed a finger along the seam in her skirt. Did she? She considered how shocked and hurt she had been yesterday. "Why did you never tell me about your past?"

The question seemed to sap the strength from him, for he sank onto the top step of the porch a few paces away. "I thought about telling you plenty of times. You and others in the town. But always, the timing didn't seem quite right. I think, looking back, that partly it was shame that kept me from the confession. But also, I knew in my heart that past was decidedly behind me."

"Until it wasn't." There was a bitterness in her words that surprised her.

He scrubbed a forefinger and thumb across his brow. "Trust me, there's no one who regrets more than me that I didn't speak of my past sooner. You have my sincerest apologies. But I can understand how this would be a barrier for you." He lumbered slowly to his feet and started down the steps, shoulders slumped.

Her heart thudded. Had they come this close only to have a relationship fall apart before it had even begun? No. She refused to lose him over something so trivial. "I do."

He stopped. Faced her. "What?" He climbed the steps to stop before her.

"I do want to be your wife." She waved a hand. "We had no understanding, and you owed me no explanation of your past. I trust there's nothing else I ought to know?"

He shook his head. "Nothing you don't know already."

"Then it's forgotten." It made her feel quite free to let go of the hurt.

Massaging his hands into his shoulders, he paced a few steps along the porch. "I appreciate that. I guess I just worry that you would be choosing me simply because you didn't have any other choice. Or experience with anyone else."

Aurora gritted her teeth. She wasn't going to sit here and beg him to court her. Yet, she did have other choices. "In case you have forgotten, I'm going to dinner with Kane Carver on Friday."

Preston plunked his hands on his hips and pivoted. His narrowed gaze probed her expression. "I've not forgotten."

Aurora rolled her eyes. "I only agreed to go with him . . . well, because . . ." She waved a hand. "That woman plastered herself all over you." More heat filled her cheeks.

A tiny smile tugged at one corner of Preston's lips. "Did she? I didn't notice. I was too busy being jealous of the fact that Kane Carver got up the courage to ask you to dinner before I did."

Aurora allowed the slimmest of smiles. "So my plan worked, then, did it?"

Preston wagged a finger at her. "Do you know, when he asked for my permission to call on you, he said that Joe told him I was like your pa?"

Aurora gave him a dismissive look. "Trust me when I say that I have never thought of you as my pa." She flapped a hand before her face. It seemed that today was her day to be overheated.

Preston dropped to one knee before her, capturing her hands in his. "So here's the short of it. We've established that we both have feelings for each other. That's a good place to start. But I don't want us to rush. I know I hurt you with my disclosure yesterday, and I certainly want to give you time to make sure this is what your heart truly wants. Maybe it would be good for you to go on to Seattle and get your music degree. We could write to each other. Get to know each other. I mean, we know each other, but get to know each other in a more . . ." He cleared his throat. "Intimate way. The way a man and wife ought to know each other."

Aurora cocked a brow, feeling her amusement mount. There was no way the man had meant that statement the way it sounded.

Preston's face blanched. He shot to his feet, holding out his hands. "No! Not— No! I just meant . . . sharing our dreams with each other, sharing insights we have from the Scriptures, talking through expectations of marriage. That sort of thing." He blew a frazzled breath.

Aurora pressed her lips together, pondering his wishes. Did he truly love her if he would encourage her to leave town? And if she did leave town, she would be leaving him in Wyldhaven with Poppy Scarlatti. Preston might not have designs on that woman, but there was no question in Aurora's mind that Poppy definitely had designs on Preston.

There was also her distinct lack of peace about leaving for the university.

She rose and strode to the end of the porch and back. She had thought that if there came a time when she and a man confessed their love for each other, all problems would dissipate. She'd never considered that professing love for another could raise a whole passel of problems. He'd said that he wanted her to be sure that he was what her heart truly wanted, but maybe he also wanted to give himself time to be sure *she* was what *he* really wanted?

If it were up to her, they would walk down the aisle tomorrow. There was no question in her mind what she wanted. But Preston was a man of deliberation. And if he needed time to make sure this was the direction he wanted to go, she would gladly give him that. She would try to be thankful that, where this morning she'd had no hope, she now had at least a glimmer.

She stopped before him and looked into his face. Took in the tiny white scar beneath his eye and the line of stubble that accentuated his rugged jaw. Took in the green of his soft eyes as they searched her own.

"What is it?" he asked.

She shook her head. "I'm just relishing the fact that we are even here having this conversation. I had given up hope."

He raised one hand and tucked a strand of her hair behind her ear. "So? What do you say?"

She pushed out a breath and inspected the yard, as though it might hold the answers. "Before you got here today, I had decided that I was going to leave a week earlier than I had planned. I have been praying for weeks for the Lord's guidance, yet I can't say that I definitively know what He would have me do. In the absence of His direction, I will defer to yours. Since you think we should take things slowly, I will keep to my plans and go to Seattle. And you, dear Parson, have permission to write me letters." She batted her eyelashes in exaggerated coquettishness.

He chuckled. "I like the sound of that. I do have one request."

"Oh?" She raised her brows.

"Send Kane Carver packing."

Aurora couldn't withhold a burst of laughter. "Why, Parson Clay, that wouldn't be a note of jealousy I detect in your voice now, would it?"

He curved one hand around the side of her face, and his thumb swept a caress along her cheekbone. The smile he gave her was wry. "It just might be. I'll put all the details in my first letter."

Aurora threw back her head on a laugh, and such joy filled her as she had not experienced for years.

Preston's amusement shone in the depths of his eyes. "Have dinner with me? Tomorrow evening at Dixie's?"

Her breath hitched as she searched his face. "Are you ready for the whole town to be talking about us?"

He grinned and tilted his head toward the main ranch house. "I think we might have already lit that fire."

A quick glance revealed Liora, Ada, and Eliza peeking at them through the kitchen window.

When she returned her focus to Preston, he was smiling broadly. "I'm ready to face the talk if you are."

She nodded. "I'm more than ready."

He gave a dip of his chin that indicated his pleasure. "Well, all right, then."

Chapter Sixteen

Sheriff Reagan Callahan strode up the street from where he'd just dropped his horse in the livery. He pushed into the jailhouse and hung his hat on the peg by the door.

Zane Holloway, a former US Marshal who had given up the job after marrying Reagan's mother, rose from behind the desk. He was now simply a deputy in town, though everyone still called him Marshal. "So? Anything?"

Reagan reached for the coffeepot on the woodstove. The coffee had boiled so long that it was a thick sludge when it drizzled into his cup. Just the way he liked it. He angled Zane a look. "Can't say."

"What do you mean you can't say?"

"I mean, she met two men that she took some food to. But there is nothing criminal in taking men some food, though it is suspect that she rode all the way to Cle Elum to buy it."

"Did she talk to them?"

Reagan slurped the coffee and winced as it burned all the way down. "Yeah, but I wasn't close enough to hear what was said."

Zane paced. "I don't like it, Reagan. If we lose this money, it could mean the end of the bank before it's even started. And you know that Olann has already extended loans to several. People are counting on that money. Doc has even borrowed a sum to build a house."

"I know." If Zane wasn't going to sit, Reagan certainly was. He was tired after spending the whole day in the saddle. He sank into the desk chair and propped his boots on the corner of the desk. "I don't like this tension any more than you do. I still can't believe Zeb announced the bank's opening in the papers."

Zane huffed. "All he thinks about is promoting the town. Not keeping it safe."

Reagan gave Zane a droll roll of his eyes. "That's what he pays us for."

"Yeah." Zane gripped the back of his neck. "Next Wednesday can't come soon enough. At least once the bank is open, we only have to keep people from breaking in. But this business of the money being on the open road . . . That's likely to give me angina before this is through."

"Ma's cooking hasn't done that already?" Reagan teased.

"Careful, or I'll tell her you intimated as much."

Reagan dismissed their joking with a swipe of his hand. "For now we simply need to keep an eye on her. She did stop a couple times on the way back to town and looked like she was praying."

Zane scrutinized him. "Looked like?"

Shrugging one shoulder, Reagan took another sip of coffee. "She's a brand-new convert. Maybe she's just not used to talking to the Almighty yet. She sure did look uncomfortable though."

"Or it could have just been your suspicions making you think so."

Reagan nodded. "That's a possibility, yes."

Zane sighed and reached for his hat. "Well, since you're back, I think I'll take myself home to sample some of your mother's fine cooking."

Reagan smirked as the door closed on Zane's parting words.

He blew out a breath. "Lord, we really could use a little providence to help us keep this town and its people safe. Especially in the next few days. Please give us wisdom, and protect those in our care."

Weariness draped him. He glanced at the empty jail cells, then rose to his feet. There was nothing keeping him here. He might as well head home and enjoy an evening with Charlotte.

Poppy arrived back in Wyldhaven Monday evening.

As she had ridden back to town, a thought had struck her. And even now it still had her smiling as she stepped into the entryway of the boardinghouse.

Cora Harrison, the pretty girl who manned the desk, looked up with a warm smile. The girl's gaze took her in from head to toe, and a note of curiosity gleamed in their depths. "Good evening. You are just in time to catch the last few minutes of the dinner hour."

"Perfect! I'm famished!" Poppy swept past the desk and into the dining room, feeling the girl's eyes following her all the way. A glance over her shoulder proved her instincts correct. She turned and faced the girl full on, propping her hands on her hips. "Can I help you?"

The girl tilted her head. "It's a small town. And I heard that you rode out this morning. I confess that my curiosity has me wondering where you spent the day. But I know it's none of my concern."

"Indeed, it's not." Poppy cocked a brow at her.

The girl had the presence of mind to look chagrined. She dropped her gaze to the desk before her. "Yes, ma'am. Enjoy your dinner."

Poppy studied the girl for a long moment. Would that be the end of it? Perhaps she should have responded with a little more friendliness. Too late now. She would just have to keep an eye on her. If she took to gossiping, Poppy might have to put a stop to it.

She turned her back and sank down at one of the tables.

Dixie Griffin, the boardinghouse owner, finished setting plates before two burly loggers and then stopped by her table with a coffeepot in one hand. "Good evening. Tonight's choices are pot roast or fried chicken."

Poppy decided on the pot roast, and as Mrs. Griffin headed for the kitchen to fetch it, Poppy returned her thoughts to her earlier realization. She hadn't liked how Preston and the local sheriff seemed to be on such friendly terms at the gathering yesterday. And that was even after Preston's shocking confession to the congregation. Had he been putting the sheriff on her scent? She wasn't certain. If the sheriff had learned of her history, wouldn't he have her followed? She'd kept an eye on her backtrail all day and hadn't noticed anyone. Yet she'd had a . . . sense of being watched—a feeling she couldn't pin down. Because of that feeling, she'd paused twice and looked to the heavens, eyes closed as though in prayer. She'd felt like an idiot. But if someone was watching her, maybe they would believe the ruse of her newfound faith . . .

It was a realization about that which had made her smile as she came into the boardinghouse. If she was going to continue that ruse, she had better study up on what it actually took to look like a Christian.

Mrs. Griffin arrived at her table and set the beef before her. The tantalizing aroma made her stomach rumble. Mrs. Griffin did not seem to notice, or if she did, she politely ignored it. "Can I get you anything else?"

Poppy laid her serviette in her lap. "No, thank you. This looks wonderful." But as Mrs. Griffin started away, she thought to ask, "Oh. You wouldn't have an extra Bible I could borrow by chance, would you?"

Mrs. Griffin's eyes sparkled with joy. "I believe I can find you one, yes. Mr. Hines stocks a few in his mercantile."

"I'll stop by there then." Poppy gave her a nod. "Thank you." Hang fire. She didn't want to spend any of her few remaining dollars on a Bible.

"There's no need. I've been meaning to get a few to keep in the rooms anyhow. I'll make sure to bring one by in the morning. I have to tell you, we are all just thrilled by your confession of faith. Please know that if you ever have questions about anything, I'm happy to chat. Anytime."

Great. Just what she needed. People wanting to nurture her made-up faith. She forced a smile. At least she wouldn't have to spend any of her money. "That would be wonderful. And as for the opportunity to ask questions, I may just take you up on that."

"Please do. I'll leave you to eat now." The woman gave her a parting smile and went to the other table.

Poppy tucked into the food, and only in that moment realized just how hungry she truly was. She'd skipped her noon meal in order to bring her men their supplies.

But thankfully, her plans were coming together.

Now, all she needed was to figure out what pressure she could put on Preston that would convince him to work with her.

There had to be something.

Maybe another visit with him was in order. In fact, there was no time like the present!

She smiled. Why hadn't she thought of this sooner?

Preston was pouring himself a cup of tea when a knock sounded on his door.

He closed his eyes. Great. He'd just gotten Tommy off to sleep. If this was someone who needed him to ride out to the camps, he'd have to wake Tommy to go with him, which meant that all day tomorrow Tommy would be a bear to get along with.

He opened the door. Blinked.

Truly, seeing Poppy on his stoop was the last thing he'd expected. Would he ever get used to seeing her around town? He thought of Aurora's questions about her and wondered how long his old friend would be staying.

She shifted, sending her skirts swaying as she tucked her hands behind her back and looked down. "I'm sorry to show up on your stoop so late in the evening."

He stepped onto the porch and motioned her to a spot near the rail. He wasn't about to invite a fox inside. Not to mention the impropriety of it. "What can I do for you?"

She darted him a look. Pushed out her lower lip. "So stiff and formal. Is that any way to treat one of your oldest friends?" She reached to rest one hand on his forearm.

Gripping the back of his neck, he paced several steps from her. Far enough to free himself from her touch. "I don't mean to be stiff, Poppy. Sorry. I'm only tired. How can I help you?" He tried to inject kindness into his tone. After all, the good Lord would want him to show love and mercy to this one who claimed she'd found her way to Him—despite Preston's doubts over the claim.

Poppy shifted to lean against the rail, but thankfully didn't come closer. There was a long moment of silence. Finally, she pushed out a little breath. "I'm getting a Bible in the morning. I wondered if you had advice on where I should start reading."

The words were spoken so softly, he turned to study her profile. He hadn't expected that.

Angling him a look, she waited. Her eyes were large and dark in the moonlight.

He couldn't quite read her. If she were serious about this godly transformation, he would be overjoyed. He still couldn't bring himself to believe it. Yet she'd walked up the hill in the dark to ask him where to start reading her Bible? "John is always a good place to start."

With a nod, she lifted her skirts and took the steps from the porch to his yard. She paused to look back at him. "Thank you. Will it be hard to find?"

Again, she'd taken him by surprise. Was that really the only reason she'd come to see him? His hope once again lifted its head. "Not at all. There's almost always an index in the front of the book that will tell you the page number to go to. John is the fourth book in the New Testament—second half of the Bible."

She started back toward town. "Okay. Thank you. I won't keep you any longer."

There was a catch in her voice, and he heard a sniff. Had he hurt her? "Poppy?"

She paused.

Now what? He couldn't invite her to stay. But neither did he want to quench the Spirit's work in her life if that truly was happening. "You are welcome to come ask me questions you might have about the Bible, anytime. But—daylight hours are better, if you can."

Even in the darkness, he could see her shoulders relax. She nodded. "Thank you. I appreciate that. And yes, I understand."

As she resumed her way toward town, her step seemed lighter.

He remained on the porch. Turned his gaze upward to study the spangle of stars in the dark dome of the sky.

Lord, if ever there was a time when I needed special wisdom directly from You, this is it.

Chapter Seventeen

uesday morning, as Belle helped Ma in the kitchen, she couldn't help but worry over the days ahead.

Thankfully, Zoe's injured ankle had only been a severe sprain, according to Doc. She would recover well, and in fact was already at the schoolhouse this morning, with her foot propped up on a stool that Belle had carried in for her. She'd gone to the school early to do some extra preparation since the students had missed the whole day yesterday.

As Belle whisked a little milk into the eggs she was preparing to scramble, she couldn't withhold a smile at the memory of Taulby Eklund showing up on their stoop first thing with an offer to give Zoe a ride to the schoolhouse. His wagon, with a mound of hay covered in a quilt, had been fixed just so for Zoe. She wondered how long it would take her sister to recognize that the new man in town was already more than half in love with her.

Belle sniffed. Would serve Wash Nolan right if he returned from his adventures to find Zoe the wife of another man!

Ma finished laying the last of the sticky buns into the baking dish. "These are ready for the oven. I need to run and milk the cow since Zoe wasn't able to do that before leaving this morning."

Belle popped the sticky buns into the oven. "I'll finish breakfast and make sure the kids are up and ready for school on time. Since we are running behind, I can pack their lunches after they leave and walk them to the schoolhouse later when we go to town for our shifts at the boardinghouse."

Ma made a little sound of relief. "Yes, that is a good solution."

Just as Ma bustled out the kitchen door to go do the milking, there came a knock on the front door. Belle smiled. That would be Mr. Harrow. And it would be good for him and Ma to have some quiet time together. She hurried to open the door and pointed him toward Ma, who was just disappearing into the barn at the far end of the yard. "Ma just went to milk the cow. Breakfast will be ready in a few minutes."

"I'm sure she could use some help." Mr. Harrow started across the yard, but paused and looked back at her. "You look like you have the weight of the world on your shoulders. Everything okay?"

Belle hesitated.

It was their current lack of a ridable horse that had her concerned. After school each day, Aidan delivered the mail to the camps for Mr. King. She and Ma and Zoe had been so thankful when he'd secured that job a few months ago. But now, without the horse, there was no way he would have time to make it to all the camps each day. Not having a horse would cost him the job. And they desperately needed the money he made from those runs. They would have to get another horse. But with funds as tight as they were, she wasn't sure how they would manage it.

Yet she wasn't certain she should tell any of this to Mr. Harrow.

She wished she knew for certain what his intentions toward Ma were. If he were going to be part of their family, she would feel more comfortable talking through their situation with him. But he and Ma's relationship was still so new, she didn't want to burden him with their problems if he wasn't going to be part of their future. Besides, she supposed that talking to him about their issues ought to be Ma's responsibility.

On the other hand, she knew her mother. Ma was the type who mainly sat back and let life happen. With the horse lame, Ma would realize they needed another, yet she would ponder and plan and postpone a purchase because of their tight finances, and the delay would only cause their finances to grow even tighter.

Belle relinquished her thoughts, suddenly realizing that Mr. Harrow still watched her patiently. She assessed him.

He smiled. "Whatever weighs on you will likely feel less burdensome when shared."

She swallowed. Plunged ahead. "What are your intentions where my mother is concerned, Mr. Harrow?"

"Ah." He thrust his hands deep into his pockets. "I'm sorry to have caused you concern on that account. I—"

"Please forgive me," Belle interrupted. "I believe I've given you the wrong impression. It's not you and Ma I'm concerned about, really. But since what I am concerned about involves our family, I feel I need to know the one before burdening you with the other, if that makes sense."

"It makes perfect sense." The man rocked on his toes and cast a glance over his shoulder toward the barn. "For my part . . . that is, your ma is . . . very special to me."

A swath of red crept over his collar.

"However, we've not spoken of the future, so I can see why you'd be reluctant to confide in me." A small furrow puckered a line between his brows. "Moving ahead from a first love, isn't easy. Though, if your mother feels even half for me what I feel for her, I think we'll work it out." He smiled sheepishly, as though realizing he hadn't meant to say so much. "I'll just—" With a thumb gesture toward the barn, he started to turn away.

"It's the horse," Belle blurted, before she could second-guess. She didn't want the man to feel she didn't trust him. If, as she suspected, he was indeed to one day be her pa, she wanted to get off on the right foot.

He looked at her, waiting patiently for the rest of the explanation.

Belle laid out her concerns.

"Ah, I see." He pondered for a moment, seeming to go to a far-off place. Finally, with a blink, he came back to the present. "If you'll allow me some time to ponder, perhaps we can come up with a solution at breakfast?"

Belle nodded, already feeling relief to have someone else helping her search for a solution. "Yes. That would be fine."

"All right. I'll just go chat with your ma now." He started toward the barn but then stilled and turned back to her with a smile. "If you would take a moment to pray for God's leading for all of us, especially in the next few minutes, this old man would surely appreciate it."

Belle's eyes widened. Did he mean . . .

There was a sparkle of mischief in his gaze. He gave her a wink.

He *did* mean it!

Feeling like a warm blanket had just been wrapped around her, Belle gave him a nod and a smile. "Will do. See you in a few minutes."

Excitement jolting through her, she headed back to the kitchen, praying Ma and Mr. Harrow would find joy and happiness with each other.

The eggs sizzled as she poured them into the already heated skillet. "Girls! Aidan!" she called as she stirred the eggs and peeked at the nicely browning buns. "Breakfast in fifteen minutes. Up and at 'em." She paused to listen and was gratified to hear a couple of thumps and a groan or two that indicated the kids were indeed waking up. But then immediately her worries rose to the fore again.

Ma and Mr. Harrow would obviously have other things on their minds today. But . . . Belle shook her head. A decision needed to be made and be made today. She needed someone who knew horseflesh—who knew the horses in this area in particular. Maybe someone had an older nag they could buy for a song? If it could even get them by for a couple months, that would be a huge help.

Her thoughts flitted to Kane Carver. She flapped a hand before her face and strode to open the kitchen window. Somehow the room had suddenly grown very warm.

The twins bustled in.

"Mmm. Sticky buns!" Sharon exclaimed with an appreciative inhale.

"Yes!" Aidan did a little dance of excitement.

Shiloh gave a smile, though she was less enthusiastic. She strode to the cupboard, removed the dishes, and started setting the table.

Belle's jaw went slack. Well, there was a first time for everything. When was the last time Shiloh had pitched in to set the table without being told?

Sharon paused by her side and looked up. "Do you think Zoe's going to be okay?"

Belle stirred the eggs and nudged Aidan to get the milk from the ice box, then bent so she could look Sharon right in the eyes. "Yes. I'm sure she's going to be fine. Doc said she would be. Don't you go worrying about her. You just worry about studying the lessons she teaches you." Belle gave her sister a wink.

"I'm ever so thankful she only hurt her ankle."

"Yes. I'm sure we all are."

"Do you think Lilac is in pain?" Sharon fetched the silverware and set it near each plate that Shiloh had already laid out.

How Belle loved her sister's soft heart. "Maybe for a few days, but Doc looked at Lilac and said he felt she would make enough of a recovery to live pain-free." Belle noticed that both girls had grabbed enough for a place setting for Mr. Harrow without even asking. The realization filled her with a sense of happiness. Things were going to work out fine.

And, Lord willing, their family would soon be complete once more.

Susan Kastain felt lighter than air as she and Elijah left the barn carrying the bucket between them.

Not only had he come to the barn to see her first thing, but he'd insisted that she teach him the ins and outs of milking a cow. However, as she'd bent over his shoulder and reached to adjust his hands on the udder, he'd done more watching of her and leaning close to bump her teasingly, than he had in paying attention to her milking lessons.

Even now he leaned close and covered her hand on the bucket handle with his own. "A fellow could get used to this country life, Mrs. Kastain. He truly could."

His caramel-and-cream gaze settled on her, warming her rather much more than it ought for the fact that they'd just been in the smelly barn with a cow. She tore her gaze from his. "You'd miss your clocks. And your busy city life."

"Not nearly as much as I miss you when we're separated."

She pinged him a glance. "Oh, do go on with you."

His thumb caressed her hand. "I'm serious, Sue. Marry me?"

She stopped so suddenly that some of the milk sloshed out of the pail. Slowly, she lifted her gaze to his. His eyes were gentle and full of light. "I mean it. I'll go to Seattle, pack up, sell my shop, and be back here just as soon as you say you'll have me."

Her heart frolicked so, that she feared it would never settle back to its proper place. "Truly?"

He nodded. His lips pressed into a hopeful twist as he appraised her.

Susan felt as though the Lord had just poured a double portion of blessing into her life. "Oh, Elijah, I just wasn't certain how we would work things out. I don't want you to feel that I cost you everything, yet I can't imagine moving the children to Seattle."

"How could I feel that you cost me anything when I'd be gaining such a family as yours?" He set the bucket down slowly and stepped around it to grip her shoulders. He looked intently into her eyes. "Wyldhaven is growing, from what I've seen since I've been in town. There's a spot next to the post office where I could set up a small shop. Even loggers have timepieces that need fixing. So what say you? Marry me and let's spend the rest of our years blissfully in love with one another."

She laughed nervously, hardly able to believe that he'd asked her so soon. She certainly hadn't been expecting it this morning. "Just you wait until Aidan is sick with the sniffles and comes crawling into bed with his ice-block feet in the middle of the night. Or until the twins go at each other over a hair ribbon or a dress they both want to—" She stumbled to silence because she suddenly realized he was shaking his head at her.

"Nothing you attempt in order to scare me off will succeed, dear Susan Kastain."

She laughed. "But the ice-block feet nearly did, did they not?"

He chuckled softly. "If anything could have made me flee for safety, that would have been it." His hands tightened gently on her shoulders. "Say you'll have me, Susan, and make me the happiest man in the world."

She swallowed. Searched his face. His expression revealed only sincerity. "You're certain? Taking on responsibility for five children won't be easy."

"God never promised us easy. Only a blessing when we do things the right way. But . . ." For the first time the hopeful light in his eyes waned. "I didn't think I'd need to convince you."

Susan quickly reached out to touch his arm. "Please don't misunderstand me. I'm as thrilled as a hen in cracked corn, but I don't want to be selfish and jump into a relationship that might not . . . suit you in the long run."

Elijah reached one hand to cup her face. "Dear Susan. Nothing could be further from the truth. You, and your children, are just exactly what I want."

Tears blurred her vision, and she turned a kiss into the palm of his hand. "Well, all right then. My answer is a most emphatic yes."

"Glory be!" Elijah scooped her up and twirled her in a circle.

"Oh my! Elijah, I'm much too old for this!" She laughed as he settled her back to the ground.

Still smiling, he bent toward her ever so slowly. "Maybe you're right. I think I felt something pop in my ankle." He winked. He used a fake limp to inch closer, bringing his face to within a breath of her own.

With a chuckle and a smack to his chest, she said, "Be serious and kiss me." She held her breath as his lips gently brushed hers. The world spun, and she took hold of the front of his shirt.

His hands at her waist steadied her.

Cheering erupted from the porch, and with a laugh Susan turned to find three of her offspring leaping and dancing, and Belle leaning against the rail with a smile of welcome for Elijah.

Beside her, Elijah loosed a breath. Eyes fixed on the children, he bent and whispered in her ear. "I guess this means we don't have to talk them into this?"

She laughed and leaned her back against his chest, cradling the arm he wrapped around her. "It seems they are fully on board." Tilting her head against his shoulder, she looked up at him. "Shall we go tell Zoe?"

"Yes!" All four children barged off the porch and headed their way.

Aidan snagged her hand. "Right now!"

Belle smiled her approval and reached for the bucket of milk. "I'm right behind you just as soon as I stow this in the ice box and save the sticky buns from the oven."

It did Susan's heart good to see Sharon and Shiloh each take one of Elijah's hands.

As they started for the schoolhouse, she met Elijah's gaze above the children's heads. He gave her a wink of reassurance, and she realized her heart hadn't felt this light for many a year.

Chapter Eighteen

oppy was still asleep late Tuesday morning when a knock woke her. She padded across the room, tugging her housecoat about herself and pushing her tangle of hair from her eyes. She inched open her door and peered out.

Dixie stood on the landing, holding a book in her hands.

Poppy felt her brow furrow as she looked from the book to Dixie and back again. Surely the woman hadn't woken her to bring her the Bible?

With a hesitant smile, Dixie held the leather volume toward her. "I'm sorry to wake you."

"It is rather early." Only then did Poppy realize she truly had no idea what time it might be. She'd paced her room late into the night considering and tossing aside idea after idea on how to get her hands on the bank's money.

Dixie opened her mouth but must have changed her mind about what she'd thought of saying, for she snapped it shut again. She thrust the book closer. "This is the Bible you asked for last night."

Poppy sighed and accepted it. "Thank you." She started to close the door, but Dixie held out one hand.

"I also wondered if you would like a muffin and maybe some coffee? Several women from town gather in the dining room on Tuesdays to have a short Bible study. We'd love to have you join us."

"I'm afraid I don't have ti—" Her subconscious pinged a reminder of the role she was supposed to be playing. "Actually, sorry. I had trouble sleeping last night, and I'm still a bit cotton headed. What time should I be down?" Blasted friendly busybodies!

"Mama!" A toddler with a head of brunette curls hurtled down the landing and threw her arms around Dixie's skirts.

An older woman followed the little one, giving Dixie a look of apology. "We are going out for a walk."

"It's fine." Dixie directed a smile toward Poppy, even as she scooped the little one into her arms. She settled the girl on her hip. "Elle, this is Miss Scarlatti. Can you say hello?"

Poppy resisted a roll of her eyes, instead reaching out to tweak the toes of the little girl. "Hello there, beautiful." That much at least was true. The girl was quite striking with her hazel gray eyes, burnished skin, and dark curls.

The toddler assessed her with wide-eyed curiosity for a moment, then looked up at her mother. "Go walk?" She plunked a thumb into her mouth.

Dixie tugged the child's hand to extract the thumb and lowered it to the child's side. "Ma's working. You go on a walk with Grandma Rose, and I'll see you this afternoon before your nap."

"Okay." With one last flash of her eyes in Poppy's direction, the girl squirmed to get down and then darted to take the older woman's hand.

Dixie offered Poppy a smile. "We're still working on her manners, I'm afraid."

A memory surfaced of Babbo backhanding her across the room after a similar incident when she'd been about three. Poppy blinked back to the present, realizing Dixie was still talking.

". . . so glad you're going to join us. We start in half an hour at eleven.

"I'll see you then." Poppy closed the door. She wished she could go straight back to sleep.

But if she were to keep up her ruse, she supposed this was a good way to do it.

As she filtered through her trunk for a clean dress, she considered on the questions that had plagued her into the wee hours.

Ought she to have asked Preston, once more, to join her team? She still could hardly wrap her mind around this new leaf he seemed to have turned over. Surely, if she just asked him in private, he would confess to her that he was on a long con?

Though . . . he hadn't that first day. And his actions at the church on Sunday certainly weren't those of a man trying to hide anything from anyone. Yet that could in and of itself be part of a con, couldn't it?

She blew an unladylike sound.

No. The risk was too great to press him for more right now. She needed to let her own religious "conversion" do its work and see where things took them. Simply being near him would reveal things he wouldn't expose if pressed.

She would bide her time.

But my, how she hated biding her time.

With a frustrated grunt, she snatched the Bible from where she'd dropped it on her bed and hurled it into the corner near the floor. The pages splayed open, fluttered, and then settled.

She sank down by the trunk, blinking tears from her eyes. She would not fall apart.

She simply wouldn't.

Belle set the milk bucket into the ice chest, took the sticky buns from the oven and the eggs from the stove, and then hurried outside to follow her family. A thrill of excitement that she hadn't ever expected to feel on this day coursed through her.

Skirts hoisted, she angled a glance toward the sky. "Thank You, Lord." She knew this feeling of acceptance could only be a miraculous gift from heaven. She wasn't surprised that the younger children had accepted Mr. Harrow so readily. She only hoped that Zoe could feel the same measure of excitement that she was feeling. She and Zoe, being the oldest, had felt Pa's suffering and death perhaps more keenly than the other children.

She caught up to her family just as they strode up the church-cum-schoolhouse steps.

Aidan barged ahead and burst through the doors yelling, "Zoe! Have we got news for you!"

They were all laughing as they stepped around the partition at the back of the building. Belle was the first to notice Zoe's look of shocked despair.

Wide-eyed and with her foot still propped on the stool, her sister searched her out. "Is it Wash? Did something happen to the train?"

Belle stretched a hand of reassurance toward her. "No. I'm sure Wash is fine. This has nothing to do with him." She turned to look at Ma and Elijah, wanting them to be the ones to spill their news.

Ma strode down the center aisle and bent to look Zoe in the eyes. Resting her hands on Zoe's shoulders, she stood at arm's length. "Mr. Harrow has asked me to be his wife. What do you think about that?"

"Oh! Ma!" Zoe struggled to stand, balancing on her good foot. She pulled Ma into an exuberant hug. "I'm so happy for the both of you. I had a strong feeling about you two from the moment we met you, Mr. Harrow."

Over Ma's shoulder, Zoe's sparkling gaze settled on the man. She motioned him toward her. "If you don't mind helping a poor crippled girl out"—she laughed—"please come closer so that I can squeeze your neck."

It warmed Belle's heart to see Mr. Harrow wrap both his arms around her sister and rest his cheek against the top of her head. "I thank the good Lord that He gave you an adventurous spirit that sent you to my shop that day. And I also"—he reached out and ruffled Aidan's hair—"thank the good Lord that Aidan knocked Washington Nolan's watch into the creek so that it needed fixing."

Zoe laughed. "Unfortunately, he knocked more than just Wash's watch into the creek." She gave an exaggerated shiver with her arms wrapped around herself.

Everyone laughed. Aidan, looking sheepish, kicked at the leg of the nearest desk.

Belle decided to save him from his discomfort. "Zoe, we better get and let you start classes. Would you like me to ring the bell for you on our way out?"

Zoe checked the pocket watch on her desk. "Oh my! Yes. I'm two minutes late."

Belle followed Ma and Elijah down the aisle as Shiloh, Sharon, and Aidan settled into their desks. She gave the bellpull several strong tugs and then descended the stairs—against the flow of students dashing up them—to follow Ma and Mr. Harrow back to the house.

As they settled down at the breakfast table and Ma heaped Mr. Harrow's plate to the brim with warmed-over eggs and sticky buns, Belle's contentment gave way to her concerns of the earlier morning.

After they said a prayer, Mr. Harrow cleared his throat. "Susan? Belle tells me that Aidan may lose his job if he doesn't have a horse to ride?"

Ma gave her serviette a snap and spread it on her lap. Her aggravated gaze shifted to Belle for only a split second before falling to her plate. She lifted her fork and dabbled in her eggs. "Yes, I suppose that is true. But I'm not sure there's much we can do about it. We'll lose Aidan's income, and I don't see how we can sell Lilac, lame as she is, so we'll still have the cost of her feed. But the children have had enough loss, and I'm glad we don't have to put her down." She waved her fork as though to dismiss the concerns. "The Lord has always taken care of us." She offered a forced smile and tasted the eggs.

"I don't see how Aidan will be able to get another job with no horse to ride." Belle clamped her teeth together. She had not meant to blurt her thoughts.

Ma gave her another stern look. It was patently obvious that she didn't want to burden Mr. Harrow with this.

"I'm sorry. I don't mean to sound impertinent, Ma."

Ma sighed. "I don't think of you as impertinent, child. I'm just not certain what the solution is. Nor should Elijah bear the burden of fixing this." Pink tinged her cheeks. "At least not yet."

"Nonsense. I'm more than happy to lend my mind to coming up with a solution. In fact, I think I might have one." Mr. Harrow downed the last of his first sticky bun and licked sugar from his fingers. "I must say that's the best thing I have eaten in a very long time." He picked up another.

Belle watched him, noting Ma doing the same.

"What solution do you propose?" Ma asked.

Mr. Harrow lifted a shoulder. "Why, to get another horse, of course." He pegged Belle with a look. "Do you know anyone who deals in horses around these parts?"

Of course Kane Carver was the first to come to mind. Belle worked some moisture back into her mouth. "I know someone who trains them. He may know of one that is for sale somewhere."

"Right, then." Mr. Harrow nodded. "I say we pop by to see him today."

Belle looked to Ma, wondering if she would protest. But instead of finding the stubborn look she had expected, Belle was surprised to see Ma studying Mr. Harrow with a light of thankfulness and relief in her eyes.

She smiled. It was good to see that look in Ma's eyes again. She gave Mr. Harrow a nod. "We could stop by and see him on my way home from my shift this evening?"

"That sounds fine. I'll meet you ladies outside the boardinghouse kitchen. What time should I be there?"

Belle felt a tremor of anticipation, even as she considered how it would be good to have someone with her, to stand as a buffer between herself and these confounding feelings for a man who had only been offering kindness and nothing more. "We get off at six this evening." A quaver jittered through her. Just the thought of seeing Mr. Carver again had her on edge.

Ma rose from her seat. "Speaking of which, we'd best get going or we'll be late."

Mr. Harrow stood politely. "If you don't mind, I'm going to stick around and do a little work on the porch and steps."

With a hand flying to her lips, Ma's eyes misted.

Mr. Harrow looked taken aback. He studied Ma uncertainly. "Unless you . . . don't want me to?"

Ma couldn't seem to find her voice.

Belle swallowed, knowing that Pa had been the last person to work on the porch. She held her silence, giving Ma time to find the words, and quickly stepped to the other side of the sideboard that separated the dining area from the kitchen and set to putting together lunches for the children.

After a long moment, she heard Ma take a breath. "No. It's fine. It's just that William was the last . . ." Ma waved a hand.

"Don't mind me. I've been thinking those boards needed fixing for quite some time. So yes, please do."

Belle snuck a look at Mr. Harrow's expression. He was looking at Ma with a furrow in his brow. "I don't want to overstep."

Ma went to him and smoothed her hands across his chest. She looked up into his face. "You are not overstepping. All of this . . . letting go and moving forward is just going to take me some time to adjust to."

Settling his hands at Ma's back, Mr. Harrow peered down at her. "Well, don't let me rush you. I want you to feel perfectly at peace with all of this."

"I do. Honestly, I do." She rose on her tiptoes, and Belle averted her eyes.

She carefully tucked a serviette across the top of each of the children's tin pails, and if she clanked them together a little more loudly than normal as she gathered them, well, it was only to remind Ma and Mr. Harrow that they were not alone.

Ma glanced her way and stepped back with a sheepish smile toward Mr. Harrow. "We had best get."

Yes, they had. Belle blew at a strand of hair that dangled in her face. Hopefully, the family would get past this awkward phase sooner rather than later.

urora felt like skipping and dancing as she traversed the road toward town with Liora, carrying baby Law, walking beside her. Today was her turn to lead the Bible study, and normally that would have her more nervous than a fly in a crate full of frogs, but today she couldn't find a hint of room for nervousness.

Her heart was too full of joy and elation.

She could hardly believe that Preston had finally confessed he had feelings for her. In light of that, spending a year attending school in Seattle while they sorted out the future was nothing. She would endure the months with great happiness.

Liora glanced over and gave her a wink. "You haven't stopped grinning since yesterday."

Aurora chuckled. "I know! I don't think I have ever felt this happy. We still have so many issues to work through, but I'm simply thrilled that we've started the process." She reached for baby Law. "Here, let me carry him for a while."

"Thank you. That lad has been putting on the pounds." Liora shook out her arms as Aurora relieved her of Law's weight.

Aurora smiled and held Law before her, giving him a jostle. She spoke to the baby in a high-pitched tone. "Have you been getting so big? Yes, you have!" She blew a sound against his belly and then held him away from her again. "Yes, you have!"

Law slurped on his fingers and giggled, blue eyes sparkling at her from above his chubby cheeks.

With a sigh of satisfaction, she tucked the baby into the crook of one arm.

They crested the hill just above town, and Wyldhaven stretched before them. On this side of town, a new section of rowhouses had gone up in the last month. And the sound of hammering could be heard from where several men worked at the construction of the mill across Wyldhaven Creek. Sunlight glinted off the burbling waters, and Aurora hoped that adding a waterwheel to the stone building wouldn't change the landscape of the creek too much. She loved to wander the mossy embankments where forget-me-nots and ferns grew liberally. Her gaze swept to the other end of town, where the livery towered beyond the new bank. "My, before we know it, Wyldhaven will be a bustling metropolis."

"Did you hear that Charlotte has finally gathered enough money and that the lumber for boardwalks is going to be the first thing Mr. Eklund produces at the mill?"

"I hadn't heard! Do you suppose we'll be able to talk them into building a walk up the hill to the church? That would certainly save many of the ladies' hems on Sunday mornings."

Liora gave her a side-eyed look. "I know someone who has some pull with the parson. Perhaps she can make it happen."

Warmth filled Aurora's cheeks. She flapped her free hand before her face, looking away from Liora. This was a new phenomenon. Being teased about a relationship with the parson. She rather liked it.

Liora looped her arm with Aurora's. "Don't let my teasing get to you. But it does my heart rather a lot of good to be able to tease you about a relationship that I know you have longed to commence for so many years."

Aurora nodded, feeling no need to hide anything from Liora. "I have at that. I can still hardly believe he stopped by yesterday."

Liora shook her head. "I can hardly believe that it took him so long!"

"What do you mean?"

Her friend offered a slight roll of her eyes. "For several months at least, everyone in town has known that you and the parson had eyes for each other."

"I hardly think that can be true. I'm not sure when his feelings changed. But I can't say that I'm sorry they did."

Liora gave her a squeeze. "You both deserve the greatest of happiness."

They took the stairs up to the boardinghouse porch and made their way inside and to the table in the corner of the dining room, where they had their Bible study each Tuesday. Law set to fussing, and Liora took him up the stairs to Dixie and Doc's home, to feed him.

Aurora was thankful for the few minutes to collect her thoughts. She had been doing so much woolgathering on her way into town that she hadn't refreshed her memory on what she wanted to say today.

Dixie bustled from the kitchen with a tray filled with muffins and cookies. Susan Kastain was right behind her with both tea and coffee service.

Dixie nudged a couple of chairs farther apart and inserted another between them just as Charlotte Callahan and Jacinda Holloway strode up. "The new woman who is staying upstairs is going to join us for Bible study today."

While Dixie's tone made it clear she was entirely thrilled about the prospect, Aurora felt her face blanche. "Really?" Her voice squeaked, and she cleared her throat.

The eyes of every woman around the table fixed on her.

"Sorry. It's just that . . . I have to confess, it surprises me that she would want to come."

Charlotte gave her a wide-eyed warning with a little shake of her head.

Horror filled Aurora, but it was too late to retract her words.

From behind her a husky voice drawled, "Don't worry, carissima. It surprises me too." Poppy gave a sultry laugh.

Feeling her humiliation blaze, Aurora faced her.

Poppy wore a red watered silk gown that accentuated every aspect of her femininity. Did the woman ever wear any color besides red?

"I'm sorry . . . I just . . . Please don't think that we aren't happy to have you join us. You are very welcome." Even Aurora recognized her words were a lame bandage for the damage she'd created. She stretched a hand to direct the woman to a seat, determined to try to make up for her mistake. She might doubt Poppy's sincerity, but this was a good sign. If she were sincere enough to attend Bible study, the Word of God could change her—if she let it.

Frustrated with herself for voicing her suspicions that the woman might have ulterior motives, Aurora stepped to the end of the table, where the Bible study leader always sat.

Liora rejoined them a few moments later, and they all sank into their seats. They each enjoyed a muffin and a drink and then finally, when Aurora sensed everyone was ready, she set aside her plate and cup and tugged her notes from her reticule.

The women quieted and focused on her.

"What I want to say today is very short." She tried not to let Poppy's assessing scrutiny make her nervous. "The story I would like for us to read is about Paul and Silas when they were imprisoned by the Philippian jailer."

She turned to the sixteenth chapter of Acts and read the story of how Paul and Silas were beaten unfairly and imprisoned.

"Yet despite all this they chose to have a joyous attitude. Instead of grumbling about how unfair their treatment was, the Bible says they sang hymns to God, and the other prisoners were listening. Though we can't know for sure, I have to wonder . . . if they had grumbled and complained instead, would God have sent the earthquake that freed them?"

"That's a very good question." Belle looked surprised at her own outspokenness. "I don't mean to interrupt, but I'd never quite thought of that aspect before. I think had I been in their shoes, I would have felt quite justified in having a bad attitude." She gave a self-deprecating grin and a shrug of one shoulder.

Glad that Belle had participated, Aurora smiled at her. "I think it's likely we all would have." She swept a glance at the women. "As to whether it would have made a difference, perhaps that's a question we can ask the Lord when we reach heaven someday." She assessed her notes. "What we can know is that the Lord did send an earthquake that freed them. Paul and Silas and maybe many of the other prisoners could have escaped, but they didn't. They stayed where they were. Again, a sign that they cared more for those around them than for themselves, because the jailer was tasked with guarding them at the expense of his own life. He planned to kill himself, supposing everyone gone, but Paul called out to him not to harm himself. Had Paul and Silas grumbled and complained and been fixated only on themselves, I think they might have chosen to flee that day. But instead they chose to walk in the way of our Lord, and because of that, the Philippian jailer and his whole household were saved." She looked up and smiled. "I guess my challenge for us today is to ask ourselves, when things don't go our way, what good influence might we have on those around us if we choose to have a positive attitude even in difficult circumstances?"

Charlotte nodded. "So much easier said than done, isn't it, ladies?"

Agreement made the rounds of the table.

"Yes." Aurora nodded. "I think we all struggle with that. Especially during difficult times. I'm not certain I would have the fortitude to sing in such a circumstance."

Jacinda Holloway raised her hand, and Aurora acknowledged her with a tip of her chin. "I think the Lord gives us strength at just the right time that we need it. I know you'll all remember when I was taken captive and chained in the cave outside of town. Still to this day, I'm not sure how I made it through that time, except the Lord helped me in the exact way I needed. If I hadn't taken that knock to the head and gotten amnesia, I'm not sure if I would have been able to remain calm or what would have happened. But looking back on it, I know that despite the difficulty of the situation, the Lord was watching out for me."

Poppy leaned forward and assessed Jacinda with a searching look. "You were taken captive and *chained* in a cave?"

Jacinda nodded. "Several years back now."

Poppy's eyes widened. "My! That's terrible! Where did this happen?"

Jacinda pointed. "Just a mile south of town on the west side of the road. There is a cliff behind a large patch of huckleberry bushes. And the cave is about halfway up the cliff. There is a narrow little trail that leads up to it." She shivered. Gave a laugh. "Trust me—I wish I could forget how to get there."

To Aurora's surprise, Poppy reached out a hand and settled it on Jacinda's forearm. "That must have been a trying ordeal. I'm sorry you had to go through that."

Jacinda gave her a smile. "While I wouldn't want to go through it again, the Lord did use that whole situation to bring good into my life. I'm not certain I would be married to my husband today if I hadn't been taken captive." She returned her focus to Aurora and spread her hands. "I guess my point is that it might be singing, and it might be a knock on the head that gives you amnesia, but the Lord knows just how to help us make it through difficult circumstances that we might not see coming."

Aurora nodded. "I agree. What we need to do is prepare our hearts in advance to allow the Lord's strength to work in us."

The women all agreed.

Aurora smiled. Spread her hands. "That's all I have for today. Who would like to close in prayer?"

Charlotte volunteered, and only a moment later, as the women rose and set to gathering their dishes onto the trays for Dixie and Susan, Aurora watched Poppy Scarlatti. She remained in her seat for a long stretch, staring into the depths of her empty teacup, lost in thought. After an extended period, she blinked a few times, as though coming back to the present, looked up, smiled softly at Aurora, and then rose and set her cup onto the tray.

Dixie smiled and said something to her that Aurora couldn't catch. Poppy offered a few words, and then with a nod of parting to several other ladies, she made her way from the room.

Just before she crossed the threshold into the entryway, she paused and looked back. To Aurora's surprise, the woman's lips were pinched and her jaw was set just so as her narrowed gaze slipped over Aurora for the briefest of moments. Then with a flip of her head, Poppy departed.

A shiver snaked the length of Aurora's spine.

Kane Carver was surprised when he looked up from the horse he was working with in the corral to see Aurora McClure walking toward him.

Lifting his hat, he swept a sweaty arm across his forehead and tied off the colt. Placing both hands on the top rail, he leapt over the fence and landed softly just as she came to a stop.

It surprised him to realize that he hadn't thought of her even once this morning. No indeed, for his thoughts had been filled with visions of heart-wrenching, teary blue eyes and blond curls. A decisive chin smudged with lead from pencil sketching. And small hands quickly gathering paint supplies upon his intrusion. Guilt rushed in on the heels of the recognition.

"Aurora." He gave her a nod and worked the handle of the yard's pump. He likely smelled only a sight better than the horse he'd been working with all morning. When the water poured from the spout, he scooped a double handful and sluiced it over his face and arms. Then taking up the scrap of toweling hanging on the corral by the pump, he dried off as he looked at her. "Happy to have you drop by. What can I do for you?"

Rocking on her tiptoes, she looked everywhere in the yard but at him. She jutted her chin toward the Appaloosa colt. "He's beautiful. Whose is he?"

Kane turned to study the beast, feeling a measure of pride in the animal's sleek lines. "He's mine. I rode to an auction out past Cle Elum last week and won the bid. He sure is pretty, but . . ." He laughed. "That colt surely does have a mind of his own. That is, until Tommy Crispin gets in the corral with him. Then he's like butter on a biscuit—soft and malleable." He smiled at her.

Humor softened her gaze. "Tommy does have an amazing way with them, doesn't he?"

Kane nodded. "Nothing short of miraculous, if you ask me."

He studied her. Wondered why she'd come. In all the months he'd lived here, she'd never dropped by, leastwise not unless Maude was home. But she knew that Maude had taken a job with Mr. Hines and was in town working at the mercantile today. The only explanation for why she'd stopped by now would be that she was here to see him. And judging from the way she didn't want to look him in the eye, he had a feeling he was about to get passed over.

Surprisingly, he felt no pain or remorse in the realization. He rehung the towel and then simply waited, giving her time to formulate her thoughts.

Finally she looked him in the eye. "I'm afraid . . . that is . . ." She blew out a little breath and shifted uneasily. "Preston came by to see me."

Ah. So it came down to that, then. He'd always wondered about the two of them and had thought Preston's reaction to his request to call on Aurora a bit odd. Here, then, was the explanation.

Her lips pressed into a firm line before she blurted, "I'm awfully sorry to do this to you, but Preston and I . . . well . . . I've been halfway—no more than halfway—in love with him for years. And he's just come 'round and asked me to dinner. I didn't feel . . . you see, we didn't feel it right that I keep my dinner engagement with you for later in the week." Her gaze flicked to his. "I'm ever so sorry, Kane. The last thing I want is to cause pain."

Kane propped his hands on his hips and worked his teeth over his lower lip for a moment as he studied her. "Actually, I have to say that I'm surprised to realize I'm okay with that."

Relief sagged her shoulders. "You are?"

He nodded, feeling a smile well up from inside him. He hadn't realized it, but ever since he'd bumped into Belle Kastain in the wildflower field above town, the scheduled dinner with Aurora had felt like a weight on his shoulders. Only now that he was relieved of it did he recognize the fact. "Truly, I am. I wish you all the best with the parson."

A shimmer of gratitude glazed her eyes. "You will make someone a fine husband one of these days, Kane Carver. You truly will."

Feeling an unfamiliar embarrassment, he stepped to the corral and scratched the colt—which had come to hang its head over the fence—between its ears. "I suppose only the good Lord knows about that." He swept his hand down to pat the horse's broad cheek.

"Thank you for letting me off easy."

He nodded. Swiped at a trickle of sweat on his temple.

Aurora lifted one hand and then walked away.

And as he watched her go, he couldn't even summon up a hint of regret. He smiled. The good Lord surely did work in funny ways sometimes.

Chapter Twenty

Taulby Eklund sat at his desk for a few minutes to do some paperwork and assess some orders.

He had several men working on splitting by hand the pieces that would be needed for the wells of the waterwheel that would later power the blades of his mill. He'd already ordered the metal rims for the frame of the wheel and the gears for the internal mechanisms. Those should arrive on Saturday's train.

This part of the process had been slow, and he itched to get the mill up and running. Yet nothing would be profited from rushing these foundation steps. He wanted to be sawing lumber for years to come, and each breakdown would mean loss of income both for himself and the workers. While quality parts cost more here at the outset, he prayed they would save him more in the future.

He glanced at the clock. First thing this morning, two men had arrived looking for work. In the thick of instructing his workers on the shaping of the boards for the wells, he had asked the two to return. They were due to arrive in ten minutes.

He stretched his sore and tired shoulders. He'd been bent over, hammering down decking, for much of the morning. Ten minutes was perfect. Just enough time to step to the boardinghouse to grab a cup of coffee. And maybe he'd catch a glimpse of a certain pretty redheaded teacher. He smirked at himself with a roll of his eyes. He would see her soon enough when, after classes, he picked her up to give her a ride home.

He thanked the Lord for the providence that had made him ride that way on his trip to the mill yesterday and at just that exact time. A few minutes earlier or later and he might have missed her entirely. Despite his offer to put the horse down, he was thankful they'd declined. Never had he faced such a task before, and he wasn't sure if he could have followed through.

He left his office and crossed the bridge that stretched over Wyldhaven Creek. The boards dipped and swayed beneath the weight of his tall frame. After the boardwalks the women of the town were wanting, one of his first projects would be to build a new bridge, before this one collapsed under someone and killed them.

Despite knowing that Zoe wouldn't be up and walking around yet, he couldn't resist a peek up the hill toward the in-need-of-a-coat-of-paint church. They must be on recess, because several children played tag in the yard. He stopped himself from going to say hello. The woman would think he was stalking her if he didn't back off some. He shook his head in disparagement.

Dixie Griffin greeted him as he stepped into the boardinghouse.

"Good morning, Mr. Eklund. How goes the work on the mill this morning?"

"Coming along, ma'am. If you'll forgive me for being a bit short on time, I wondered if for a cup of coffee, I could trouble you? I have with some men an interview in just a few minutes."

"Certainly. Right this way." She preceded him into the dining room and motioned him to a seat at one of the smaller tables. "I'll fetch your coffee in a mug that you can take with you."

Taulby gave her a nod of thanks and settled onto one of the too-small chairs. Across the room a woman in a red dress eyed him above the pages of a book she pretended to read.

He gave her a nod, but she quickly averted her gaze to her pages.

Taulby couldn't withhold a smile. A fine-looking woman she was, but that right there probably left him out of the picture. And there was something . . . standoffish about her.

Her gaze flicked to him once more and widened at finding him still watching her. With a crimp of her brow, she refocused on her book.

He bit back a chuckle, wondering what her interest in him might be. Maybe only curiosity? His large stature tended to draw attention.

Dixie returned with a large mug. "Here you go, Mr. Eklund. And for five cents a week, you can consider this your personal mug. Simply come to the back door of the kitchen and we'll refill it any time you need more."

Bless the woman!

He thanked her, paid for two months up front, and returned to the mill.

The two men looking for work waited for him on the partially constructed steps of the mill building. They appeared to be having words with each other but snapped into silence immediately upon seeing his approach.

"Gentlemen." Taulby stretched a hand toward the partially finished portion of the building that would serve as his office. "Please, in here, join me."

Once seated behind his desk, with the men on the two stools he'd placed for them, he tilted back in his chair and assessed them. Neither man looked like he'd ever done much work with his hands. One was hardly out of his teen years and looked like he'd been living half near starvation for a good decade. The other, only a little older, had more meat on his bones, but his hands were just as soft.

Taulby blew out a breath. To run this mill successfully, neither man seemed to be the type he would need. "I'm Taulby Eklund. Your names are?"

The bearded one offered that his name was Tom Smith and the other was John Jones.

Taulby withheld a snort. Names like that meant they were both likely running from something. "Either of you worked before at a mill?"

Both men shook their heads.

"Mason work?" He would need masons to help finish the walls unless he did it all himself.

Again, both men shook their heads.

The bearded one spoke up. "We're newly from Boston."

At the mention of Boston, the younger man shifted and darted his partner a look.

His friend didn't seem to notice. "Back there we did a little bit of this and that. But nothing like working in a mill. We're both good workers though. We'll give you our best effort."

Taulby studied the younger, quieter man. What was it that had him on edge about these two?

The younger man returned his look steadily and must have finally felt that Taulby was waiting for him to speak, because he offered, "Yes, sir. Just as he said. We'll work hard."

Taulby wasn't so sure. "What to this area brings you?"

Both men shifted and spoke at the same time.

"Just traveling a little."

"Seeing the country."

Taulby sipped his coffee. Further pressing them wouldn't likely get him closer to the truth. "If I hire you, how long in town will you be?"

The men exchanged a look. The bearded one spoke. "We like it here. Real well. Beautiful country. We're thinking about settling down and making this our permanent home. You know, if we can get work."

Taulby loosed a sigh and studied the creek out his office window-that-wasn't-a-window-yet. He did need more stones hauled out of the creek. And it wasn't a job he relished. Even if he only got a few weeks of work from these two, it would save him hours of time, and they did not need special skills to extract rock.

He returned his focus to them. "All right. Some things I have that you can do. You're hired. A trial you are on, understand?"

The men nodded. "Yes, sir."

"Thank you, sir."

They rose, and the younger shuffled his feet. "We wondered, sir, if we could get paid at the end of each workday, at least for a few days?"

Taulby rubbed his fingers along his jaw. An unreasonable request it was not, he supposed. If they had traveled from Boston, as stated, it might have been some time since they'd eaten a proper meal. That would explain their gauntness. "That I can do. Three dollars a day. But you have to work hard and be consistent."

Both men's eyes widened.

"Yes, sir! Three dollars a day sounds fine."

"Right now, you can start. Since it's noon, I'll pay half today."

They agreed.

"First I'll show you the stones needed. Then"—he fished in the front pocket of his vest for fifty cents and handed each man a quarter—"before work you start, you go to the diner. Good food to fuel good work, yah?"

The men looked a little awed. "Thank you, sir."

Taulby nodded. "Come. Let me show you."

He led them down to the creek, but what he'd just gotten himself into, he couldn't help but wonder.

Aurora paced her room, trying not to be nervous on Tuesday evening. Pressing one hand to her middle, she pulled in a long, calming breath. Tonight could signify a beginning to a lifetime of love and friendship, or it could abruptly bring their fledgling relationship to a crashing halt. Because on her way home from Kane Carver's, she'd been worrying over her lack of peace about going to Seattle.

As she'd walked through the field, she'd seen the caved-in gopher hole and been reminded of what happened to Zoe, and a thought had swept over Aurora with such overwhelming clarity today that she'd nearly been bowled over by it. And on its heels, the first wave of peace she'd felt in quite some time had rolled in. Finally she felt like the Lord was giving her some direction.

She'd decided that she would press him again about allowing her to minister with him. Ministry was his calling, and if they were to make something of this relationship—to become one— it would also be her calling. Coming to terms on this would be the first hurdle they needed to cross.

When she heard the clop of hooves and squeak of wheels in the yard, she took one last look in her mirror. With a nod, she gave herself a mock chuck on the chin. She could do this.

Preston knocked on her door, and she opened it with a tremulous smile. "Good evening." She was still a bit in awe of the fact that he was here. Taking her to dinner!

Preston bowed over her hand, letting his gaze slip over her. "Good evening. I don't think I've ever seen you look prettier."

Glancing down at herself, she smoothed her hands over the front of the blue bombazine dress. She hadn't been at all sure what to wear, but Liora had urged her to choose this one, and from the look in Preston's gaze, she must have chosen wisely. "Thank you."

In the yard, a one-bench cabriolet waited. She recognized the horse at the front as one that Bill Giddens rented at the livery.

Preston held out a hand and helped her up to the bench, then crossed behind the carriage to climb to the driver's seat.

"I'll be the envy of every man in town tonight." He cleared his throat uncertainly.

But uncertain because he hadn't meant the words? Or uncertain because he was nervous?

"It's kind of you to say so." Aurora winced at her awkward reply, and studied her hands. It was going to take them both time to adjust to this new step in their relationship, she supposed.

After the coach had rolled out of the yard, he looked over at her. "How was ladies' Bible study today?"

"Good." She watched the green of the passing hills, then met his gaze. "Poppy attended."

One of his brows winged upward. "Did she?"

"Indeed. But I'm afraid I rather put my foot in my mouth." She explained what had happened.

Preston pondered for a long moment. "Well, none of us are perfect. You apologized, and that's all you can do. I'm sure she'll be fine."

Aurora puffed out a breath. "I hope so."

"Besides . . ." Preston let go of the reins with his near hand and reached hesitantly to take one of Aurora's. When she lifted her gaze to his, he grinned. "I don't want to talk about Poppy."

Aurora smiled and relished the feel of Preston's broad fingers warming her own through her evening gloves. A wave of shyness swept over her, yet she was also surprised to be so comfortable with the action. While she underwent a moment of angst over the unknown future, she also felt utterly and completely comfortable and at home.

She rested her free hand atop his. "Where's Tommy tonight?"

Preston clucked to the horse to urge it into an incline. "Jacinda and Zane's place. If you don't mind, I'll need to pick him up after dinner, and he can ride with us back to Joe and Liora's when I take you home."

Aurora grinned at him. "Since this is only a one-bench carriage, and that means I'll have to sit closer to you on the ride home, I can't say that I protest that necessity at all."

He threw back his head, mouth wide with laughter. And then released her hand to wrap his arm about her shoulders and tug her closer. He bent close to rumble in her ear. "Who says we have to wait until Tommy is sharing the seat with us?"

Awe washed over her. "I can hardly believe we are here."

He squeezed her. "We are here. Let us not look back."

She worried the inside of her lip, wondering if he would feel the same after she told him what she felt the Lord might be saying to her and that she still wanted to minister with him in the camps.

The cabriolet crested the hill above town. With purple-blue dusk falling and the golden lanterns hanging in the doorways of most of shantytown accenting the brighter glow of Main Street's windows, Aurora caught her breath. "Isn't it beautiful, this burgeoning town of ours?"

"It is." But Preston's gaze was not on the view that stretched before them. He was studying her.

Heat crept into her cheeks. It did her good to have him speak to her this way.

He chuckled and leaned close. "I confess, I like to make you blush, Rory."

The name jolted through her with tender familiarity. She looked up at him. It was the name he'd first known her by— back when she was posing as a boy. But also . . . "My pa used to call me his Rory-girl."

"Is that why you chose that name when you came to stay with me?"

She tilted her head in thought. "I suppose it is. I wanted a name that I wouldn't forget to respond to." She smiled.

Preston reined the horses around the corner and pulled to a stop in front of the boardinghouse. "Does it bother you for me to call you that? Bring back bad memories?"

She shook her head. "Not at all. I quite like it."

"Well, then . . ." He helped her down, looped her hand through his arm, and covered it with his own as he grinned down at her. "So do I."

Belle Kastain, who was working the dinner shift, smiled conspiratorially at Aurora as she directed them to a table. "I'll fetch you both water and then take your order. Tonight's specials are lemon-dill rainbow trout or beef stew and cornbread." With that she bustled off.

Aurora's stomach rumbled loudly.

Preston chuckled as he held her chair for her. "Next time, it seems we need to come a little earlier."

Aurora blushed. "No. Truly, this is fine." She didn't elaborate on the fact that she'd been too nervous to eat anything after the tea and cookie she'd had at Bible study this morning.

They made small talk until Belle returned, whereupon they both ordered the trout. Preston asked for coffee, and Aurora ordered a pot of tea.

As Belle hurried toward the kitchen, Preston's gaze settled on Aurora. "So did you talk to Kane yet?"

"Yes."

"How did he take it?"

Aurora thought back to their conversation, feeling her humor rise. "Surprisingly well. I got the feeling that he was even slightly relieved."

Preston reached one hand halfway across the table, palm up. When she settled her own hand into his, he gave her a wink. "That's because he lives in fear and trembling of what I might do to him."

Aurora tilted her head on a laugh. "I'm certain he does! As much as he might fear a bunny or a fuzzy red kit."

"Hey now! I can be very ferocious when I want to be. You've no idea how much self-control it took not to lay my hand to the back of his head the other day in the church."

She relished the joy of their camaraderie. "You are to be commended, Parson, for showing such great restraint!"

Preston smiled. "Indeed I am."

"Indeed you are, what?"

The husky feminine voice behind Aurora filled her with immediate angst. She started to withdraw her hand from Preston's, but he tightened his grip just enough to let her know he didn't want her to, so she remained as she was.

Her heart thudded in her chest. Poppy was not going to like this.

Poppy sidled to a stop by their table.

Aurora studied the grain of the wood in front of her for a long moment, but then chanced a glance at the woman.

Poppy's gaze, which rested on their linked hands, was almost a slit-eyed scowl.

Preston finally broke the silence with a little sound at the back of his throat. "Evening, Poppy."

His thumb slid over Aurora's knuckles, making her swallow. She was torn between relishing his caress and feeling sorry for Poppy, who was obviously upset by it.

But then, to her surprise, Poppy offered them a brilliant smile. "Evening. I can see that I'm interrupting, so I won't keep you any longer. If you'll excuse me . . ." She dropped a parting curtsy and practically skipped to a small table in the far corner of the room.

Aurora searched Preston's face.

He looked back at her steadily. One eyebrow inched above the other.

"You're certain there's nothing there?" she asked.

"The only woman I want is sitting across the table from me, holding my hand." His thumb swept over her knuckles again.

Aurora's anxiety rose. She couldn't go another moment without bringing up the subject that had plagued her all day. "Then . . . I feel there's something we need to address." She wetted her lips.

"What's that?" He took a swig from his water glass.

Aurora fiddled with her fork. "The fact that if we . . . well, one day if we—"

"Marry," he supplied for her candidly.

Was Dixie recently keeping her dining room warmer than usual? Aurora drew in a composing breath. "Yes. One day if we marry, we will be a team, correct? Like one unit?"

He nodded. "I believe the Bible backs that up, yes."

"So then, wouldn't it make sense for me to travel with you and minister alongside you?"

His thumb, which had continued to stroke her knuckles, stilled. "Aurora, I thought we settled this?"

She withdrew her hand into her lap, lifting her gaze to his. "No, I'm not certain we have."

A muscle ticked in his jaw.

She held up a palm for him to listen. "After helping Zoe, a thought occurred to me that I can't help but feel may have come

directly from the Lord. I don't foresee using a musical degree
to help people—at least, I'm proficient enough for the tasks
I've taken on. Getting a degree in music might be beneficial if
I felt called to join an orchestra, or some such. But I don't feel
that's my place. However, if I switched my focus—maybe let
Doc teach me medicine—I could be a great help to you. You
could tend to people's souls, and I could tend to their physical
wounds. It would ease some of Doc's burden, too, if I took on
some of the lighter cases in these parts. And I wouldn't have
to go away."

Preston shifted uneasily.

She took a hasty sip of her water. "I've been troubled by that.
Going to Seattle. Even before you and I spoke yesterday. I just
never really felt a peace about the conservatory. But this—the
thought of helping the sick alongside you in the camps—I truly
feel peace about this."

Preston frowned. Swiped at the drops of moisture on his
glass. "Aurora, a woman as beautiful as you? In the camps? I'd
be a fool to even consider it. The answer is an emphatic no."

She sank against her chair's slats, disappointment crashing
through her. She wasn't ready to let this go. "So you trust the
Lord to protect you but not me, is that it?"

He frowned. "Nothing of the kind. I can take care of myself.
Plus, risking my own life is a different thing. It's part of my
calling before the Lord."

"I see. And the Lord can call you to minister and risk your
life, but He can't call a woman to the same?"

His frown deepened. For a long moment he remained silent.
He turned his fork tines-down and then tines-up, repeating the
motion several times.

Belle arrived with their plates and drinks and set the food
on the table. Seeming to sense the tension that had sprung up,

she glanced back and forth between them. "C-can I get you anything else?"

Preston flicked her a glance. "This will be fine. Thank you."

Aurora offered her a tight smile that she hoped conveyed gratitude and not the irritation swelling inside her.

Behind the parson's chair, Belle pulled a face that indicated she'd have Aurora's back if she needed her. "All right. I'll check with you again in a few minutes."

Aurora watched her escape across the room to take Poppy's order, with a little envy. She would like nothing more than to escape also, or at the very least return to the camaraderie she and Preston had shared a few minutes ago. Yet they couldn't take their relationship further without working through this.

Preston cleared his throat. "Shall we say grace?"

"Please do." Aurora bowed her head and tried to be grateful for the food and circumstances. She wasn't so certain she succeeded, however.

Stilted conversation hung over the rest of the meal like a wet blanket. They chatted about a little bit of everything, but nothing of substance. And when finally, an hour later, Preston pulled the cabriolet to a stop outside her door and helped her down, Aurora still didn't feel as though anything had been resolved.

"Good night, Tommy," she offered, as she started toward the bunkhouse.

"N-night, Miss A-Aurora," Tommy replied. "I w-wait h-here, PC?"

Behind her, she heard Preston sigh. "Yes, Tom-Tom. I'll be right back."

"O-Okay."

As she tromped toward the bunkhouse, Preston took her hand from behind and gently pulled her to a stop. With a soft sigh, he gripped her shoulders. He looked intently into her eyes. "You do realize that my wanting to keep you from the camps is only because of my desire to keep you safe, don't you?"

Aurora stepped away from his touch and led the way onto the porch. "I understand that, but I can't help but feel you're being more than a bit overbearing about it."

"Overbearing?" He folded his arms. "How can it be overbearing to want your protection?"

Despair took hold of Aurora. There would be no resolving this tonight, and she felt the beginnings of a headache coming on. "Let's both give ourselves some time to think on it, shall we?" She gripped her temples between thumb and forefinger. "We can speak on the subject again in a couple days. Meanwhile, if it's all right with you, I'll ask Doc what he thinks about my idea?"

Even in the shadows beneath the bunkhouse porch, she could see his brow was furrowed. He took in the hand massaging her temples. "Headache?"

She brushed his concern aside. "Just a small one. It will pass." She searched his face, willing him to relent.

But instead of relenting, his jaw set, and she knew what he was about to say before he even opened his mouth. "I don't suppose there's any harm in you speaking to Doc, but I have to tell you that I don't foresee anything that will make me change my mind on this."

Aurora tipped her chin, anger flaring. "Well then, I don't see that we have a future, Parson Clay." She gave the formal address of his name emphasis to draw his attention to it. "I bid you good evening."

She presented him with her back and yanked open her door.

"Aurora, don't—"

It gave her great satisfaction to bang the door shut in the insufferable parson's face.

Guilt immediately overcame her for the immature action, and she pulled the door open again.

Preston was still where she'd left him, staring at her with a blank look on his face.

She clasped her hands and looked down at them. "That was uncalled for. Please accept my sincerest apology." She peeked at him through her lashes.

A muscle bulged in his jaw. He gripped the back of his neck. "I accept your apology. And I want to promise you we'll work through this, Aurora. I do. But the truth is, I'm not certain I see how we'll manage. At least not unless one of us relents." He gave her a pointed look that made it clear he did not plan to be that one.

With all her hopes for their future deflating around her, Aurora felt her shoulders sag. "Perhaps we should sleep on it? Can we talk again tomorrow?"

He shook his head. "Tomorrow I have a funeral at Camp Sixty-Three, followed by a wedding at Camp Sixty-Five in the evening."

"I see." Aurora pressed her lips into a tight line to keep herself from spilling more of her disappointment. She laced her fingers before her.

With a puff of breath, Preston reached out and took her hands. He rolled her little finger gently between his thumb and first finger. Tilted his head down to look her in the face. "I could do Thursday morning if you can meet me for breakfast at the boardinghouse?" He cocked one brow. "How does eight o'clock sound?"

She nodded. Swallowed. Willed herself not to think about how handsome he was when he looked at her like that. Focused on their clasped hands instead. "Yes. That will work." She took a calming breath and blinked away the threatening tears.

But her disappointment could not be denied. Shouldn't their declarations of love for each other have smoothed the seas for clear sailing?

"Aurora." Preston cupped her face and tilted her chin so she met his searching look. "Would you let me pray for us? If the Lord wants us together, surely He can help us figure this out, yes?"

The words were like a balm to her weary heart. "Yes. Let's pray."

Preston's voice rang low and mellow as he asked the Lord to help them hear His plan for their future, closing with, "And may we ever live to serve each other and not ourselves. Amen."

He released her hand but not her gaze as he backed toward the porch steps. "I'll see you Thursday. Until then, I'll hold you here." He clapped a hand over his heart. And then he disappeared into the darkness.

Aurora shut the door and leaned against it, working her teeth over her lower lip. The prayer had helped calm her.

But she was definitely going to do some praying of her own.

Because if ever they were to have a happy future, Preston was going to have to learn not to be so high handed.

Chapter Twenty-one

With her shift finally over, Belle removed her apron and massaged some kinks from her shoulders. Ma gathered the children, who had been doing their homework at a table in the corner of the boardinghouse kitchen, and they stepped onto the street.

The evening was warm, and an orange-and-crimson sunset stretched across the western sky, filling Belle with awe at the Creator's painting. She took in the colors, memorizing them for her next palette. Above her head, soft strawberry-pink clouds shot through with streaks of apple red floated like fluffs of cottonwood. Closer to the horizon, a swath almost the exact shade of Zoe's hair was rimmed with a glow the color of Dixie's lemon meringue pie and softened with strokes of Ma's peach preserves.

"Belle," Ma called.

Belle returned her focus to the earth and realized her family was all staring at her. "Sorry." She hurried forward to where Mr. Harrow waited for them by a wagon.

Exchanging a soft smile, Mr. Harrow and Ma gave each other's hands a quick squeeze, then Ma started for home with the children while Mr. Harrow helped Belle climb aboard the wagon.

They were headed to see Kane Carver. Just the thought startled a barrage of butterflies in Belle's middle. She did her best to relax and focus, instead, on the beautiful evening, but despite her resolve, her hands clenched so tightly in her lap that her fingernails pressed into her palms. Thankfully, Mr. Harrow seemed content to drive the wagon in silence, and Belle only had to give succinct directions once in a while.

As they rounded the last corner and approached the cabin, Belle swept the place with an artist's scrutiny. The Carvers had done a lot of work to the cabin they rented from Kin Davis, who was out of town in Seattle. Kin had only been a boy when he lived here with his pa, who had later passed away, but at that time the cabin had been not much more than a canted pile of logs with large gaps. Since the Carvers had moved in, they had shored up the walls and added fresh chinking. The porch was brand new, with a peeled-log railing that gleamed like browned butter in the waning light.

The golden light spilling from the windows cast rectangular swashes of light across the hard-packed dirt in front of the cabin.

"Whoa." Mr. Harrow pulled the wagon to a stop and hopped down.

As Belle waited for him to make his way to her side, she turned her focus to the corral. An Appaloosa colt that Kane must be training kicked up its heels and whinnied loudly as it darted around the perimeter of the enclosure.

Just as Mr. Harrow reached her side, the cabin door opened, and Kane stepped onto the porch, wiping his hands on a serviette. "Good evening!"

Belle missed Mr. Harrow's hand and practically fell off the wagon. She was only saved from splatting on her face by Mr. Harrow's quick grasp of her waist.

Brow's lifted, he looked down at her. "You all right?"

Feeling her humiliation rise, Belle smoothed her hands over her skirt. "Yes. Thank you." She tucked her hands behind herself and clasped them tight. *Breathe. Just breathe.*

She looked toward the house once more, feeling Mr. Harrow turn to do the same.

Kane's gaze swept Belle from head to toe and back again, and even from this distance she could see the flash of his white teeth as he smiled in the darkness of the porch.

Heat blazed through her cheeks. So he hadn't missed her clumsiness. She turned her attention to how the shadows of the window's crossbeams angled against the plain of the land.

She heard, more than saw, Kane stride down the steps and reach a hand to Mr. Harrow. "Name is Carver. Kane Carver."

Mr. Harrow accepted Kane's clasp. "I'm Elijah Harrow." He tipped a nod toward Belle. "I presume you know that this is Belle Kastain."

Kane's grin widened as his focus transferred to Belle. "Yes. Miss Kastain and I have met." Feeling the impact of his searching gaze all the way to her toes, Belle lowered her focus to the ground once more. She resisted the urge to shield herself behind Mr. Harrow.

The porch creaked, and Maude Carver stopped at the top of the steps. "Kane, why don't you invite everyone inside? I've set a couple extra places."

Kane stepped back and swept a gesture toward the stairs. "Yes. Please do join us. Maude makes the best stew this side of the Mississippi."

Belle felt her embarrassment compound. They should have realized they'd be interrupting dinnertime. "We really don't want to disturb your dinner. I'm sorry we arrived at an inconvenient time."

"Nonsense. We've got plenty. Besides, conversation is always better over a good meal." His hand remained stretched in indication that they should lead the way up the steps. His gaze settled on her, warm and inviting.

Mr. Harrow placed a hand to her back and nudged her forward.

As she stepped inside the tiny cabin, Belle felt conspicuous. There was hardly any place to turn, and her skirts took up most of the available space.

Maude motioned to two chairs on the near side of the table. "Please make yourself at home."

Seth Carver, the youngest of the three siblings, sat on the opposite side of the table. He gave them a nod. "Evening."

Mr. Harrow and Belle returned his greeting as Mr. Harrow held Belle's chair, and they sat.

To Belle's consternation, Kane stepped in behind them and sank into the seat at the end of the table, just to her right. He smoothed his serviette into his lap, and his smile was as large as a cat licking cream as he said, "We were just about to say grace." He held his hands out toward Belle and his brother.

With a twist of her lips, Maude sank into her seat at the head of the table, nearest the kitchen. "Fortuitous that you both arrived just when you did." She quirked a dark brow at her brother, and Belle heard him give a soft chuckle.

"Indeed."

"Best we dig in," Maude continued. "Stew and biscuits are always better piping hot." Her gaze shifted to Belle.

Belle realized that everyone had taken hands, including the fact that she had already taken Mr. Harrow's hand, but Kane's hand still stretched across the corner of the table toward her, palm up—and empty.

She took a breath. Met his gaze.

In the depths of his chocolate-brown eyes, there was a soft understanding, even if it was accompanied by a teasing glint.

Across the table, Seth shifted and cleared his throat.

She was holding up the prayer.

Belle snapped her hand into Kane's and was thankful for the excuse to immediately close her eyes.

The fingers that closed around hers were broad and rough. Callused. A working-man's hands. Just like Pa's had been. The kind of hands that could be trusted. The kind of hands that made a woman feel safe. Unaccountably, she felt tears prick the backs of her eyes. Not since Pa had she sensed this much of a connection to a man. Not even Mr. Harrow, whom she'd been surprised to accept and love so easily. How was it that she barely knew Kane Carver yet felt so at ease, and all at once discomfited, by his presence?

Seth cleared his throat a little more loudly this time, and Belle came back to the present. The prayer had ended, and her fingers were still nestled in Kane's. She snatched her hand into her lap, her embarrassment ablaze.

Mr. Harrow passed her a plate. "Biscuit?" A sparkle of amusement glinted in the man's gaze, but his quick wink set her at ease. He slurped noisily from his spoon, drawing everyone's attention to himself. "My, this is a delicious stew, Miss Carver. What is your secret?"

"Basil and plenty of tomatoes." With a quick little glance in Belle's direction, she continued to ramble about how the potatoes from last year's crop had been so plentiful that she'd had plenty of opportunity to perfect her recipe.

Belle appreciated how Maude had joined in to remove the focus from her.

Mr. Harrow waited until everyone had almost finished eating before his gaze settled on Kane. "So Belle tells me you are the man to see if we need a horse?"

Kane glanced between the two of them. It was obvious he was trying to discern how they were connected.

Belle dabbed at her lips with her napkin. "Mr. Harrow is soon to marry my ma," she offered quietly.

"Ah!" The relief in Kane's exclamation had Belle hiding a smile behind another pat of her serviette.

"We wondered if you knew of a horse for sale in these parts?" Mr. Harrow asked. "We'd like a good strong animal with plenty of years left—"

Belle laid a hand on Mr. Harrow's arm. She'd better jump in before he committed them to an animal they couldn't afford. She'd talked to Ma, and they'd decided they couldn't spend a penny more than ten dollars. Even that would leave them without any savings. Belle's stomach crimped at the mere thought. What would they do if another expense arose?

Realizing every eye around the table was settled on her and that she'd once again left them waiting, she despaired. If she didn't gather her thoughts and act like a normal-thinking human being, Mr. Carver was going to take her for a fool. "I'm not certain if you heard, but our horse, Lilac . . . had a bad fall the other day. She survived but can no longer be ridden."

Kane dropped his spoon. It clattered against his bowl. "Oh no. I'm so sorry."

"Thank you. Zoe was riding across the field, and a gopher tunnel gave way beneath Lilac's hooves. There was no way Zoe could have known it was there. Thankfully, Mr. Eklund arrived soon after." Belle left off the story there. They didn't need to know all the details. "My youngest brother, Aidan, needs a horse for his job. But we can't . . . that is, we want a horse he can ride, but, well . . . a great deal depends upon the price, you see."

Kane's gaze settled on Mr. Harrow for a moment before he slathered some butter on his biscuit. "I understand. There are a few available horses in the area. However, it will help me to know how much you can afford."

Swallowing her trepidation over the low amount, Belle quietly offered, "Ten dollars." She pretended great interest in her stew, knowing how unlikely it was that they'd find a decent horse for that price.

Mr. Harrow cleared his throat. "Belle means to say a hundred and ten dollars. Or more, if it's required."

Belle choked on the last bite of her broth, but Mr. Harrow went on eating as though nothing out of the ordinary had just happened. She turned her gaze on the man. They had never in their lives owned such a fine horse. How much money did this man her ma was set to marry have?

Kane seemed to take it all in stride. He tipped his head toward the corral outside. "The Appaloosa colt you saw when you arrived, I'm still training him, but he's going to be a fine horse when I'm done. Lots of spirit. I could let him go for . . . a hundred and twenty-five."

Even as Belle's stomach sank at the price, she noticed Kane's gaze ping off Maude's. Maude's lips pinched into a thin line, but she held her silence and poked at her stew. Could such a high price not be enough to cover what they'd put into the animal?

Kane shifted and pressed ahead. "In the meantime, while he's still in training, I'd be happy to let Aidan ride one of our other horses on the days he needs to do deliveries."

Wiping his fingers on his serviette, Mr. Harrow swallowed the last of his biscuit. "That sounds fine." He reached into an inner pocket of his vest and withdrew a billfold. He extracted several bills and slid them across the table to Kane. "There's a little extra there for the remainder of his training, boarding, and the expense of his feed until we take him home."

Kane tried to slide a portion of the money back. "I'm a man of my word, Mr. Harrow. I named the price I meant."

"Yes, I know." Mr. Harrow held up one hand. "But it simply wouldn't be the right thing for us to buy a horse and then expect you to complete the training and feeding of it at your own expense. Please, take it. Truly"—he looked up and met Kane's gaze—"the cost is no hardship."

Belle felt as though her head were spinning.

Maude looked considerably relieved and pinned Kane with a pointed look. A jut of her chin seemed to indicate he oughtn't reject the extra money a second time.

Somewhat hesitantly, Kane drew the bills toward himself once more. "Well, all right. I'll make sure the horse is as gentle as a kitten before I complete his training, sir."

Mr. Harrow nodded. "I'm sure you will. Now" —he pushed himself back from the table—"I fear we've intruded on your hospitality long enough. Belle? Shall we head for home?"

He pulled out her chair, and she was still too stunned to do anything but follow his lead.

"Good night, everyone. Thank you for the delicious meal."

Belle reminded herself of her manners. "Yes. Thank you." She dipped a shallow curtsy to Kane and his siblings, then hurried to step through the door Mr. Harrow was holding for her.

Mr. Harrow helped Belle to the seat and snapped the reins to set the horse and wagon moving before he offered quietly, "Perhaps we could keep the amount we paid for that horse just between the two of us? At least for a while?"

Belle swallowed. Nodded.

He'd just handed over two hundred dollars! More than she and Ma together made in two months at the boardinghouse.

Poppy grinned as she lay on her bed in her room and stared at the ceiling. She really oughtn't smile based on the way Preston had flaunted that lass in her face. He'd wanted her to know that he'd moved on and there was no longer anything between them. She'd gotten that message plain.

Nevertheless, she couldn't help but smile. For the solution she'd been searching for had suddenly been revealed to her, and she knew clear as a cloudless day just what she needed to do now.

A little more patience and her plan would be complete. She had the approximate date of the arrival of the money. Now she just needed to wait. She would watch the bank and have her plan in place.

How providential was it that the sheriff's mother had mentioned being chained in a cave just outside of town? Tomorrow she would do a bit of exploring. But to escape town without being followed, she would need a diversion. That part would be easy.

She would find the location. Then as soon as they could move, she would be ready.

Now she put her mind to coming up with an escape plan. And maybe, just maybe, she'd be able to help Preston see the difference between a girl and a woman.

She laughed. Rolled over on her bed and traced a finger along the counterpane.

Yes. Maybe she would.

Chapter Twenty-two

Taulby Eklund paused before the small scrap of looking glass hanging outside his kitchen door. He adjusted his string tie and cocked an eyebrow at his tousled blond hair. Never could he seem to keep it from going every which direction. No amount or brand of hair cream had been able to tame his stubborn Swedish curls.

He blew out a breath. Perfect hair wasn't likely to make a difference. No matter that he'd been picking Zoe up and giving her a ride to school for a couple of days now, she didn't seem interested in anything further. He had a feeling a fellow must be in the picture that he didn't know about. Nevertheless, he would keep being a gentleman and bide his time. Maybe at some point the tide would turn in his favor. At any rate, the journey would be pleasurable. Zoe Kastain was a woman most fascinating.

She was ready and waiting when he arrived at the Kastain place. Her sister handed him the stool for Zoe's injured foot. Zoe didn't weigh any more than a trifle. He easily hoisted her to the seat.

He tried to make conversation with her as he drove the wagon toward the schoolhouse, but she remained quiet. Distracted.

"Everything is all right?" he asked.

"Pardon? Oh yes. I apologize. I haven't been very good company for the past couple days, have I?"

Taulby gave her distraction a pass with the swipe of one hand. "Seems you've had on your mind many things. But on my account do not worry. Just if ever you need anything to talk about, I'm a good listener, yah?" He gave her a friendly bump of his elbow.

She smiled, but the distance remained in her expression. "I appreciate that, Mr. Eklund."

"No need for such formality. Please, Taulby, you can call me." He held his breath wondering if she would reciprocate the offer.

She hesitated, and he thought she would ignore his gesture of friendship. But then she offered that beautiful blue-eyed smile. "And you can call me Zoe."

Taulby grinned. Somehow he was suddenly feeling like all was right with the world. Too bad the schoolhouse wasn't farther away because, already, they had arrived. He helped her down and got her situated, and then, feeling like a spring calf ready to kick up his heels, he headed for the mill.

The two men he'd hired the day before stood, seemingly in a deep discussion, in the mill yard. Something about the tension in the line of their shoulders arrested Taulby's awareness. What did they have here? Suddenly, the bearded one, Smith, shoved the other man, Jones, in the chest. He went down hard.

Jones didn't take kindly to being pushed and came up swinging.

"This you must stop!" Taulby yelled.

But neither man seemed to have heard him. They tumbled over each other, teetering on the brink of the creek, both giving as good as they got.

Taulby hurried the horses, but by the time he parked the wagon and dashed across the Wyldhaven Creek bridge, the sheriff, the deputy, and the marshal were all running their way.

Taulby reached the fracas first. "*Sluta!*"

The men ignored him.

Taulby realized he'd spoken the word in Swedish as he ducked a fist. "Stop!" He pushed Smith back and pressed a hand against the other man's chest, standing between the two like a referee at a boxing match.

"You are crazy!" Jones leaned around him to shake a finger at Smith. He tried to push past Taulby.

"Whoa. Whoa. Whoa." The sheriff approached Jones from behind and captured the man's arms. "What's going on here?"

Taulby blew out a breath and shrugged. "Arrived only just now. These two dummkopfs, I hired yesterday." He hoped the glower he gave both men conveyed his displeasure with their conduct. They'd been good workers yesterday afternoon. He hoped he wouldn't have to fire them.

Smith didn't seem ready to let the matter drop. With a curse, he lunged toward his partner. "Give it back, you blasted fool!"

To hold him now required both the deputy and the marshal.

Taulby plopped his hands on his hips and scowled at his two newest employees. "What here is going on?"

"He took my pocket watch." Smith strained toward the other man.

Jones produced a fob and dangled it from its chain. "I was only checking the time! Wanted to make sure we arrived at work on schedule."

Taulby narrowed his eyes. Something false rang in the man's words.

Smith snatched the watch and thrust it into the front pocket of his vest. "Well, next time I'll thank you to ask when you want to see it." He looked sheepish as he glanced at those gathered. "It was my father's."

As fast as it seemed to have escalated, the tension evaporated from the two men's stances. The sheriff and his men relaxed as well. They released the two men and glanced between them.

"Everything going to be okay here, then?" the sheriff asked.

Both men nodded.

The sheriff fixed his gaze on Smith. "You pressing charges for him taking your watch?"

"Nah. We're fine."

Sheriff Callahan's eyes narrowed. "I need you both to know that I run a clean show here. Any more fighting and you both will be escorted out of town. Understand?"

The men nodded.

But Taulby was not willing to let it go so easily. "And I a clean business run. Tolerate I won't, any more such behavior as this. To work get, both of you."

Looking like two chastised schoolboys, both men waded into the creek and started extracting stones.

Taulby stretched a hand toward the sheriff. "About this, I am sorry."

The sheriff clasped his hand in a firm grip. "We appreciate the fact that the mill is going to be a boon for Wyldhaven. But let's try to keep any trouble to a minimum."

Taulby nodded. His irritation rose. Just what he needed. These two employees causing him trouble in the town. "Yah, Sheriff. Completely, I understand."

As the three lawmen started back toward town, Taulby blew out a sigh and headed for the mill office. Somehow this day that had looked so promising now felt a little gray.

Poppy smirked as she led her mount out the back door of the livery on Wednesday morning. She couldn't resist a peek around the side of the barn. On the far end of town, Smith and Jones whaled on each other, rolling and tumbling on the shore of the creek. The town's three lawmen already barreled toward the fight.

With a chuckle, she swung into the saddle. It was always so satisfying when a plan fell into place. She had better not waste her men's efforts.

A click of her tongue set her horse at a smart trot out of town, and she left the roadway as soon as she found a feasible spot to cut back into the forest.

The sheriff's mother had said the cave she had been held in was to the south of town and partway up a cliff.

Poppy had surreptitiously asked for more details from the old liveryman and felt certain she wouldn't have much trouble finding the cave.

She followed the man's instructions to the letter and, sure enough, exactly where he said it would be, she came out at the base of a cliff. The patch of huckleberries was larger than she'd expected. She grunted. Finding a path through this tangle would take her longer than she'd anticipated. She eyed the brush critically. Her gaze snagged on what appeared to be a sparser area, but when she stepped forward and parted the branches, nothing but more thickly interwoven shrubs lay beyond.

There was no other recourse than to work her way down the brush line in a thorough search. Branches scratched her arms, and a little farther on, one even sprang back to whack her in the face. With a curse, she dabbed at the scratch. Her fingers came away dotted with blood. She swore again. Now she would face a barrage of questions over how she'd scratched her face. She attacked the bushes with new fervor, determined not to let them get the best of her.

Frustration had her nearly at a boiling point by the time she found the little path that led back to the base of the cliff. A rocky ledge angled up the cliff face, and taking up her pack,

Poppy pressed her back against the wall and reminded herself not to look down as she inched her way up the incline.

When she reached the cave, it was not merely a shallow indent in the rock face, as she had imagined, but a full-fledged, narrow-mouthed, black-as-sin hole that taunted her with its perfection.

She lowered herself gingerly to her hands and knees and peered into the dark maw. Her heart thudded in trepidation. What if something was living in there? She rolled her eyes at herself and tugged her pack from her back and dug inside for the supplies she'd need.

Striking a match, she then lit the lantern and thrust it into the mouth of the cave as far as her arm could reach. The light might as well have been draped in black cloth. Grunting in frustration, she inched ahead keeping the light thrust before her. Her heart hammered so fast that she felt a sweat break out and trickle between her shoulder blades. Unable to see for more than a few inches in front of her, she felt like she could be creeping forward into the heart of the mountain eternally. But then, as soon as that thought had made itself known, the lantern lit up the brown tones of a sheer wall that blocked her from going farther. She had reached the end.

She turned to the right and, just as Jacinda Holloway had described, found the chains and manacles still hanging from the wall.

Despite her continued discomfort with the darkness, Poppy gave the chains a flick with one finger, and a huge grin broke out on her face. All the day's exasperation came to fruition in this one moment of perfection.

This was just exactly what she needed.

Aurora dragged herself into the Rodantes' kitchen the morning after her dinner with Preston.

Liora was already standing before the stove stirring a pot of porridge. She looked up and paused. "Everything all right?"

Despite her resolve to keep it together, Aurora felt tears welling in her eyes. "I'm not certain that Preston and I will be able to make a courtship work."

"Whyever not?" Liora plunked her hands onto her hips.

Aurora dabbed at the moisture beneath her eyes with the pads of her fingers. "We got into an argument. He doesn't feel that a woman's place is beside him in ministry. If we marry, he expects me to stay home and keep house, rather than travel with him to the camps to work."

Liora gave the porridge another stir and then tugged the pot to the coolest part of the stove. She crossed the room and handed Law to Aurora. "Take him for a moment, if you don't mind, while I finish setting the table for breakfast."

Aurora snuggled the baby against her shoulder, watching Liora cross the room with bowls and spoons. She hadn't missed the way her friend had not responded to her complaint. "Do you think I'm being unreasonable? All I asked was that he allow me to travel with him to the camps to minister alongside him."

She watched Liora's shoulders rise and fall on a breath. "You and I, Aurora, are very familiar with what rough places the camps can be. I'm certain he only wants to protect you."

"And what better way for him to protect me than with me fast by his side!"

"Yes, but try to see it from his perspective. He won't want to be taking you into a place where he may be *required* to act for your protection."

Aurora felt her hopes deflate even as she realized that baby Law had tilted his head back to examine her intently. She took a moment to gather her thoughts as she smiled down at him and made faces. My, he was going to be a lady killer with all that dark hair and those amazing blue eyes. After a moment, the baby chuckled and reached up to pat Aurora's cheek. She captured his chubby fingers in her own and returned her focus to Liora. "I guess I thought you would be on my side."

Liora gave her a pinched-lip look as she crossed to the stove and hefted the porridge pot. "I am ever on your side. As I am ever on Preston's side. I am friends of you both." After setting the porridge on the table, she stepped onto the porch and clanged the triangle that would let the other women know breakfast was ready. When she returned to the kitchen, she slipped one arm around Aurora's shoulders and tilted their heads together.

Aurora felt the comfort of a friend's embrace.

"Don't let this disagreement, dear Aurora, come between you and the parson. You both have so much to offer each other." With that she straightened, took Law, and crossed to the table, where she sank onto her seat and settled the baby on one knee.

Joe stepped into the room, still buttoning one of his cuffs. "Morning, ladies." He bent over his wife.

Liora lifted her cheek to accept his kiss. Joe also bussed a kiss against his son's downy curls, making Law giggle with the noise.

The other women arrived, and everyone sat at the table. After grace, Aurora ate her porridge mechanically. She helped with the dishes and then returned to her room in the bunkhouse, where she flopped onto her bed and stared at the ceiling.

"Lord? Am I being unreasonable? The camps can be dangerous, I suppose. But surely not for a respectable woman serving by her respectable husband's side? Besides, You haven't called us to hide in safety but to go into all the world and share the gospel."

It was as though those words ignited a fire in her soul. A burning desire to be in ministry as a helpmate and not hiding in the background. She sat up and looked at the mirror across the room. She gave herself a nod of encouragement.

She would go right now and speak to Doc about becoming a nurse. The territorial university didn't offer training for that, but if Doc couldn't teach her everything she needed to know, surely he would know a place where she could attend classes.

In the meantime, she would pray that the Lord would work on Preston's heart to see that a woman was more than just a housekeeper but could also be a partner and a helper.

oppy was ready. Her plan was in place. She met her men outside of town in the edge of the forest. She smirked as they approached looking dog tired. "How was work?"

Smith snatched his hat from his head and crumpled it in his hands. "That little stunt you had us pull almost got us fired."

Poppy waved a hand of dismissal. "It doesn't matter. Your task there is done. Soon I'll have a different job for you to do."

Jones shuffled his feet. "When will that be? Because if it's all the same to you, until then I'd like to keep working at the mill. He pays well."

"You and me both," Smith mumbled under his breath.

Poppy didn't miss the proclamation. Her hand flew. A resounding crack reverberated through the morning as her palm connected with Smith's cheek.

Startled, the man rocketed back a couple steps, blinking at her in shock.

Poppy raised a finger. She glanced between the two men. "Don't either of you ever forget who your real boss is. Or what you owe me."

The men exchanged a glance, and Poppy could almost see them recollecting how she had saved them from jail by bringing them west with her.

She forced herself to relax, seeing that she again had the upper hand. She would relent a little. "Now I am fine with you working at the mill for a few more days. Just so long as you're ready the moment I call for you."

Both men nodded.

Smith pressed the heel of his hand to his jaw and worked it back and forth. "We'll be ready."

With a nod of satisfaction, Poppy headed toward town.

She had prepared as best she could.

Now all she had to do was wait. And listen.

Breakfast in the boardinghouse sounded lovely.

Sheriff Reagan Callahan was in his office on Wednesday morning with his boots propped on the corner of his desk, sipping a cup of coffee, when suddenly Parson Preston Clay burst through the door. Reagan lurched upright, barely able to keep from spilling coffee all over his chest.

"Parson? Everything all right?" Reagan set his cup on the blotter.

The parson paced from the door to the metal bars of the cells and back again. "I have an idea. But I need you to hear me out."

Reagan nodded for him to continue. He glanced over to see Tommy peering through the window. He smiled and gave Tommy a wave. The parson had obviously instructed Tommy to remain on the porch.

"You know how I mentioned to you that the woman, Poppy Scarlatti, is the daughter of the mob boss I worked for back in Boston? And how I was worried about the bank money?"

Reagan's unease mounted. "Yeah. I take it you don't believe her confession of conversion?"

The parson blew out a heavy breath. "I would love nothing more than to believe her, but the Word declares we will know believers by their fruit. I was just in Dixie's boardinghouse for breakfast. And I noticed Poppy in there too."

Reagan folded his arms and frowned. He wasn't quite sure how Poppy and Preston having breakfast at the same time had brought the man to his office. "Go on."

The parson massaged his hands into the muscles of his shoulders as he continued to pace. "I could be wrong, but it seemed that Poppy was straining to listen to the conversations of everyone around her. I think she's trying to overhear information about the arrival of the bank money."

Reagan squinted at the parson. "Seems a little farfetched, don't you think?"

Preston sighed. "I do admit that my past experience with her might have me seeing things that aren't there. But in this case, don't you think it would be better to be safe than sorry?"

He did have a point there. Reagan downed another bracing gulp of coffee. "Yes."

"Good. I do too. And that got me to thinking . . ." Preston spun on one heel and stopped, facing Reagan.

"Yeah?"

"You are not going to like it."

Reagan studied the man over the rim of his cup. "We did follow her the other day. She met with two men in the forest just outside of town. Interestingly enough, the same two men just got hired by Taulby Eklund down at the mill."

"They'll be working for her then, mark my words on that. But do you want to hear my plan?"

"Listening never cost a man anything."

Preston forged ahead. "Her eavesdropping got me to thinking. If she's going to eavesdrop, why don't we give her a conversation worthy of eavesdropping on? Well, by *we*, I mean you and your deputies, of course." The parson raised his palms in deference. "I don't want to be part of it, because I don't want to know when the money is arriving for the bank. Above reproach and all that. But without a safecracker, she'll need to hit the shipment before it reaches town. That must be what she's hoping to learn. I just thought if you fed her a little misinformation, it might be the ticket to protecting the money until it reaches the bank."

Reagan tilted his head with a grin. "Now, Parson, you wouldn't be advocating deception, would you?"

The parson didn't smile as Reagan had thought he would. Instead, he looked solemn. "I do admit that I have pondered that quite a bit. But in some instances when a deception is for the greater good of humanity, I feel it is justified. Like Rahab who hid the two spies and lied to save their lives, I feel, in this instance, the greater good will be served by this plan. I know there are plenty of people—children, even—whose lives may be at stake if that money doesn't come through. One of my parishioners out at Camp Sixty-Five has secured a loan from Mr. Olann to build an orphanage for children in the camp. They currently sleep under nothing more than a bit of canvas stretched between a few trees. Sickness is rampant among them. The orphanage building is severely needed. But the contractor has refused to start construction until he has the money in hand. Not only that, the piece of property she secured has been promised to someone else if she doesn't come up with the money on time. And there are other such cases that I know of. So . . ." The parson shrugged. "Maybe the information Poppy overhears doesn't have to be an outright lie?" He waved a hand. "I'll leave the details up to you boys. Just . . . try not to harm her, aye?"

Reagan pondered. It actually wasn't a bad idea. In fact, it was a downright good idea. And it would help them clarify whether Poppy was indeed a bad player or converted, as she claimed. If they let it slip that the money would be at a certain place at a certain time, and she showed up hoping to steal it, that would prove she wasn't who she claimed to be. "I like your plan. I'll talk to Zane and Joe, and we'll put something into play."

The parson tipped his hat. "I best get going. Have a busy day ahead of me." He gave a wave of farewell and stepped onto the porch, then pulled the door shut.

Reagan stared after him with a shake of his head. The parson was in many ways the quietest, most withdrawn man, and yet the deepest-thinking man Reagan had ever known.

He reached for his hat. He needed to find his deputies.

When Aurora arrived in town on Wednesday morning, Doc was emerging from the boardinghouse with a huge yawn.

"Good morning, Doc."

He tipped his hat and stepped out of her way. "Morning, Aurora. Dixie just headed into the kitchen." He started toward the livery.

She fell into step beside him. "Actually, it's you I'm here to see today."

He hesitated and turned to face her with a frown. "What can I do for you? Someone sick out at the Rodante place?"

"No, no. I'm actually here to ask you about becoming a nurse."

Doc's brows nudged upward. He pushed the brim of his hat back with one finger. "Come again?"

Aurora smiled. "I'm sure you may have heard that I was accepted to the Territorial University of Washington's music conservatory. However, I'm considering transferring to a medical training and wondered if you knew of a good program to attend? I know that many times you have lamented not having more medical help in this area. And since I'm strongly leaning toward a switch in my focus, I wondered what advice you could give me?"

Doc folded his arms and shifted, still looking down at her with surprise on his face. "Don't get me wrong—I could definitely use the help. I just have never heard you say before that you were interested in medicine."

Aurora folded her hands together and glanced toward the church up the hill.

Doc followed her gaze, and understanding lit his expression.

Aurora shifted. "You're right. The thought actually came as a surprise to me as well. But I've been praying for direction, and when the idea presented itself the other day, it simply felt right. After I get some education, I could take on some of the less urgent cases to lighten your burden." She didn't add that she also wanted to travel with Parson Clay and help him minister in the camps. But just the thought of it made the heat of frustration flush her face. She glanced down at her clasped hands.

"I don't think the university offers a nursing program yet."

Aurora nodded. "Yes. If I change my direction and focus on medicine, I would need to drop out of the university."

"The best way I can think for you to get such training would be to work under a doctor. But I have heard of a nurses' school in New York. Would you want to travel that far?"

Aurora's eyes widened. All the way to New York? She worried her teeth over the inside of her lower lip. "If you felt that was the best place for me to gain experience in nursing, I would be willing to travel that far, yes." Just the thought of going that far alone made her mouth dry with trepidation.

Doc angled himself to where he could look up the hill toward the parsonage. For some strange reason, he seemed a little uneasy as he said, "If you wanted, I'd be more than happy to give you the training you need. That way you wouldn't have to travel all the way to New York."

Relief and hope burgeoned. Aurora raised her clasped hands beneath her chin. "You would?"

Doc nodded. "I would love to train you, especially to work with women's maladies, if you felt that would be an area of interest for you."

Aurora felt her anticipation climb another notch. Surely Preston could not deny her the opportunity to help sickly women. And if she were working specifically with women, he oughtn't be so worried about her safety. It was the perfect solution. Not only that, it was also one that appealed to her. "I would love that."

Gripping the back of his neck, Doc gave another glance toward the parsonage. "But will the parson?" The question was obviously rhetorical.

Aurora notched her chin up a degree. "When can I start?"

Doc blew out a whistle that all at once portrayed *why not* and *what am I getting myself into.* "Today, if you are of a mind to."

Excitement shot through Aurora. "Today? Really?" She gave a little hop. "Yes! That sounds fantastic!"

"All right, then. My wagon is in the livery." His gaze swept from her head to her feet. "I suppose that dress will do for today. But tomorrow you might want to wear something with a little less"—he slanted his arms out from himself, indicating the angle and circumference of her skirt—"expansive."

"I'll bear that in mind." She hurried to keep up with him. "So where are we going today?"

"Yes. Where *are* you going today?"

Aurora and Doc froze at the sound of Preston's voice coming from behind them. Aurora spun to face him, sensing Doc doing the same. Standing on the steps of the jailhouse with Tommy by his side, Preston had his hands propped on slender hips. His gaze drilled into Aurora's.

She suddenly felt a little breathless. "I thought you were going out to the camps today?"

He motioned toward the livery. "On my way to pick up our horses. I just stopped to speak to Reagan for a few minutes." His searching look transferred to Doc.

Flynn cleared his throat and fiddled with the handle of his medical bag. "Aurora asked me about becoming a nurse. I told her I'd be happy to give her some training to work with women."

Preston's shoulders slumped, but then he descended the steps with Tommy following, and they all continued toward the livery together.

Tommy skipped ahead, chattering something to Doc about the colt he was working with at the Carver place.

Aurora searched what she could see of the side of Preston's cheek. She couldn't quite tell from his reaction what he was feeling except to know that he wasn't too happy with her. Yet she couldn't figure out why that would be. She'd told him she planned to speak to Doc today.

Inside the stable, Doc set to hitching his horse to his wagon while Tommy and Preston stepped into the stalls that housed their horses. Aurora paused in Preston's doorway and watched him heft first the saddle blanket and then the saddle onto the horse.

Finally, she asked, "Are you upset with me?"

Preston glanced at her over his shoulder as he tightened the cinch. "I thought you were going to talk to him about it. Not start training right away. I thought we'd have a chance to speak more on this tomorrow at breakfast."

Aurora studied one of her fingernails. She supposed that was what they'd agreed upon. "I'm sorry. You're right. His offer for me to start training right away took me rather by surprise, and I responded without fully thinking things through. Do you not want me to go?"

Preston propped one arm on the saddle and faced her. "I don't want to prevent you from doing what you feel is right. I think I was just a little disappointed that we didn't talk about it first." Preston stepped to her. He rested a hand on her shoulder. "Aurora, my aim is not to stifle you. I only want to keep you safe. I trust Doc not to put you in a dangerous situation. But please, just be careful? Wise as a serpent and harmless as a dove and all that, okay?"

His words filled Aurora with a warmth that started in the region of her heart and spread to every extremity. But confusion and hope also filled her. Was he changing his mind? She examined his countenance.

His thumb stroked along the length of her jaw. "I spent several hours last night praying about our conversation. And I feel the Lord impressed upon me that you are right."

Aurora felt her jaw go slack.

Preston's lips thinned into a barely perceptible smile. "I can see that I've surprised you. Perhaps that is an indication that I am often more set in my ways than I realize." He chuckled softly. "At any rate, I wanted you to know that you have my blessing to pursue this nursing path with Doc. I will pray for your safety and trust the Lord to keep you in the palm of His hand."

Aurora stepped forward and threw her arms around him. "You've no idea how much good it does me to hear you say that.

My only desire is to follow the Lord in ministry where I feel He is leading. And I truly felt peace for the first time only after this idea of nursing came to mind."

Preston's arms encircled her, warm and sturdy. "Your big heart is one of the reasons I fell in love with you."

Aurora could have stood in the shelter of his arms all day, but Doc, and her new future, were waiting. She eased back and smoothed her hands across the lapels of his jacket. She looked up into his face. "I'll see you tomorrow at breakfast?"

Preston tapped the end of her nose. "Indeed. I'll be looking forward to it."

"As will I."

Tommy appeared, leading his mount. She left them to mount their horses then and allowed Doc to help her onto the seat of his wagon.

Chapter Twenty-four

A t breakfast on Wednesday morning, Poppy Scarlatti watched as the last of the few remaining tables emptied and the dining room grew quiet. Discouragement sloped her shoulders. She had truly hoped to overhear something interesting with regard to the bank money this morning. She knew the nature of small towns where nothing was kept secret for long. And she knew if she kept listening, she would eventually hear something. But would it be in time for her to act?

At least for this morning, it looked like she was out of luck. She reached for her reticule to fetch the money to pay for her meal, but before she could even extract it, the town's three lawmen entered the dining room. They lingered by the door, speaking in low tones.

Poppy stilled and returned her purse to the table.

Dixie bustled in a few seconds later. Her steps stuttered, and then she hurried forward. The sheriff said something too quietly for Poppy to hear, and then Dixie led the three men to a table. "It's not often that I see the three of you in here together."

Thankfully, the table she led them to was somewhat close to Poppy.

"We have a little business to discuss," the oldest of the three said. His gaze darted to Poppy then, and he cleared his throat softly, as though he wished he hadn't blurted that out.

Poppy's excitement surged. She was about to learn something. Finally!

Dixie stopped by her table and asked if she needed anything else. Irritated with the fact that the interruption was keeping her from potentially hearing vital information, Poppy quickly asked for another cup of coffee, more to get rid of the woman than because she actually wanted more. Tugging her book closer, she focused her gaze on the pages—and her ears on the conversation at the next table.

The three lawmen huddled over their table to lean close to each other.

The youngest man, the one in the long duster with the soft curls of dark hair, spoke in a low voice. "The logs Charlotte ordered from Camp Sixty-Five for the boardwalks are set to arrive at the mill on Friday."

As Dixie refilled her cup, Poppy's disappointment reared its head, but then her curiosity piqued. Why would three lawmen state that they had business to discuss and then set to talking about something as benign as logs to be made into lumber for boardwalks? She was careful to keep her eyes on her book and sip her coffee, as though merely enjoying a leisurely morning, but her mind worked faster than the wheels on a steam locomotive.

The sheriff shifted in his seat, making room for Dixie to lean past his shoulder to fill his cup. "We sure that, uh, Eklund is prepared for that . . . shipment to arrive?"

The oldest man, who now sat with his back to Poppy, nodded. "Spoke to . . . the man in charge just this morning. He said everything is prepared and ready for the . . . arrival."

The sheriff dipped his chin. "The shipment—ah, logs—are arriving via the road from the camp at eight o'clock sharp. We will all need to be on hand, just to make sure everything goes smoothly."

Poppy felt a prickle of awareness slide along the back of her neck. They were not talking about logs for the mill. Lawmen wouldn't need to be on hand for something like that. They were speaking in code! Excitement caused the hand holding her coffee mug to tremble. She carefully set the cup on the table and tucked her hand into her lap.

Friday! If the money was to arrive that day, then Saturday would be the perfect day for her heist.

That gave her a day to finalize her plan and a day to pull it off. By this time on Sunday, she could be on her way back to Babbo with enough cash to finally make him proud of her. And if all went according to plan, Preston would be going with her. Maybe not willingly, at least not at first. But with time she could remind him what he'd been missing all these years.

She mentally ticked through a list of everything she needed to finalize. She'd found the perfect location for step one, and securing the leverage to ensure Preston's cooperation wouldn't be hard. It was just a matter of packaging each step of her plan into one smooth process. And finding the patience to wait until Saturday evening. She really couldn't have asked for a better day, however, because the town was likely to be loud and bustling on that night. Having the noise of the alehouse just a few doors down from the bank would help disguise any noise they might accidentally make while breaking in.

Poppy smiled and took a final sip of her coffee. She loved it when things started falling in place.

Aurora's day passed rather quickly, for a line of patients already waited for Doc when they arrived at the first camp. Doc had a small tent that was nothing more than a shelter with a table and chair beneath it.

The first patient was a woman who had accidentally cut her foot while hoeing her garden. Doc showed Aurora how to clean, stitch, and bandage the foot. The woman deposited two bits into Doc's hand and limped out of the tent.

Doc washed his hands in a basin and pegged Aurora with a look. "She's lucky. Any deeper and it likely would have cut some tendons. But I think she'll recover without incident."

The next patient was a logger with a smashed hand. Doc showed her how to apply plaster of paris. After the logger came a woman with her small son in tow. Doc diagnosed him as having pneumonia and gave the woman some acetylsalicylic acid to give the boy in a tea. Before Aurora knew it, they were packing up and headed for the next camp, where they treated a spider bite, a broken leg, and a woman with a persistent cough that Doc feared was incurable. He gave her some powders for pain.

After the woman left, Aurora searched his face. "What's wrong with her?"

Doc shook his head grimly. "When she first started coming to me, I thought she might have pneumonia. But none of the treatments I gave her for that worked. I believe she may have cancer, though she doesn't have the money to travel to a hospital where better diagnostics are available."

Tears pricked the backs of Aurora's eyes. "That's very sad."

Doc released a sigh. "If there's one thing that is true about this profession, Aurora, it's that you will see a lot of sadness. If your heart can't handle it, then this is not the profession for you."

Aurora pondered his words throughout the rest of the day. Yet despite the dread of constantly facing tragedy on a day-to-day basis, she found that joy over those she *could* help overwhelmed the trepidation.

She thought of one of her favorite verses from 1 Peter:1, where the author reminded the readers that even though they faced trials, they could claim joy inexpressible and full of glory because of their salvation!

It was such a joy she felt now. And she could only feel that it must be confirmation that she was finally moving in the direction the Lord wanted her to.

She breathed out a silent prayer as Doc drove the wagon down the hill to the Rodantes' spread to drop her off. *Thank You, Lord, for Your guidance and direction. May I ever be faithful to serve in the ways You ask of me.*

Doc pulled the wagon to a stop and hopped down to cross to her side. As he helped her down, he smiled. "You did really well today."

"Thank you. I found it quite fulfilling."

His smile widened. "So you'll be coming back to help me again tomorrow?"

She chuckled. "I will. What time should I meet you in town?"

"Same time as today should be fine." He climbed back to the driver's seat.

"Doc?"

He hesitated. "Yes?"

"Thank you for allowing me this chance."

"I should be the one offering my thanks. Dixie's been after me to find some help, but I've been too busy to put much effort into it. She'll be relieved to know I'll have someone to share the burden of care." With a tip of his hat, he flicked the reins against the horses' rumps. "See you tomorrow."

Aurora lifted a hand of farewell, feeling a well of excitement rise inside her.

For the first time in her life, she couldn't wait to see what adventure tomorrow might hold.

Aurora leapt from her bed the next morning, filled with excitement about the prospects for the day ahead.

She remembered Doc's advice and donned her plainest skirt, along with a serviceable blouse. She also chose her most comfortable boots—the ones Preston had ordered custom made for her by Bill Giddens the year she'd come to town. They'd seen many a year of wear and were no longer pretty, but yesterday she'd worn her newer store-bought pair, and by the time she'd removed them, her feet had been screaming for freedom. If she spent even half the time on her feet today as she had yesterday, she would be thankful for the broken-in, comfortable, ugly pair.

She whistled a tuneless song as she rushed to milk the cow and hurry the bucket inside.

Liora smiled at her. "You sound happy today. Breakfast is almost ready."

Aurora gasped. "Oh dear! I forgot to tell you. I'm having breakfast with Preston in town this morning! And then I'm spending the day training with Doc."

"Training with Doc?"

"Yes! I'm going to become a nurse. I've been praying long and hard about what the Lord would have me do, and I feel this is my calling."

Liora smiled. "That's wonderful. You'll do a marvelous job. And did I hear you right? Breakfast with Preston? That sounds promising."

Aurora puffed out her cheeks on a breath. "I hope so. We had a good talk yesterday. Thank you for your advice not to give up."

"Of course. And as for breakfast . . ." A swipe of Liora's hand showed her lack of concern. "That's fine. It's only eggs and biscuits. In fact, grab that small pail, and I'll pack you some for your lunch."

"Oh, that's a good idea. In my excitement, I quite forgot to plan for lunch. Doc shared his with me yesterday, but I doubt he'll want to do that every day." She laughed.

Liora pointed to the bowl of fruit on the sideboard. "Take an apple too."

Aurora picked up a golden-red orb and appraised it. She rolled it through her fingers, remembering.

"What is it?" Liora asked.

"Nothing." Aurora smiled at the memory that had overtaken her. "I was just reminiscing about the morning I met Preston all those years ago. A boy was about to pound me into dust over an apple. I've come a long way since then."

Liora gave her a side-armed hug. "You sure have. And now look at you! Going back to help those very people. I'm so proud of you!"

"It's kind of you to say, but"—Aurora rocked on her toes, embarrassed—"it's nothing. At any rate, I'd better get going." She placed the apple in the bucket next to the biscuit sandwiches and hefted it. "Thanks for lunch!"

"Of course. Have a good day."

Birds chirped in full chorus as she trod toward town. The road had a small embankment on either side, carpeted in verdant grass. Beyond that, forest rose on both sides. The sun warmed the trees enough to raise a fog, and drops of dew glistened on blades and leaves and needles.

Aurora inhaled deep. Exhaled slow. It was the kind of morning that made one thankful to be alive. She would have loved to linger and simply soak it all in, were it not for how much she looked forward to breakfast with Preston. She couldn't wait to tell him about everything she'd learned yesterday.

She skipped for a couple steps. It made her feel a bit childish, but it wasn't like anyone would see her. She was out of sight of the Rodante spread and only halfway to town. With a giggle, she skipped a few more paces. She still almost had to pinch herself over the simple fact that she was having breakfast with Preston! That glorious realization only added to her euphoria.

She angled a look at the rectangular strip of blue sky outlined by the tall trees above her head and raised an arm in praise. "Oh, Lord, You are amazingly wonderful and glorious!" She spun in a circle, lunch bucket swinging by her side—and froze.

On the embankment, a man ran toward her on tiptoes! He wore a bandana that covered most of his face.

Her euphoria fled, creating a vacuum that sucked in terror. *Run!* Her mind shouted the word at her, but her feet were leaden weights.

The moment the man noticed that she'd seen him, he gave up all pretense of quiet and surged forward. Brush crackled beneath his boots.

With a cry, Aurora hurtled her lunch pail at his head.

The man put up one arm and deflected it. "Get her!" he bellowed.

The sound of other footsteps and labored breathing came from behind her. Fingers grazed her arm.

Aurora sprinted. Fear pulsed with every beat of her heart. The wood that had a moment ago seemed so peaceful and serene now seemed sinister and black. A glance over her shoulder showed that the other footsteps belonged to another man who rushed at her from the opposite side of the road.

She opened her mouth to scream, but a hand clamped off the sound. She tasted dirt and sweat and minerals as a tackle took her to the ground. Air left her lungs when the man's weight crashed upon her. The hard dirt of the roadbed ground into her cheek.

Her assailant cursed and cracked something against her skull.

Pain splintered through her.

A pair of boots stepped into her vision, then her view faded to black.

Chapter Twenty-five

Seated at a table in the corner of Dixie's Boardinghouse, Preston glanced at his pocket watch for the third time. If he were going to make it to Camp Sixty-Five to help the elderly Mrs. Wharton slaughter her sow at the appointed time, he needed to get going. But worry niggled at the back of his mind. It wasn't like Aurora to be late. Nor was it like her to miss an appointment.

Dixie stopped by his table. "Everything okay?"

Preston felt his brow slump as he tucked his watch back into his vest. "I was supposed to meet Aurora here for breakfast, but she's late. You haven't heard from her this morning, have you?"

Dixie shook her head. "No. I'm sorry."

Doc stepped into the room just then, searching as though looking for someone. Seeing Dixie next to Preston's table, Doc approached. "Either of you seen Aurora this morning?"

Preston's stomach crimped. "I was just asking Dixie if she might have heard from her. She was supposed to meet me here half an hour ago."

"Just running late maybe?" Doc studied Preston's face.

Preston shook his head. "It's not like her. I'm worried."

Doc thumped him on the shoulder. "I have to go past the Rodante place anyhow on my way to the camps. Why don't you tie your horse to the back of my wagon? We'll likely bump into . her on the way."

Preston was already rising. "Yes. Thank you." He handed Dixie the coin for his meal.

"I'll have the ladies pray," she said.

He nodded his thanks as he followed Doc to the livery, grateful that Tommy was at the Holloways' for today. It only took him a moment to saddle his mount, and then he tied it off and climbed up next to Doc.

Doc snapped the reins and set his team at a smart clip out of town.

The farther along the road they traveled without encountering Aurora, the greater Preston's concern. *Lord, please be with her. Just help her to be all right. That's all I ask.*

The road remained empty all the way to the Rodante spread. Dread mounting, Preston jumped down and followed Doc to the door.

Liora opened it before they'd even reached the top step to the porch. Preston swept his hat off, seeing Doc do the same beside him. Through the doorway, he could see Law playing on a small quilt on the floor behind her.

Her gaze slipped over Preston, and a groove formed between her brows. "What's the matter?"

"I was supposed to have breakfast with Aurora."

Liora nodded. "She left about an hour and a half ago." Her eyes widened. "She never arrived?"

Preston exchanged a look with Doc as the bottom dropped out of his stomach. He lost the strength in his legs and sank onto the bench by the door. He propped his head into one hand, trying to think. Willing himself not to dissolve into panic. She'd left here but never arrived in town. Yet they hadn't seen any sign of her on the road between here and there. What did that mean?

Every answer he thought of terrified him worse than the last.

Why hadn't he insisted on coming out to pick her up? After all his concern about her safety in the camps, the short distance she routinely walked from the Rodantes' to town hadn't even given him pause. And that may have cost him the most precious thing in the world—the woman he loved.

Doc dropped a hand against his shoulder and squatted beside him. "You going to be okay?"

Preston pulled in a deep breath, then pushed it out between pursed lips. If something had happened to her, he wouldn't be the only one to feel pain. He had to pull himself together and be strong for the townsfolk who would need him. He gave Doc a nod. "We'd better check the road between here and town again. If something happened to her, surely there will be a clue."

Doc nodded. "Agreed. Maybe we somehow just missed her."

Preston doubted that was the case, but he appreciated Doc trying to keep him encouraged. "Yeah, maybe." He stood and turned to Liora. "Until we figure out where she might be, it's probably best if you and the women stay inside. We'll let Joe and the lawmen know just as soon as we get back to town."

Wide-eyed, she nodded. "Okay. We'll be praying."

"Yes. Good. We will too." An urgency propelled him forward. "Flynn, I'm going to ride so I can search the embankments. It's probably best if you hurry straight to town to let Reagan and the boys know she's missing."

Doc nodded and leapt onto the wagon seat as Preston untied his mount. "Will do." And with a shout, he set the team at a gallop back toward town.

Preston's horse balked at the clatter, but he reined it into a circle and clicked his tongue. They trotted after Doc.

Preston prayed from the depths of his soul like he hadn't prayed in a long time. No words seemed able to form. Instead it was as though his heart strung together one long wail for the Maker to pay attention.

Dismounting, he led his horse as he scoured first one embankment, then the other, bending to examine the road for tracks in between. But the dirt was so hard packed that nothing seemed to have marred it save the slight indentations that formed the grooves cut by many a wagon wheel.

The sunshine of the more open plains surrounding the road gave way to the shade of the forest, and still Preston had found nothing. The going was slow as he searched carefully in the dimmer lighting.

Just ahead he saw a squirrel sitting on a stump, chomping on an apple it held in both paws. Preston stopped, frowning. His horse bumped into him and whickered. He took another step, and the squirrel abandoned the apple to dart into the trees. Preston bent to pick it up. The squirrel hadn't eaten much, and he could see that the apple wasn't a wrinkly, pitted wild type, but instead was perfectly round with shiny red skin. Heart hammering, he surged ahead, searching the ground more fervently. It only took him a moment to find the small, galvanized pail that lay on its side, hidden by the tall grass on the embankment next to the road. Whatever food may have been in it had long since been packed off by critters. Only a few crumbs remained as evidence that the pail had contained anything.

Heart sinking, Preston picked up the bucket. Along here the woods were thick with underbrush, and there wasn't any sign of Aurora nearby.

Hoofbeats sounded, and Reagan and the other lawmen galloped into view, followed by Doc, who was now mounted on a horse. He must have left his wagon at the livery.

Preston held up the bucket. "This is all I've found. I presume it must have been her lunch pail. Did you see anything?" Though he knew the chances were slim, he allowed himself to hope they might have good news.

But just as he'd suspected, Reagan shook his head. "No."

Shoulders slumping, Preston studied the vast forest that stretched in either direction. "She could be anywhere by now."

Reagan tipped his hat back and scratched his head before resettling it. "Know anyone who might want to harm her?"

Preston's thoughts immediately jumped to Poppy. His heart kicked against his sternum. Things like this didn't happen in Wyldhaven. At least not since they'd run Lenny Smith's outlaw gang out of town. But this was just the kind of tactic Poppy and her father employed. What would she want with Aurora though? Simple revenge against him for moving on with another woman? Would she stoop that low? Surely not. They'd not been in contact for years.

"Parson?" the sheriff prodded.

Preston sighed. "I might. Though I hardly fathom what reason she'd have to hurt Aurora."

Doc held up a hand. "If you are thinking of that new woman, Poppy, I thought of her too. I went in to ask Dixie if she'd seen her, and she was there, sitting in Dixie's dining room just a moment ago. And Dixie says she's been there for quite some time."

Preston thought back. Yes. She had been there earlier when he'd been waiting for Aurora. Disappointment surged. And yet . . . "She might not be directly involved, but she could still know something. Those two men—the ones you saw her speaking to who were recently hired at the mill—I'd bet they didn't show up for work today!"

Zane, who had been studying the trees on either side of the road, turned his mount now to look at Preston. "You sure that's her lunch pail?"

Preston studied the bucket in his hand, then shook his head. "Can't say for certain."

Joe nudged his horse closer to the bank. He leaned forward and propped an arm on the pommel, reaching out a hand. "Let me see it."

Preston handed the bucket to him. After a few seconds of scrutiny, Joe looked at Reagan. "I'm certain this is from our kitchen. It has the same small dent in the side."

Preston's eyes fell closed. Though he'd been certain it was hers, the confirmation drove a nail through his heart.

Zane cleared his throat. "Joe and I can stay here and search the woods while you fellas go check at the mill to see if the two new men are there. If not, then maybe we speak to Poppy anyhow, because of the way Reagan saw her talking to them the other day."

"Yes. Let's go." Preston was just happy to have a task. He swung onto his horse and urged it down the embankment. But his disappointment grew yet again when they arrived at the mill to find the two new hires arriving from downstream with a large wheelbarrow full of rocks.

Taulby Eklund confirmed that they'd arrived for work on time that morning. And by the number of rocks they were pushing, they had to have been working steadily for quite some time.

Upon questioning them separately, the men both swore that they'd been working together to extract rocks from the creek all morning, and their stories matched.

Preston's hopes deflated. "Now what?" he asked Reagan.

Reagan used his bandana to wipe sweat from his brow. "Since our only other suspect has been sitting in plain view in the diner all morning, we need to ring the church bell to call everyone. Then we organize search parties."

Preston blinked hard to keep tears at bay as he kicked at a clump of grass with one boot.

Calling for a search party was never a good thing. Never a good thing at all.

He should have ridden out early to pick her up instead of waiting for her in the boardinghouse. This was all his fault.

Kane Carver led the Appaloosa colt out of his yard and down the path toward the Kastain place. The horse was in no way ready yet. But Kane figured it would be good to give the animal some time in the locality that would eventually be its new home.

He rolled his eyes at himself and grinned. The horse probably did not need to spend time in the Kastains' barn, but it wouldn't hurt his feelings any to have a conversation with Belle. It was only after he was halfway to their place that he realized Belle might be at work today. He paused. Maybe he should just return home. But it really wouldn't hurt the horse to have some time on the lead and experience a fresh environment. He decided to proceed.

A little farther ahead, he came to the bridge that spanned a small tributary of Wyldhaven Creek.

The colt tossed his head at the sound of the trickling water.

Kane urged him forward, speaking to him in soothing tones.

Tentatively, the horse followed him. But the moment his hooves thunked against the boards of the small bridge, he whinnied and threw back his head, trying to make an escape.

"Whoa, boy. Whoa." Kane reached a hand to gently pat the horse's cheek. He murmured soft nonsense until the animal calmed.

He was just starting across the bridge again, when his eye caught on something in the brush upstream. He squinted for a better look. There was something . . . He couldn't quite make it out. But it didn't look like it belonged out here. He'd better take a closer examination.

Tying the colt off to a tree, Kane pushed through the brush.

Odd. Someone had left a perfectly good wheelbarrow right here on the bank of the creek. He could see that several rocks had been extracted from the creek bed, because where the rest of the creek was covered with stones, this area had bare patches. However, the wheelbarrow remained empty.

With a shrug of one shoulder, he returned to the colt. Perhaps someone was using the wheelbarrow to haul stones back to their place. Maybe they had other duties today and simply would return later for their tools. But it wasn't usual for someone to leave a wheelbarrow in the woods—especially one as nice as that one. That was a good way to have it stolen. Perhaps it belonged to the Kastains? They lived the closest to here. Maybe young Aidan had gotten distracted with play and forgotten to take it home. He would ask him.

After untying the colt and coaxing it once more to the edge of the bridge, Kane was happy to see that the animal was less hesitant to cross this time. Once they reached the other side, Kane stopped to feed the Appaloosa a piece of apple. He lavished praise on it, patting its neck in affirmation.

He had just reached the Kastain place and led the colt into their yard, when the church bell peeled from town.

Looking concerned, Belle stepped onto their porch, drying her hands on a towel.

Ah! So she wasn't at work after all. His heart gave an unaccountable thump.

Her gaze landed on him, and her brows shot upward. "Oh, hello." Her focus flickered to the Appaloosa. "Are you done with his training already?"

"No. I just thought . . . it might be good to bring him by. Familiarize him with his future home." Then, since he was a man of truth, he added, "At least that's the excuse I gave myself." He grinned, hoping she plainly understood the real reason he'd come. It was gratifying to see the blush that shaded her cheeks as she studied the towel in her hands. To let her off the hook, he thumbed a gesture toward the sound of the still-ringing bell. "Do you know what that's all about?"

"No." She shook her head, a groove forming on her brow. "They must be trying to call everyone to a meeting. Likely an emergency of some sort."

Kane tucked his lower lip between his teeth. She was probably right. Whatever it signified couldn't be good, and here he was dallying over an enjoyable conversation when he ought to be taking action. He turned a glance toward the barn. "I could hitch up your wagon, providing you think it might be all right for me to leave the colt in one of your stalls?"

Belle scuffed one toe at the edge of the top step and worked her fingers into a knot with the towel. "We don't have a wagon. We just walk to town. But please do feel free to leave him in a stall. Ma and Mr. Harrow went for a walk with Aidan, but I'm sure they'll hear the bell and return posthaste. I'll gather the girls."

He gave her a nod and headed to the barn. He could bring the colt with them to town, but as skittish as he still was, that probably wasn't the best idea. Besides . . . He grinned. It would give him an excuse to return after they found out what was going on in town.

It only took him a moment to fork some feed and fill the stall's water bucket. And by the time he stepped from the barn, Mrs. Kastain, Mr. Harrow, and Aidan were bustling into the yard, and Belle was urging her twin sisters off the porch.

"Come on, girls," Mrs. Kastain urged. Her gaze landed on him, and she froze for half a second, before giving him a cautious nod. She nudged the twins ahead of her. "We'd best hurry." Her gaze flicked to her oldest daughter. "Belle, if you don't mind, bank the fire, would you, dear?"

"Yes, Ma." Gaze lowered, Belle returned into the house.

Mrs. Kastain looked at Kane. "Mr. Carver, would you mind waiting for Belle and walking into town with her?"

Kane tipped her his hat. "Not at all, ma'am." And as the little family hurried from the yard, he couldn't help but grin. Mrs. Kastain was all right, in his book. All right, indeed.

It was only once he was standing alone waiting for Belle that he remembered he hadn't asked Aidan about the wheelbarrow.

Chapter Twenty-six

Aurora sat in the silence with her breath wheezing loudly in her ears. A blindfold covered her eyes, a gag pinched at the corners of her mouth, and her hands were tied behind her back. The ground beneath her was cool and hard, yet she could feel the warmth of the sun on her face. If she moved even slightly, however, the warmth dissipated. Wherever she was, it was cool and damp, so the sun probably didn't reach here too much.

Though they hadn't bound her feet, Aurora trembled at the thought of moving.

She'd still been woozy from the knock on the head, but as they'd left, she'd clearly heard one of the men cackle and say, "Wouldn't move too much if I were you. There's a drop-off that likely wouldn't kill you, but you'd be maimed, and that's certain."

His partner had issued a whistle. "Sharpest rocks I've ever seen at the bottom."

After they'd gone, she'd tried to push her blindfold off using one shoulder, but it was tied too tightly and wouldn't budge. Besides, every time she moved, she could feel the gag cutting into the corners of her lips.

So now she sat still and willed herself to breathe through the panic that hammered at her mind. Where was she? In a cave? In the middle of the forest? Could wild animals find her? What would she do if a bear or wolf or cougar came along?

She couldn't move for fear of falling. Was she near a gulch? A cavern? A cliff? Or had they only told her that to frighten her into remaining still?

The worries bombarded her until she felt lightheaded. She realized she was breathing much too fast and forced herself to calm. She inhaled long and slow, then pushed it out even slower. Again. And again.

Finally she felt calm enough to think. What tools did she have at her exposure?

Her ears.

She tilted her head to listen.

Somewhere far off, a trickle of water sounded. But there was a hollow echo to it, as though it were surrounded by a great enclosed space. She shivered at the picture that gave her. She remembered hearing a creak, like that of a hinge, along with the clanking of chains when the men had left. What had that been? Other than the sound of the water, she couldn't make out anything else.

Her feet were another tool.

Gingerly, she felt all around herself in a circle. Her feet didn't encounter any space or drop-off, but the men had said not to move *too* much. Danger could still be near.

Something squeaked, and air puffed against her cheek.

Aurora screeched, and it was as though the air around her exploded with sound. Squeaks and trills and high-pitched chatter permeated the air. Something winged past her ear. Something else buzzed her hair.

Panic once again in full surge, Aurora collapsed onto her side, pressing herself as close to the ground as possible.

Heart pounding in terror, shoulders heaving, she felt a swirl of dizziness.

Sobs convulsed her shoulders.

Why had God allowed this to happen to her? Especially just when she'd finally felt like she was on the right path?

Preston sat in a too-small desk at the front of the church, waiting for the sanctuary to first empty of students and then fill with townsfolk.

Zoe Kastain did an admirable job of keeping her students calm as she dismissed them, telling each to meet their families outside.

He traced the grain of the wood, feeling like every thought was too far away to grasp. This couldn't be happening. Not when he'd just finally found the courage to make Aurora aware of his heart!

God, please keep her safe. He felt like he'd been repeating that same prayer all morning. But he supposed the Creator understood his angst.

Footsteps marched smartly from the back door and stopped by his side. He looked up.

Mrs. Hines plunked her stubby hands on her ample hips. "What is it, Parson? Why are we all being summoned?" Her voice was strident. Demanding.

He had no patience for the woman's theatrics today. If he told her anything, she would immediately go outside and set to repeating it to anyone who arrived, and the story would likely change slightly with each telling.

"Please, Mrs. Hines. If you'll just wait, then we can tell everyone all at once what has happened." He stretched a hand, urging her to take a seat in one of the desks. "If you'll have a seat, we're just waiting for a few more to arrive."

She gave a little huff but did as he asked. He wasn't sure if his restraint could have sustained anything else.

He rubbed a hand over his face. Thirty minutes. That was the normal waiting time in an emergency such as this. Anyone who couldn't get to the church inside thirty minutes would simply have to hear the news from someone else once they arrived. Yet today the time crawled by like a snail.

Someone eased into the desk next to his, and he glanced over. Did a double take.

Poppy blinked at him guilelessly. Her red lips pursed softly. "What's happening, caro?"

There was a false innocence in the words that filled him with rage. Preston's fist closed so tight that his forearm ached. "Did you do this?"

"Do what?" She quirked a brow, glancing around the church as though searching for what he might be talking about.

Preston was weary of her games. Of the distrust that swelled in him every time she was near. "If you had anything to do with this, Poppy, please just tell me. She means everything to me."

"She? The girl you had dinner with?" Her eyes widened. "Oh dear. Did something happen to her?" She covered her red lips with one hand.

Preston scrutinized her. Her expression exuded innocence. Her posture showed nothing but concern. Yet everything in him screamed that he shouldn't trust her.

What he wouldn't give in that moment to have just a portion of God's omnipotence. Maybe just enough to look into the heart of one person to discern if they were being truthful.

She leaned across the space between them and laid her hand on his forearm. "You must be in such distress. You really don't look well. Is there any way I can help?"

Her touch filled him with revulsion. Preston extracted his arm from beneath her fingers. "Last chance, Poppy. If I find out you had anything to do with this, I won't be responsible for my reaction."

She placed the hand to her chest. "Me? Something to do— I'm crushed that you would ever suspect me. I don't even know what it is that I supposedly have done. I thought Christians were to be forgiving and accepting. Especially of their own." Large tears pooled on her lower lids.

Preston eased out a slow breath. Was he being too hard on her? She really hadn't done anything suspicious since arriving in town. And she was right about how Christians should treat others. He wasn't handling this very well. She had an alibi, as did the two men he suspected worked for her. Maybe all his doubts truly were unfounded.

Yet that didn't make him feel any better. Because if Poppy and her men weren't involved, then it meant they had utterly no leads.

She continued to pout, wounded and petulant.

He cleared his throat, still unwilling to let her off the hook. "If you did this to somehow try to step in and fill her place, it's not going to work."

Her mouth gaped open. "Thinking somewhat highly of yourself, aren't you? I've done nothing but try to be your friend."

Preston pinched the bridge of his nose. "You're right. Forgive me. I'm not handling this well."

"What *this*?" Exasperation filled her expression.

Reagan stepped to the front and called the room to order.

Preston motioned for Poppy to listen. She would hear the answer to her question soon enough.

Silence fell across the room, and Preston could almost sense the townsfolk holding their breaths.

Reagan slid the brim of his Stetson through his fingers, meeting the gazes of several before he cleared his throat. "As you all know, we don't call emergency sessions like this lightly, but Aurora McClure left the Rodante spread this morning and never arrived in town."

A gasp rose up.

Reagan held up a hand. "We found her lunch pail. But that is all. She's out there somewhere, and we've called you all here to organize a rescue. Did anyone besides Liora see her this morning?"

Preston surveyed the room hopefully. But they all shook their heads. No one had seen her.

Defeat weighted his shoulders.

Reagan looked grim. "All right then. My mother, Mrs. Holloway, is at the back with a map of our area. If you can take some time to help us search, please see her. We'd like to send people out in teams. She will assign each team a certain sector. We meet back here at dark. If someone finds her, we'll ring the church bell again to let you know to stop searching."

As all around them the people rose and formed a line in front of the desk where Jacinda handed out assignments, Poppy leaned close to Preston. "Don't worry, caro. I will help look for your love. I'm sure that God will not have abandoned her. You do still believe in this God you claim to serve, yes?"

Preston lifted her a look. *The God you claim to serve.* It was as though her words were a shot across his bow. Yes. He did serve God, but she was right. He certainly hadn't been acting much like it. God had never promised him a perfect life with no pain. Only that once he made it to the other side of this earthly walk, all pain and sorrow would no longer exist. On this earth, however, he'd been *promised* tribulations. He was only told to take heart because God had overcome the world! It was the attitude with which he responded to pain in this life that made the difference.

So now he had a choice. He could believe that God's Word was true and He made no mistakes. He could keep his faith on its firm foundation and know that no matter what pain God might ask him to walk through here on this earth, it would be trivial compared to the blessings to come. Or he could turn his back on all that and sacrifice an eternity of pure joy, bliss, and health for a few years of holding a grudge.

He surged to his feet. "Excuse me, everyone?"

The room fell to silence, and all turned to look at him.

"If you'll allow me a moment, I'd like to say a prayer for Aurora and for all of us. For our success, and for our safety and hers. But mostly I want to encourage us all to keep our trust in the Lord no matter the outcome of today's search." He felt lighter already.

Nods and murmurs of agreement encouraged him.

And as Preston prayed for everyone's safety and that they would find Aurora healthy and whole, but that they would also accept God's answer and not waver in their faith, sheer peace swept over him. Because one thing he knew to be true—if the worst happened and they only found Aurora's body, he believed beyond a shadow of a doubt that her spirit would continue living with her Lord for eternity. His heart panged him at the prospect, but if that was all the hope he ever had, it would be enough.

Please, God, let it be enough.

Poppy pondered as she walked toward the livery to fetch her horse after receiving her assignment. She'd been partnered with a man named Nolan and the girl, Cora, from the boardinghouse. And she would go out and do her part to look like she was diligently searching.

But none of that was what had her mind spinning in a thousand directions. No. It was the fact that, beyond a shadow of a doubt, she suddenly knew that Preston had indeed been duped by this proclaimed faith of his. What kind of person prayed that God would help them be accepting of whatever outcome He'd already ordained? That was just crazy talk. If he truly loved the girl, oughtn't he to be scrambling and doing everything in his power to find her? Railing at the heavens if she wasn't found?

And of course she wouldn't be found! She was hidden too well. Poppy smiled, but it faded quickly.

Just when she thought that she had Preston right where she wanted him, he'd pulled out that prayer. She blew out a sigh. For the first time she wondered if maybe her plan wasn't going to work after all?

It had to work! It would work!

She would let him stew for a couple days, worrying about the safety of the woman he loved. And then she would pull her ace.

Once he knew the girl was alive, Preston would do anything to keep her that way. He'd be happy to help her crack open the safe. And she might even allow him to remain here instead of forcing him to return east with her.

She grew tired of this religious idiocy. He could have the silly little strumpet, for all she cared! All she needed was the money.

Still, a shard of jealousy shot through her.

It was then that Poppy realized . . .

A chuckle slipped free as she swung her saddle onto her mount.

Preston could pray all he wanted to for the safe return of his love, but it was Poppy who was standing in God's way of answering that prayer!

She grinned. *So much for your all-powerful God, aye, Pres?*

She was utterly abandoned. Darkness settled around Aurora so thick and black that it could almost be felt.

Thankfully, the bats seemed to have calmed down now. But in the stillness and the quiet, tears dampened her blindfold.

Her arms, tied behind her as they were, cramped. And lying flat against the ground as she was, a damp chill had crept over her. If only she could bring her arms around to the front, that would ease her discomfort considerably.

She swiped her tears against a shoulder and sat up. If she could get her arms around her hips and under her legs, she could get her arms to the front. It took great effort, but using her head for balance, she finally managed to get herself to her knees. She held her breath, listening. Would the bats come at her again?

Thankfully, all remained silent.

She angled herself backward as far as she could and worked her bound wrists down past her hips. She was ever so thankful for the plain skirt she'd donned this morning. If she were wearing a bustle or a hoop, she never would be able to manage this.

The bindings cut painfully into her skin, but she only had a little farther and then she would be past the hard part. Gritting her teeth, she pushed through the pain and finally was gratified to feel her arms slip past the widest part of her hips. A sob of relief shook her as she sat for a moment with her hands beneath her legs. And then as quickly as she could, she brought them out from under her legs and clenched her jaw through the pain that cramped her arms.

For a long moment, she curled her arms against her chest and simply breathed, thankful to be in a more comfortable position.

Then realization struck her. She reached up and yanked the blindfold from her eyes.

She blinked for a moment and felt her face to see if another covering remained. But no, her eyes were cleared. And that was when all hope abandoned her. Because it was just as dark around her now as it had been a moment ago with the blindfold on.

Despair crashed over her. Where was she?

Chapter Twenty-seven

Peace was still his primary emotion as Preston paused, with the sheriff, next to Jacinda Callahan's table at the back of the sanctuary.

"Did we get every sector covered?" Reagan questioned his mother.

Jacinda studied the map that she had been carefully marking all morning. She tapped a fingernail against one spot. "I had a thought. And I saved this section for you."

Reagan leaned forward to examine the area she pointed to. "A thought?"

Jacinda's gaze flickered to Preston for a moment before resettling on her son. "I heard that the new woman in town might . . . have a reason to make Aurora disappear?"

Preston's heart thudded in anticipation of what she might say. Could this be an answer from the Lord? A blessing because he'd made the right choice?

Reagan lifted Preston a look. "We've already checked on her. But both she and the two men I suspect work for her have an alibi."

Preston nodded. "But what were you thinking?" He held his breath in anticipation.

Jacinda Callahan drummed her pencil against one palm. "It's just that the other day at Bible study, I brought up the time I was taken captive. And Poppy seemed . . . more than a little interested in the cave where I was held."

Preston's gaze slammed into Reagan's. There was only a heartbeat before they were both moving.

"Do you know the way?" Preston asked as they rushed down the church steps toward their horses.

Reagan nodded. "Zane showed me where it was after I got home from my wedding tour."

Preston yanked his horse's reins free, remembering that Reagan had been out of town when his mother had been captured. He was ever so thankful for a diligent lawman who'd been interested enough in the case to learn more, even though the situation had been resolved long before his return to town.

"Ready?" Reagan asked.

"I'm right behind you." Preston swung into his saddle and put his heels to his horse, sending it out of town at a gallop behind Reagan.

It wasn't too far out of town when Reagan left the main road and headed back into the forest. They had to go slower now, and every moment that passed was like a knife twisting in Preston's chest.

Reagan pulled his horse to a stop in front of a large patch of huckleberry bushes. He tied his horse off and motioned for Preston to follow. "This way."

Preston withdrew the pistol he carried in his saddle bag, tucked it into his belt, and trailed after him.

They pushed through the huckleberries to a little trail that angled along the base of the cliff. And after a moment, the trail cut up the face of the rock wall at an angle.

Preston's heart hammered with hope. How like God it would be to give him an answer to his prayers just after he'd surrendered his will to God's! This had to be it. *Please, Lord. Let this be it.*

About halfway up the cliff face, the angle of the trail leveled off, and a cave mouth opened into the face of the wall.

Reagan squatted down and peered into the blackness. He held a finger to his lips. Leaning close to Preston, he spoke quietly in his ear. "There might be guards."

Preston nodded and gestured that he would follow Reagan. Reaching under his coat, he withdrew his Colt.

Reagan lifted his brows. "You know how to use that thing?" he whispered.

Preston nodded. Would that his life experience had never made it necessary. Yet at one time, a gun had been second nature to his hand. "I promise not to shoot you in the back, if that's what you're worried about." He smiled. "But if you like, I can go first."

Reagan gave a shake of his head and then ducked low to enter the cave. Preston moved right on his heels. They skirted as close to the walls as they could to avoid being outlined against the light pouring in behind them.

Reagan crawled a few steps, then paused to listen. Silence was the only thing that greeted them. After a few more paces, he paused again.

The slowgoing stretched like a torturous eternity. Everything in Preston wanted to push past Reagan and rush down the corridor.

Instead, he cried out to the Lord again for Aurora's safety.

This would all be over soon now. He felt certain.

He just needed to be patient for a few more minutes.

Aurora worked the gag down around her neck. It was damp and disgusting, but at least she could breathe easier now, and blessed moisture returned to her mouth. That helped, at least somewhat, with her thirst. Even though her eyes had been open for several minutes, she still couldn't see anything. She worked her lips over the bindings that tied her wrists, searching for the knot that held them. Based on the taste and feel, the binding seemed to be thin leather strips. She was gratified to finally feel a series of small knots in them. She worked at the knots with her teeth, but the going was slow and clumsy because the knots were on the opposite side of her fingers, which made them hard to reach. And the darkness didn't aid in getting them untied either. Still, she had nothing better to do, so she worked.

The first knot came free, and she gave a little cry of joy. And set to work on the next one.

She wondered if anyone had missed her yet. It was hard to discern the passage of time, sitting here in the dark. Nor did she know how long she'd been knocked out.

She hoped people weren't too worried. But on the other hand, she did hope they would come looking for her. And yet if the men who had taken her captive were nearby guarding her, anyone who came for her could be injured.

That was the last thing she wanted!

Lord, please just keep everyone safe. And please help me find my way home.

Another knot came loose just then, and a surge of hope spurred her to set to work on the next.

Preston willed himself to breathe easy as he scooted along behind Reagan. After a moment Reagan reached a hand to still him. In the dim light that streamed from the opening far behind them now, Preston saw Reagan lift one finger.

He longed to cry out Aurora's name, but he forced himself to take a slow breath instead.

There was a *snick*, and a blazing light flared. Preston squinted against the blinding brightness of it.

And then discouragement crashed through him.

For as Reagan held a match above his head, Preston could see that they had reached the main part of the small cave. It continued no further.

And it lay empty.

Aurora wasn't sure how long she had worked at the knots. But finally she felt the bindings around her wrists loosen and realized she had untied the last one. She tugged them off and massaged her wrists with relief. She was free.

Except, she still couldn't risk movement, because of the blinding darkness.

She sat with her arms wrapped around her knees and rocked, willing herself to warmth. Surely there had to be a way of escape. The men had put her here. So there had to be a path, didn't there? But what if someone was standing guard? She trembled. She would have to figure that part out when the time came.

The first step was to investigate her surroundings. She crawled on her hands and knees and gingerly worked herself forward, patting the ground before her as she went. It was only a moment before her hand slipped through thin air.

Terror clamored for her mind as she imagined how close to a cliff edge she must be. How deep was the canyon? How close had she been to the edge all this time?

She backed up and turned to her right a couple degrees. There, too, her hand encountered nothing but air. Again she backed and turned and again found no ground. When she felt like she had likely turned in a full circle and all around her the ground dropped away sharply, she slumped against her ankles. Hopelessness crashed over her. It was as though she were on a tiny island surrounded by a sea of blackest space.

Exhaustion pressed across her shoulders like a lead quilt. Slumping on her side, she curled tightly into herself, rested her head on one arm, and closed her eyes in sleep. Maybe when she woke, she would find herself in heaven.

Preston never recalled feeling so discouraged before. It was fully dark now as he and Reagan reined their horses back into town. After they'd found the cave empty, Reagan had wondered aloud at the fact that the cave's chains were missing. Apparently, there had been several rusty chains in the cave the last time he'd been there. But not having been to the cave for months, there was no telling when the chains had been taken. Perhaps some children had found them and carried them off at some point.

After leaving the cave, he and Reagan had thoroughly searched the forest in every direction of their sector. They had come up empty. Now, as they pulled up to the church and tied off their weary mounts, several other men already waited for them on the porch.

Preston looked at them hopefully, but all shook their heads. No one had found Aurora.

Poppy, Cora, and Butch Nolan arrived right after Reagan and Preston. Butch settled a meaty hand upon Preston's shoulder, looking grim. "No luck for us. Anyone else have any luck?"

Preston sank onto the top step and held his head in his hands. "No." He roughed his fingers against his scalp, trying to think what else they might do. "No one found her." The words echoed hollowly through the darkness.

The feeling of peace that he'd felt after his earlier prayer had fled. Yes, God was in control. And yes, he still believed that Aurora would find herself immediately in the presence of the Lord should she be taken from this earth. But the fledgling faith that he'd seemed able to grasp hold of earlier had dissipated like a distant memory that eluded his clutch.

Hope deferred makes the heart sick. If ever there was a verse he could comprehend the meaning of, it was that one in this moment.

God, I have no words. How should I pray? Your will be done? I don't think I can say that and truly mean it.

A sob racked through him, and he had a feeling he didn't do as good a job of suppressing the sound as he would have liked.

Please, God . . .

Words for prayer still failed him. He felt spent. Useless. Lifeless. Like a dry twig planted in a waterless wasteland.

A chill breeze picked up. He shivered. And that increased his concern further. Aurora was somewhere out there. In this cold. Nights in these mountains could drop many degrees. And this time of year, it wouldn't be unheard of for nighttime temperatures to drop to freezing.

His heart wailed within him, though this time he let no sound escape.

He rested his head in his hands once more.

I am weak, Lord. So weak. Please . . . I . . . need Your strength.

He felt someone sink onto the step beside him, and a firm hand settled against his shoulder.

He lifted his head.

Reagan thrust a cup of coffee toward him. And then held out a plate with a sandwich. "You'll do her no good if you don't keep up your strength."

Preston accepted the food and ate mechanically. It may as well have been sawdust for all the taste that he recognized. But as though the kindness of the action had fueled something inside him, he suddenly found words to pray.

Oh God, oh God, oh God, I have no hope but You. Please, Lord, keep her safe and warm. More than that, if You will that this search come to no good end, please don't let me lose my faith over this. Somehow give me the strength to keep trusting You.

He didn't feel much better, but something inside him eased a little.

After another bite, he dropped the remaining quarter of a sandwich back onto the plate and angled Reagan a look. "What do we do now?"

Reagan shook his head and swept a hand over his hair to grip the back of his neck. "We'll likely do more harm than good traipsing about out there in the dark. Too much danger to the searchers. We'll have to wait until morning to go back out again."

Preston swallowed the lump of emotion swelling in his throat. He blinked at the sandwich without really seeing it. "I don't know if I can live without her, Reagan."

Clearing his throat, Reagan thumped his fist against his shoulder a few times. His focus remained on the darkness of the church yard as he spoke. "The Lord watches over the way of the righteous. He has not abandoned Aurora. Nor has he abandoned you, my friend." Reagan rose. "I'll take your horse to the livery and see he's taken care of."

Preston gave a nod of thanks.

He heard footsteps come to a stop behind him.

"W-we go h-home n-now, PC?"

Tommy was distressed. Preston could tell by the increase in his stuttering.

Wearily, Preston pushed himself to his feet. But he didn't have the strength to do anything but drape his arm around Tommy and pull him to his side. He jostled him gently, a gesture he hoped conveyed to Tommy that he was here, even if he didn't have words.

How could he go home to a warm cabin and rest, when the woman he loved was in danger somewhere?

He examined the hills surrounding the town. They were vast, dark, fathomless. Chiseled against the midnight dome awash in the glow of a swath of stars. Was she even out there? Or had her life already been taken from her? He felt the helplessness of his limitations flood him in an overwhelming wave.

Beside him, Tommy studied the stars. His voice was soft when he spoke. "I c-cried out to G-God for help."

The words from the Psalm he'd helped Tommy memorize washed over Preston like a soothing balm. The first few verses filled his mind.

He spoke the words aloud. And Tommy joined him as they stared up at the spangled sky together.

"I cried out to God for help; I cried out to God to hear me. When I was in distress, I sought the Lord; at night I stretched out untiring hands, and I would not be comforted. I remembered you, God, and I groaned; I meditated, and my spirit grew faint. You kept my eyes from closing; I was too troubled to speak. I thought about the former days, the years of long ago; I remembered my songs in the night."

Preston trailed off, too choked up to continue. Songs in the night. How many times had God brought something good from some pain or darkness in his life? He'd gone to jail. That had been one of his darkest hours. And yet from that night God had raised the song of his salvation.

Couldn't God also bring a song from this night of deepest darkness?

He realized that Tommy hadn't stopped speaking the passage, and forced himself to pay attention.

"I will 'm-member the deeds of the Lord; yes, I will 'm-member your m-miracles of long ago. I will c-consider all your works and m-meditate on all your m-mighty deeds. Your ways, God, are h-holy. What god is as g-great as our God? You are the God who p-performs m-miracles; you display your p-power among the p-peoples. With your m-mighty arm you redeemed your p-people." Even Tommy trailed away then, his voice gravelly with emotion.

Another sob claimed Preston as the truth hit him. Yes. He was only a man. He could not see all, know all, be all. But he knew the One who was and could be all those things. Who had been all those things for many in the past.

And until that One was no longer needed, Preston would not rest. He would not be comforted.

He would pray.

All night if he had to.

But he would barrage the heavens, asking the only One who could make a difference to move on Aurora's behalf.

He jostled Tommy again and spoke quietly. "Come on, Tom-Tom. Let's get home. God knows where Aurora is. All we can do now is leave her in His hands."

Tommy nodded. "I c-cried out to God with my v-voice."

And somehow, as they walked slowly toward the parsonage, Preston felt very blessed to have the prayers of one so trusting and full of faith going out on Aurora's behalf.

Chapter Twenty-eight

After getting Tommy to sleep, Preston paced the interior of his little house and prayed. Allegra sat by the front door, tongue lolling as she watched him curiously.

He prayed like he had never prayed before. In one corner, he lifted his hands and beseeched the heavens as he bounced on his toes, eyes closed. Then he strode to another corner and implored from there. He would have cried out with a loud voice if he hadn't been thoughtful of Tommy's slumber. Instead, he contented himself with fervent whispers.

In the living room, he quoted Scriptures, reminding God of all His promises.

Near the kitchen stove, he quoted Scriptures, reminding himself, through prayer, that God was ever in control.

He stood at his window, looking down on the dark, silent streets of Wyldhaven, and cried out for faith, comfort, safety, and rescue for Aurora.

He knelt by his settee and soaked the cushions with his tears. He knelt at the hearth and wet the stones with the same.

In the wee hours, he grew weary. His body begged for rest, and yet he felt no release from this task the Lord had given him.

He rose and put on a pot of coffee, continuing to pray and pace while it brewed. And when it was ready, he poured himself a cup and continued to walk through the house, sipping from his mug and hammering the heavens with his request.

One request.

God, bring Aurora back to me. You are our only hope.

Aurora awoke from the cold. Her body trembled so violently that her calf cramped. Still unable to see, she was too afraid to stand to move and get her blood flowing. Instead she rose to her knees and swung her arms first one direction and then another repeatedly—working on blood flow by only moving her torso. After she felt a little warmer, she settled back down and wrapped her arms around her knees, resting her head atop them.

How long had she been here? Time had gone all a muddle. She wasn't sure whether it was day or night. Her stomach rumbled with hunger, and thirst made her tongue not much more than a stick in her mouth.

Was this to be her end, then? She thought back over her life. If this was indeed her end, her life had not been a bad one. Other than the perilous years where she and Ma had survived in the camps, her life had been filled with much joy and she had so many things to be thankful for.

If this was to be her final few hours, she would soon meet Jesus. That thought brought a smile to her lips. What a glorious wonder that would be. To be able to throw her arms around her Savior. And behind him, her dear Papa would certainly be waiting. She remembered how he used to read her stories from the Bible and talk to her of his Savior. She wasn't as certain about Ma. She wished she had known on the day of Ma's passing the things that she knew about Jesus now. There would've been so much she could have shared with her mother on that final fateful day.

Yet now as she thought of heaven, she knew that simply seeing Jesus would be enough.

Did she have regrets? She regretted never getting to be a mother. She regretted not getting to spend more time with Preston. She regretted never getting to be his wife and never getting to pursue nursing. But in the scope of eternity, those were small things. Her regrets would fade the moment she stepped across heaven's threshold.

But she wasn't there yet. So she would endure for a few more hours. And she would do her best to endure with joy.

She still had no idea why those two men had grabbed her. They had not offered her any explanation. At first she had feared they intended to take her innocence. But neither had touched her in that way. At least not while she had been conscious. She shuddered.

This despair, this darkness, was too much to bear alone. She pressed her forehead against her knees and cried out to the Lord again.

Father, I need You. Do You see me sitting here alone in the darkness? Please give me the strength to face what lies ahead.

The song "How Can I Keep from Singing?" entered her thoughts. They had not sung it at church for a long time, yet now it came to her as though she were reading it from a page.

She hummed the opening bars, testing to see whether the bats would attack her again. But this time nothing stirred. She hummed a little louder. And still the area around her remained quiet. Louder still she sang, until she was singing at the top of her voice.

My life flows on in endless song above earth's lamentation. I hear the real, though far-off hymn that hails a new creation.

No storm can shake my inmost calm, while to that rock, I'm clinging. Since love prevails in heaven and earth, how can I keep from singing?

While though the tempest round me roars, I know the truth, it liveth. And though the darkness round me close, songs in the night it giveth.

No storm can shake my inmost calm, while to that rock, I'm clinging. Since love prevails in heaven and earth, how can I keep from singing?

I lift my eyes. The cloud grows thin; I see the blue above it. And day by day, this pathway smooths, since first I learned to love it.

No storm can shake my inmost calm, I hear the music ringing. It sounds an echo in my soul. How can I keep from singing?

How can I keep from singing?

Keep singing.

She raised her arms above her head and continued on, and oh the joy that filled her soul. If this was to be her end, everything would be all right. Because this earth was nothing—this walk, a mere shadow of reality. Even this overwhelming joy that she now felt was certainly only a fragment of the emotion she would experience in heaven.

She let the last notes of the song trail away and simply sat in the echo of them, basking in the love of her Father. A smile spread. Contentment surrounded her.

In that moment she sensed a change. It was imperceptible almost, and yet . . .

She searched the darkness above her.

What was it? And then she saw the shadow. Excitement shot through her. There was light! Above her a small circle had turned slightly gray.

It was dawn! And the sky was lightening. She had made it through the night!

Thank You, Jesus.

She sang on through another hymn, eyes closed in worship. And when she opened her eyes again, there was even more light.

Still not enough to totally make out her environment, but enough to fill her with hope.

She launched into yet another song, imagining herself at the front of the church, playing it on her violin. She sang full out with all her heart. Giving the Lord everything she had to offer. And this time, when she focused on her surroundings, her hands fell to her side.

There was now enough light to make out the interior of the cave where she sat. Above her a small hole that perhaps at one time had been a chimney for this cavern's inhabitants allowed a faint stream of dim light inside. Stone walls rose all around her in a dome, only broken by the small hole in the ceiling.

Aurora sat on the flat top of a large stalagmite with just enough surface area to hold her. Her eyes widened as she took in the deep black trench that encircled her perch. Across the canyon she could see a small shelf with a pathway leading off into the darkness. Leaning against the wall of the small shelf was a portable wooden bridge. She could just make it out as a lighter shadow against the darker shadow of the wall behind it. That must be how the men had gotten her out here. Then they had retreated and taken the bridge with them.

The hope that had swept in with the light dissipated as quickly as it had come. No matter that she had freed herself from her bonds and could now see, there would be no escaping from this prison.

And yet . . . She took herself in hand. Only a moment ago she had been rejoicing in what it would be like to cross the threshold of heaven. Nothing had changed.

Except for the fact that she could see.

She closed her eyes. Tilted her face upward. *Lord, help me keep my eyes on You and not on my circumstances. Like Paul and Silas, give me a heart that is willing to praise You even in the direst of circumstances.*

With that she forced herself to start another song.

God was still in control.

Heart heavy over the missing girl, Kane held his lantern out before him as he trod the path toward the Kastains' early the next morning. He planned to go out searching again today but figured it was best not to leave the colt at the Kastain place for too long—especially since Mr. Harrow had paid him extra for the care and feeding of the animal through to the end of its training.

He took the trail through the woods, by the Rodante place. He clenched his teeth as he walked the path, remembering that fateful day when he and his siblings had first been in Wyldhaven.

He had been taken very ill, and the Kastains had been kind enough to put him up in their barn. He had gone for a walk and found a woman lying dead right in the middle of this trail. Worse than that, he had been accused of killing her. Though later it had been determined that she had fallen accidentally on a knife that had hung on a cord around her neck, he could never seem to walk this trail without envisioning the woman, lying as he had found her, with that knife in her chest. He shuddered as he hurried past the spot.

He was just cresting the hill on the other side of the gully, when a sound stopped him in his tracks.

He held his breath. Listened.

There! It came again! The soft melodious notes of a . . . hymn? Who would be singing out here at this time of morning?

The sun wasn't even up yet. Dawn had barely brushed gray against the sky beyond the trees.

The melody stopped.

He shivered with a glance over his shoulder toward the place where the dead body had been. Was he hearing things?

No. The music started up again. This time, a little louder.

This path he was on was the only one that stretched through this portion of the wood. So whoever it was must be walking on the trail. Somewhere up ahead perhaps?

He waited, but the sound of the singing did not grow louder. Neither did it grow fainter. Odd. He walked a few paces. More details of the music could be discerned now.

He paused again, hands propped on his hips to listen. His heart pounded in his chest.

He could swear that voice sounded just like Aurora McClure's did when she sang the worship songs on Sundays. He lifted his lantern higher and studied the trees in the direction the sound was coming from. The underbrush was thick and did not appear to have been disturbed, but there was nothing for it other than to try to find the source of that voice.

He found a gap in the brush and pushed through. After taking several steps, he paused to listen again.

The song came from up ahead and to his right.

He hurried several more paces, ducking branches and pressing past clinging shrubs.

In places the brush was so thick that he had to retreat and come at his approach from a different angle.

"Aurora?" he called.

The singing continued.

He called again, louder this time. "Aurora!? Can you hear me?"

Aurora ceased her singing. Her heart pounded in her chest. Had she really just heard someone call her name?

She willed herself to breathe shallowly and listen past the pounding in her ears.

"Aurora?"

Yes!

"I am here." Her voice was too soft, even to her own ears. She cleared her throat and tried again. "I'm here!"

"I can hear you! Keep talking. I'm trying to find where you are."

She wasn't sure what to say. Relief at having someone finally so near had her trembling. And then a shot of terror whipped through her. The walls of whatever structure she was in made the voice outside unrecognizable. What if it was one of the men who had taken her captive returning and simply tormenting her with false hope? Maybe she should remain silent. And yet . . . What was a little false hope in the face of potential rescue?

"Who are you?"

"It's Kane Carver, miss."

Her eyes closed in relief. Kane Carver. *Thank You, Lord.* She was going to throw her arms around his neck and give him a hug he wouldn't forget after this.

"Just keep talking to me," he continued. "Are you okay? Have you been hurt?"

Aurora shook her head even as she answered him. "I'm not hurt. And I managed to untie myself. But it's dark. And I'm surrounded by a drop-off."

"Dark, you say? It's not much lighter where I am at. It's barely dawn. Can you see any light? If you can describe your surroundings, that might help me be able to find you."

Aurora searched the cavern again. The faint gray coming from above her had increased slightly. "There's a small hole above me. Yesterday I thought I felt sunlight, but that was when I had my blindfold on, so I can't be certain. Otherwise, all I see is blackness. I think I might be underground."

"All right. Sing one of those lovely hymns of yours. I know you have to be close. I just need to find the way in. Keep singing so I know where you're at."

With renewed hope, Aurora launched into another hymn.

Kane Carver propped his hands on his hips and spun in a circle, searching the area. He had come into a thick copse of trees, and here the underbrush was sparse. He could see for several paces in all directions.

There!

A few paces ahead, on a mossy rocky knoll, a hole opened in the ground. He approached cautiously, not wanting the ground to cave in on her, but his footing remained sturdy, and her song grew louder with each step.

He leaned over the opening and peered into the darkness below. Her singing stopped abruptly. "I can see you!"

Relief swelled through him. He'd found her! He flattened himself on his belly and lowered his arm and lantern in through the fissure. There was a flutter and burst of chittering as several bats scooted away from the light, but then they seemed to settle in the shadows behind a stalactite.

He swallowed and scrutinized the cavern. The floor was littered with stalagmites, one of which formed her prison. He had no idea how deep the floor of the cave actually was, because the light didn't pierce that far.

Realizing she was simply sitting quietly, waiting for him to take the lead, he grinned at her. "You have no idea how happy I am to have found you."

She smiled. "You have no idea how happy I am to be found."

His brow crimped with worry as the light glanced off a dried patch of blood at her temple. She was far enough down that he'd never be able to reach her, even if she could fit through this small hole, which she couldn't. He scanned what he could see of the walls of the cavern. "How did you get in there?"

She shook her head. "I'm afraid I'm no help. I was knocked out on the road and woke up here. But"—she pointed—"there seems to be a path over there. And there's a bridge sort of thing that I think they used to get me out here."

He hated to leave her in the dark again, but there was nothing for it if he was to help her escape. "I'm going to see if I can find the entrance. Hang in there. I promise not to leave you for long."

To his surprise, her smile remained serene. "I'll be all right."

With a nod, he pushed back from the hole and headed in the direction she had pointed him.

The brush grew thicker, and a tangle of ivy wove so tightly between several trees that he had to skirt away from Aurora's shelter. His frustration mounted when he reached Wyldhaven Creek without finding a way through the vines.

He retraced his steps and, from near the hole into Aurora's jail, held his lantern aloft to scrutinize the brush for a better route.

It was light enough now, however, that the lamp offered no aid. Yet the sun was still hidden behind dense forest. In frustration he puffed out the flame. "Hold on a little longer, Aurora. I'm still searching for a way in."

"Thank you." Her voice was soft with weariness.

He squinted through the dim morning light. There had to be a way.

And then he saw a part of the forest floor that was a fainter gray than what lay around it. Hugging the face of a large rock, the barest hint of a game trail penciled a path through the wood. "I see something!" he called, wanting to keep her hopeful.

"I promise not to go anywhere." She chuckled.

As he took the path, he marveled that she could laugh at a time like this. That was one strong woman.

He reminded himself to remain alert and guarded. Who had taken Aurora? Would they still be close by? He didn't see anyone. And the normal dawn chatter of birds filled the trees. If there was danger, they would likely be silent.

The trail angled downward, cutting into a ravine that left a wall of rock rising on his right. If he hadn't been looking for an opening, he never would have paid attention to the slight shadow that marred the rock face. But when he stepped nearer, he saw it was a gap that led into the heart of the mountain.

He paused to light his lantern again, then proceeded into the darkness with caution.

"I can see light! Is that you?" Aurora called, hope in her voice.

He winced, fearing that her call might have alerted someone, but then he rounded a blunt corner and the cavern opened before him. They were alone.

Kane released a breath. No guard?

"It's me." He lifted the lantern high above his head, and that was when he realized why Aurora's attackers had felt comfortable leaving her alone.

His heart sank.

A vast gap spanned the distance from where Aurora sat to where he stood.

The bridge she'd mentioned did indeed lean against the wall to his left, but it was made of thick timbers and heavy crossbeams. It would be much too heavy to move by himself.

Yet he couldn't leave her here alone. What if her assailants returned before he could make it back with help?

"Can you lower that bridge?" There was a tremor in her voice.

He forced a smile. No need to burden her further with his concerns. To give himself time to form a response, he paced closer, as though examining the bridge. Something clanged beneath his foot.

He looked down. Frowned. Bent to study the area with the lantern.

Chains . . .

He followed them to where they were attached high up on the wall near the top of the bridge.

His eyes widened. "It's like a drawbridge!"

That meant . . . It only took him a moment to find the hand crank that would lower the bridge.

"Hang on, Aurora. We're going to get you out of here!"

Chapter Twenty-nine

reston was still pacing and praying in the wee hours of Friday morning, when a knock sounded on his door.

Allegra leapt to her feet with a yip.

Something inside Preston surged with a joy he couldn't explain. He lurched to the door and yanked it open.

And this time his joy was not deflated. Kane Carver stood on his porch, with Aurora at his side.

"God be praised!" Preston reached for her and pulled her into a firm embrace, uncaring that Kane stood by, awkwardly studying the boards of the porch. He rocked her and turned in a gentle, joyous circle. Her head snuggled perfectly into the curve of his shoulder, and he cupped one hand to the back of her head to press her closer as Allegra cavorted at their feet.

"Hi," she said softly.

"Hi yourself." He dropped a kiss against the hair above her ear, feeling unashamed of the tears streaking down his cheeks. "I've been praying for you. All night." His voice broke. "I was nearly undone when we couldn't find you yesterday."

She eased back and looked up at him, too much peace in her eyes for someone who'd just been through such an ordeal. "God did not abandon me."

"No. He did not." Morning light illuminated her temple then, and his stomach pitched at the sight of the dried blood marring her skin. He touched her face, to assure himself she truly was here, and then nudged her through the door, leaving it open for Kane to follow. "Where were you? What happened?" He pulled out a chair at the table and eased her into it.

Allegra flopped contentedly beneath the table.

Kane stepped in and pushed the door closed.

At the stove, Preston scooted the kettle to the warmest part of the stove and added a stick of wood. He gathered a rag and a bowl.

Aurora rested her elbow on the table and gently cradled her head, as though it might be paining her.

Preston's gaze pierced Kane's.

The man shook his head. "Someone stashed her in a cavern by Wyldhaven Creek, out near the Kastain and Rodante places. It was only a miracle that I found her. She was singing."

A shiver of awe swept down Preston's spine, and despite the gravity of the situation, he couldn't withhold a smile. "Praise God. He's still in the miracle-working business." His gaze slipped to Aurora, and his smile faded.

Eyes closed, she simply sat with her head propped on one hand.

"Someone, you say? She didn't know her assailant?"

Kane shook his head. "Says she never got a glimpse of their faces. Two men chased her down." He leveled Preston with a pointed look.

Raw anger surged at the picture that formed in his mind of Aurora running in terror for her life. He realized Kane's words should have significance, but all that filled him at the moment was concern for the woman he loved. *Is she okay?* he mouthed.

Kane turned a worried gaze on her. Lifted one shoulder.

Aurora opened her eyes and straightened a little. "Might I have a glass of water?"

"Of course." Preston leapt into action. He snatched a cup from the sideboard and worked the handle of the pump as fast as he could. With the glass filled nearly to the brim, he crossed the room and handed it to her.

Her hands trembled so violently as she accepted it, that water spilled over and sloshed down the sides.

Worry slammed through him even as he reached to steady the cup for her. "Here. Let me help."

As Aurora guzzled thirstily, Kane strode past them. "I'll fetch Doc and let the town know she's been found."

Kane was almost to the door before Preston blurted, "No. Wait." Two men, Kane had said. Two men snatched her. Poppy had been seen talking to the two new men from the mill. That couldn't be coincidence, could it? Despite the fact that they all had alibis?

Kane looked at him questioningly.

"Get Doc. And the sheriff. But don't tell anyone she's been found yet."

With a frown furrowing his brow, Kane hesitated. But then he acquiesced with a nod and departed.

Aurora pushed the glass away.

Preston refilled it and set it on the table near her, then sloshed warm water from the kettle into a bowl and dipped the rag into it. He squatted before her. Pressed the rag gently to the blood at her temple. "Who did this to you?"

Though he'd meant the question rhetorically, her green gaze melded with his. She shook her head. "They wore bandanas. I only caught a glimpse before they knocked me out." She rested her hand against the back of his where he gently dabbed at her split skin. "I'll be fine."

"Marry me," he blurted.

She blinked a couple times, brows arching.

He set the rag into the bowl and put it on the table. On his knees, he scooted closer to her. Ever so gently he cradled her face in both his hands. Though he hadn't meant to blurt the request, he wasn't about to retract it. "Right now. Today, before the day is through."

She chuckled, settling her hands against his wrists. "I must have taken a bigger hit to my temple than I thought."

He shook his head in denial. "You heard me right. What do you say?"

A door creaked.

"M-Miss Aurora!" Tommy exclaimed exuberantly.

Preston's eyes fell closed for the briefest of seconds. Of course Tommy had awoken just now.

He thundered across the room and clumsily inserted himself between them to pull Aurora into an enthusiastic embrace.

With a smirk in Preston's direction, Aurora stood and returned Tommy's hug wholeheartedly, though Preston saw her wince as she did so.

Preston reached out to nudge Tommy back. "Here, Tom-Tom. Don't hurt her."

Tommy didn't seem to hear the command. He jumped up and down, hands flapping by his sides in excitement. "The angel t-tolded me you'd be okay!"

A chill swept down Preston's spine. He and Aurora shared a glance. "An angel, Tommy?"

He nodded confidently. "He was a n-nice m-man in a light c-coat. I c-cried out to God with my v-voice. Then the angel c-comed. He t-tolded me you'd be okay." He lifted his palms. "Then I sleepted."

Aurora reached to touch Tommy's cheek. "Thank you for praying for me, Tommy."

He nodded. "I'm g-glad you're okay. You want to m-make me oatmeal?"

A chuckle burst from Preston. "No, Tommy. She's not going to make you oatmeal. Go wash up and finish putting on your boots. Then you can take Allegra for a walk, and I'll make your oatmeal when you get back, all right?"

Tommy nodded. But as he tromped toward his room, he grumbled over his shoulder. "She m-makes it b-better than y-you."

Aurora leaned toward him and whispered confidentially, "Very small pinch of salt in milk that barely covers the top of the oats, boil it, stirring every so often, until it's thick, then pull it from the heat and let it set for five minutes. After that, plenty of butter and a heaping scoop of brown sugar." She glanced innocently toward the door. "I should get home. Joe and Liora will be worried about me."

He snagged her hand, relishing the feel of her cool, slender fingers, slipping between his. "Oh no you don't. Doc is coming here to see you. Besides, I don't want anyone to know you've been found yet."

Her curiosity was reflected in the gaze she shot his way.

But Tommy was back. He crossed the room and took down the lead. Ever enthusiastic about getting a walk, Allegra scrambled from beneath the table and trotted to his side. Bending to attach the leash to Allegra's collar, Tommy said, "C-come on, g-girl."

"Tommy?" Preston said.

Tommy looked over.

"Let's keep Miss Aurora's safety a secret for now, okay? Don't tell anyone."

Tommy pondered for a moment, then lifted one shoulder in a shrug of acknowledgment. "Okay. D-don't t-tell no one."

Preston's tension eased. "Good lad."

And as he went out, Preston blew out a breath of relief. His gaze locked with Aurora's humor-filled one. She wasn't fooled by the reason he'd urged Tommy out of the house. But hang it, could a man be blamed for wanting an answer sooner rather than later, to a question such as he'd asked?

He opened his mouth to urge her answer, but before he could speak, Doc stepped inside, followed by Reagan and Kane.

"There she is!" Doc exclaimed. He pointed to one of the chairs. "Have a seat and let's take a look at you."

Aurora smiled at Preston as she did what she was told.

"Well, you're smiling at least. I'd say that's a good sign." Doc bent over her to listen to her heart. "Tell me about your ordeal. Any pain anywhere?"

Preston missed her answer because Reagan and Kane stopped before him. Reagan tipped a nod to the man beside him. "Kane says you don't want the town to know she's been found? I've got searchers showing up already and am not sure what to tell them."

Preston held up a finger. "Just until we see if Poppy shows up to try to take the money at the presumably false location you slipped to her. When is that supposed to be, by the way?"

Reagan looked grim. "Thought you said you didn't want to know about that?"

Preston raised his hands. "Put Kane on me as a round-the-clock watch. I promise I won't leave his side."

Reagan gave in. "Fine. Eight o'clock this morning. On the road from Camp Sixty-Five. We've got an empty trunk heading here as we speak. Joe and Zane are keeping watch from a distance. But I put Jackson Nolan on watch at the boardinghouse and told him to let me know if Poppy left. And he hasn't said anything yet."

Preston spread his hands. "Maybe she's waiting until you get closer to town? I think she was holding Aurora as leverage in case anything goes wrong. A bargaining chip of sorts. If she makes a move, you can arrest her, and we can ask her about it. If she doesn't make a move . . ." He sighed. "I guess we'll just have to let it go. We may never know who did this. Aurora says she didn't get a look at their faces. They wore bandanas."

Reagan rubbed the back of his neck and glanced to where Doc was still examining Aurora's head. "Yeah, Kane told me. I just don't see how Poppy can be involved when she was in the boardinghouse in plain sight the whole time during Aurora's capture, and the men that we suspect work for her had to have spent that morning loading their wheelbarrow with rocks."

Kane stepped forward. "Wait a minute. Wheelbarrow? What wheelbarrow?"

Reagan explained to Kane that the men had arrived for work on time and that by the time they'd gotten to the mill to question them, they'd been returning from downstream with a full load of rocks for the walls of the mill. "They didn't have enough time to both kidnap Aurora and get back to the mill with a full barrow."

Kane's eyes widened, and he snapped his fingers. "Unless they had *two* and filled one with rocks the night before!"

"What?" Preston frowned at the man.

"I found an empty wheelbarrow right near where I found Aurora. Suppose they bought an identical wheelbarrow to the ones owned by Eklund? Those large wooden ones that are more like a cart, correct?"

Reagan nodded.

Kane pressed on. "The night before, they trundle it out to the location and fill it. The next morning, they arrive for work and pick up an empty wheelbarrow. But instead of filling it, they use the time to nab Aurora and stash her in the cavern near the creek. Then they return to the mill with the stones they harvested the night before."

Preston exchanged a look with Reagan. "That could be it!"

Reagan nodded. He clapped Kane on one shoulder. "It's brilliant. I have to go. If Poppy still thinks she has her bargaining chip . . ." He swished a hand through the air, as though indicating he didn't have time to explain all the possibilities. "I'll check with Jackson to see if she's left the boardinghouse. Don't let Preston out of your sight. We'll be back just as soon as it's over."

Preston felt his heart fall. Did Reagan really suspect that he would be involved with stealing the bank's money?

Reagan had only taken two steps when he paused and spun back to face him. "I don't suspect you, by the way. Not in the least. But this way if something goes wrong, you'll have an alibi."

Relieved to hear it, Preston gave him a nod. It probably was best to exercise the better part of caution.

Poppy stretched languidly on her bed at the boardinghouse. She relaxed against her pillows, staring into nothingness with a smile on her face.

They'd made it through the night without anyone finding Aurora. Poppy's stomach had been in knots there for a while last night. She'd known that the cavern her men had accidentally discovered while fetching rocks for the mill was well-disguised—they'd only noticed it because while working in the creek one evening, they'd seen bats flying in and out of the entrance—but it was still a great relief to reach daylight without an alarm of Aurora's rescue being sounded.

Today was the day.

She would take Preston to see his little woman. Let him speak to her. Maybe even give her some water. She had to be thirsty by now.

Then with Poppy's men standing by as insurance, she would promise him that no harm would come to Aurora as long as he helped her get into the safe tonight. He didn't need to know that she'd already instructed her men to push Aurora into the canyon. It would look like she'd slipped. Poppy would act appropriately shocked and sorrowful. Repentant.

He would be horrified for a while, but then he'd see reason and come back to her.

And they'd be rich.

Not only would she make Babbo proud, she'd get her man as well. Because she'd decided that was important to her. Once Preston's prayers weren't answered, he would see what a farce his religion was. He would give it up. Then they'd be happy. Together.

She smiled and lurched to her feet.

It was going to be a good day.

She just had a couple hours to wait.

Breakfast would fill the time nicely. One last breakfast in Wyldhaven. Indeed, she would miss the breakfasts in this place once she headed back east.

Reagan could still see Jackson whittling away at a stick on the church porch. He'd parked him there, because even if Poppy left from the back side of the boardinghouse, Jackson would still be able to see her ride away from this vantage point.

He stopped at the base of the stairs. "Anything?"

Jackson shook his head. "Ain't seen hide nor hair of her. But"—he pointed with the tip of his blade—"there was some to-do down at the mill a bit ago."

Reagan looked that way. "I'll go check it out." He tipped his chin toward the church doors. "How many people has Ma sent out to search?"

"Five or six so far. You sure I wouldn't be better served out there looking?"

Reagan shook his head. "I need you here."

Jackson shrugged a shoulder. "All right. Everything okay at the parson's?"

Reagan hesitated. Jackson had obviously seen Doc go inside with him a few minutes ago. He waved a dismissal. "Nothing to worry about. I better get to the mill."

Jackson sighed and carved another slice from his stick before turning his gaze down the hill to assess the town. "I'll be here keeping an eye out. Sure hope Miss Aurora is all right."

Reagan felt his guilt mount. He walked away before he could change his mind and tell the boy she was even now safe at Preston's house. It really was better to keep that knowledge to as few as possible. Thankfully, Kane had arrived with her when it was still dark enough that no one had been stirring yet.

He strode down the hill.

Taulby Eklund was on a ladder mortaring rocks into the mill's wall.

"Morning, Taulby." Reagan eyed the work the man was doing. Taulby was talented. The building was going to be downright beautiful when he completed it. "Jackson Nolan said there was something going on down here this morning?"

Taulby descended the ladder and wiped his fingers on a rag. "The men that I this week hired? They did not arrive today to work."

Reagan's heart hammered. "The two that got into a fight the other day?"

Taulby nodded. "Yah. Those are the ones." He plunked his fists on his hips. "None of my men have them seen."

Reagan suddenly felt a great urgency to get to Zane and Joe. He clapped Taulby on one arm. "I'm sorry about your men. If I hear of anyone looking for work, I'll send them your way."

Taulby sighed and scanned his wall with a critical eye. "For this, I thank you."

Reagan was already heading for the livery and his mount.

Poppy's men were probably even now set to attack the decoy money!

He rode as fast as he could, worried the whole way that he'd be too late to help, but when he arrived, it was to find the wagon with the empty trunk trundling casually down the road.

Ewan McGinty squinted at him from the driver's seat. "Thought you promised me that if I got out of bed early to help you with this scheme that I might get to see some action?"

Reagan scanned the road in both directions and the trees all around. "No attack so far?"

Ewan quirked a brow. "Not unless you mean an attack of boredom."

"Well, just keep your eyes out. It could still come."

But an attack did not come. Reagan rode behind the wagon all the way into town until it stopped in front of the bank. No one even attempted to approach them. Zane and Joe pulled their mounts to a stop at the other end of the street. Reagan lifted a hand.

Either they'd been too subtle with their information and Poppy hadn't caught on. Or she was innocent of what they suspected her of.

With a sigh he dismounted and handed the reins of his horse to Joe as he approached. "Take care of him for me, would you? I better go back up and speak to Preston. Seems we were wrong in our suspicions."

Ewan tossed down the reins. "And I got out of bed for this."

In the boardinghouse dining room, at the table she'd purposely chosen by the window, Poppy frowned as the wagon went by. Only the driver and one guard? A moment later, two more men rode by. She sighed. Four men made more sense, but she'd thought there would be more.

No matter. It didn't change her plans. She glanced at the clock and dabbed at her lips. It was time. Satisfaction swept through her. All her planning coming to fruition.

She couldn't wait to see the shock and hurt on Preston's face when she told him she had the woman he loved. Couldn't wait to lord her power over him and force his hand.

A tremor of excitement swept through her as she dropped her payment on the table and stepped out of the room.

Just a short walk up the hill and all her plans would fall into place.

Chapter Thirty

oc was just leaving after pronouncing that Aurora should be fine with plenty of rest, when Reagan arrived with his news. Tommy stepped in behind him and loosed Allegra from her leash, then went to the wash basin in the kitchen.

"Nothing?" Preston felt his consternation rise as he focused on Reagan. He'd been certain that Poppy would attack the decoy wagon. What was she waiting for?

Could he be mistaken about her? Had she truly changed her ways? He glanced to where Aurora sat tiredly on his settee. They needed to call this off and get her home to rest. He wasn't sure what more could be gained by keeping her rescue hidden. "I don't know what to say. Perhaps I need to repent of my suspicions where Poppy is concerned."

Aurora flicked him a glance. Her lips pinched.

But before he could open his mouth to reassure her of his feelings toward her, the door burst inward and Jackson Nolan surged through the opening. "Sheriff. She's coming! That woman you asked me to keep an eye out for—" His gaze landed on Aurora and he blinked. "You're here!"

Reagan scooped a hand through his hair. "Yeah. Sorry I couldn't say anything earlier."

"Bad lady, c-comin'," Tommy said as he sank into his place at the table. "I want oatmeal."

"Did she see you?" Reagan asked Jackson.

He shook his head. "I don't think so. I went through the church and came out the back door. She might have seen a flicker of movement on the church porch for a moment when I moved."

Preston and Reagan looked at each other for one frozen moment. "Into the bedroom." Preston pointed. "You, Jackson, and Aurora. Let's see what she wants before we decide on her innocence."

"B-bad lady, c-comin'," Tommy said again.

And then everyone moved at once. As the three of them surged into Preston's bedroom, Preston rushed to remove all evidence of Aurora's presence—the bandages, the bowl of water, and the rag from the table. Reagan shut the door with a soft click.

Preston dried his hands as he scrutinized the room for anything he might have missed. He swiped at some water on the table and pushed the chair Aurora had used back to its place. "Tommy, not a word to the bad lady. Understand?"

Tommy nodded. "I'm hungry."

"Okay. You keep quiet, and I'll make you some oatmeal."

Tommy beamed. "I paint."

"All right. You do that."

His hands trembled as he worked quickly to scoop some oats into a pan. After all his suspicions of Poppy, the fact that she would be so near to Aurora had him practically jumping out of his skin.

The knock sounded on his front door as he was pouring some milk over the oats.

"Coming," he called. He cleared his throat, hoping she hadn't heard the catch in his voice. He set the oats on the stove and moved to open the door. He did his best to look surprised to see her on his stoop. "Poppy. Good morning. How can I help you?"

"Morning." She glanced back down the path toward town, fiddling with the reticule that dangled from her wrist.

Was she nervous about something?

She returned her focus to him. "I wondered if I could come in for a few minutes?"

Preston swallowed. He hadn't let her in the other day. He should keep to his pattern. "Actually, maybe we could talk on the porch—" He blinked at the gun that had appeared in her hand.

"I think inside would be better." She smiled softly.

"Okay . . ." He stepped back and allowed her entry. Suddenly Aurora wasn't his only worry. What if something happened to Tommy?

Allegra growled.

"Down, girl." He knew Poppy wouldn't hesitate to shoot the dog if she tried anything. "Go lay down."

Poppy simpered as the dog slunk under the table and flopped down.

Tommy sat at the table with his head angled away from Poppy, like a toddler who didn't want to look at someone they were mad at.

Preston kept his hands in plain sight. This was the Poppy he knew. "I was just making Tommy some breakfast. Mind if I continue?"

Poppy assessed the kitchen and then shook her head. She nudged him toward the living room with a direction from her gun barrel, just as he knew she would. "Nothing hot for you, if you don't mind. I've no desire to be scalded. Sit."

At least there was some space between them and Tommy now. Preston did as he was told, keeping his hands on his knees so she wouldn't think he was about to try something.

"Good." She smiled at him. "I'm here to talk business."

A sadness filled him. How he suddenly wished he'd been wrong about her. "Business?" was all he said.

"I have her. Your precious Aurora. The girl you flaunted in my face the other day."

He shifted. "I wasn't trying to flaunt her."

One of her black brows nudged upward. Her red lips pressed into a pinch. "Weren't you?"

"Why didn't you tell me yesterday when I asked you? Why the pretense of looking for her?"

She smirked. "Timing, dear Preston. I needed you to be ready to rescue her. If you want to come with me, I'll take you to see her. But she won't be free until you do a little something for me."

He frowned. He hadn't expected that. If he left the house, he would be alone with her, and since his gun remained in his saddle bags, which currently hung by the door, she would have the distinct advantage.

They already had enough information to arrest her, simply with her confession of having kidnapped Aurora. But if Reagan hadn't emerged yet, he likely wanted to hear more.

"Why should I come with you? So you can kill us both?"

She pouted. "Preston. You do me great hurt. I could never kill you."

He rose, anger flooding through him. He advanced on her.

Eyes widening, she stepped to the side and pivoted, cocking the derringer. "Don't force me! I will shoot if I have to!"

Preston stopped. Reagan at least now knew that she was armed. And he'd gotten her to face away from his bedroom door, which had been his goal. "I'm not going anywhere with you until you tell me what this is all about and why you are holding a gun on me."

Poppy seemed to consider. Her derringer never wavered. Finally, she spoke. "All right. At this very moment, down on the street in front of the bank, is a trunk full of money. I confess that if I'd known how lightly it would be guarded, I would have taken my chances with an attack on the road. But I thought it would be heavily guarded by many armed men. In the end, there were only four." She gave a dismissive shrug. "My plan has always been simple. Tonight, once the money is in the bank's vault and the town is good and rowdy, we break into the bank, and you open the vault. We'll be long gone by morning before anyone even realizes the money is gone. It will be like old times. You. Me. And plenty of cash." She smiled.

"So Aurora is your leverage to ensure that I cooperate?"

She nodded. "Yes."

"And the two men who work for you, were they the ones who captured her?"

For the first time, Poppy looked a bit taken aback. "Yes. How did you know about them?"

He spread his hands and took a step toward her, offering a deprecating smile. "Poppy . . . Have you forgotten how closely we used to work with each other? I know you almost better than you know yourself." He tossed her own words back in her face.

She thinned her lips. "Touché. And yes. I have a couple men working with me. In fact one of them will be the one guarding your little woman until you've completed your part of the job."

Surely that was enough information for Reagan?

Behind Poppy, his bedroom door eased open the barest fraction of an inch.

"There's only one problem with your plan, Poppy." Preston scuffed his feet across the floor to disguise any sound his door might make as Reagan opened it.

"Oh yeah? What's that? Stand still, would you?"

"The problem is . . ."

Reagan stepped forward and pressed his gun to Poppy's head. "That you lost your leverage without even knowing it."

Poppy's hands rose on instinct. There was something about the feel of the cold metal of a gun barrel pressed behind one's ear that encouraged that. Her eyes filled with tears and searched Preston out. "How could you betray me like this?"

"How could *I* betray *you*?" If he didn't feel so sorry for the way sin had trapped her, he would have been disgusted by her.

"Drop the gun," Reagan demanded, his own weapon still pressed to her head.

At the table, Tommy rocked, rubbing his hands over his hair. "Bad lady. B-Bad lady."

Frustration glimmered in Poppy's eyes as her gun thudded to the floor.

"Don't move." Reagan ratcheted the first loop of his iron handcuffs around one of her wrists. Once Reagan had her arms cuffed firmly behind her, he nudged her closer to the door.

Preston's focus settled on Aurora, who stood in the shadows of his bedroom, eyes wide and fixed directly on him.

Keeping hold of one of Poppy's arms, Reagan bent to pick up her gun. "I'll take her to the jail, and then we'll ride out and see if we can capture her men. They may have already discovered that Aurora was rescued and fled town."

Preston nodded, but his gaze was still fixed on the woman he loved. Relieved to have the ordeal behind them, he held out a hand to motion Aurora to come.

She rushed forward, throwing her arms around him. "I was so afraid for you."

"It's over. I'm fine." He smoothed his hands over her back. "It's all right."

Sensing that the danger was past, Allegra emerged from below the table, tail wagging. Aurora bent to pat her on the head, but then immediately returned to Preston's arms—just the way he liked it.

Jackson stepped from the bedroom, and Reagan turned to look at him. "Good job. We owe you one." With Poppy's gun in his left hand, Reagan loosed her arm with his right to stretch his hand toward Jackson.

With a feral yell, Poppy lowered her shoulder and barreled toward Aurora's back, teeth bared. She intended to bite her!

On instinct Preston swung Aurora out of the way and thrust an arm to push Poppy's trajectory off course. But Allegra had seen her coming and had scrambled to get out of the way. Preston's thrust pushed Poppy right into the path of the dog.

Allegra gave a yelp as Poppy tripped over her and, off balance and with her arms cuffed behind herself, careened face first into the log wall. There was a loud crunch, and then Poppy screamed in pain.

Reagan hauled her to her feet and assessed her. Blood streamed from her nose. "Hmm, looks like you broke your nose there. That's not gonna heal up pretty, I can tell you that." Holding her arm firmly now, he assessed Preston and Aurora. "You two okay?"

"Yes." Keeping a wary eye on Poppy, Preston bent to pet Allegra. "You okay, girl?" The dog wagged her tail, and if he didn't know better, he could have sworn she grinned as Reagan hauled a cursing Poppy from the house.

Jackson scurried after them. "I'd better go ring that church bell to let everyone know you're all right, Miss Aurora!"

"Tommy have oatmeal n-now?" Tommy asked hopefully from the table.

Aurora chuckled. She held up one finger to Preston. "I'll be right back." In the kitchen, she scooped Tommy's oatmeal into a bowl, added a dollop of butter and a large scoop of brown sugar, and gave it a stir. She set it and a glass of milk on the table before Tommy. "There you go, Tom-Tom." She touched his head and bent to look him in the eye. "I love you."

Tommy nodded with a huge grin. He picked up his spoon. "I l-love you t-too, Miss Aurora."

And then she turned to look at Preston. A world of emotion shone in her green eyes. But he had something to tell her first. "I realized something during this whole ordeal."

"Oh?"

"I realized that no matter where you are, I can't protect you. That's God's job and responsibility."

She searched his face, hope shining in her eyes.

Preston crooked a finger to motion her closer. "I also I realized that more than anything, I want to partner with you in this ministry God has called us to."

With a smile, she sidled toward him. "You asked me a question a bit ago, if you'll recall."

The little torturer. He allowed his amusement to show in his eyes. "I do recall."

She paused directly before him and rested one hand on his chest, looking up into his face. "I'd like to answer you now, if you want to hear it?"

He curved his hands against the small of her back and settled more comfortably into his heels. "I most definitely want to hear it." He studied her lips, wanting to watch them form the word.

"No," she said.

Confusion crashed through him. He lifted his gaze to hers.

She giggled and leaned a little closer. "No thing on this earth could keep me from saying yes to you, dear Parson."

Relief swept in to replace his confusion. "You can't do that to me. This old heart can't take such a shock. Especially not after the day we've had. And on not a wink of sleep at that." He tickled her ribs.

She squeaked and grabbed his hands.

They both stilled, and though they remained smiling, she searched his face more somberly. "Not a wink of sleep?"

He shook his head. "I was up all night doing battle on your behalf in the heavens."

She sighed and pressed her ear against his heart. "No wonder I had such peace and found it so easy to sing those songs in the night. Kane wouldn't have found me, I don't think, if I hadn't been singing. But something compelled me to do so."

Preston led her to the settee and sank onto it, tugging her down by his side. She placed her head on his shoulder, and he rested his cheek against her hair. A bone-deep weariness sapped his strength, for the battle was over, and now it was time to rest.

Epilogue

Belle stood at the front of the church, watching Parson Clay and Aurora, who faced each other before the traveling judge.

He had come to town for the trial of the Scarlatti woman and her men, both of whom had been arrested as they'd tried to make their escape from town last fall after Aurora's ordeal.

The trials had taken place last week, and much to everyone's relief, all three participants had been sentenced to long terms in jail for their parts in Aurora's kidnapping.

The judge had remained to conduct this wedding.

Aurora looked radiant in the white gown overlaid with lace that Mrs. Holloway had made for her. The circlet of pink tulips that she wore as a crown brought out the joyous flush of her skin and the lively twinkle in the green of her eyes.

The judge motioned the couple toward a table that held three candles. The two slender outer candles were lit, but the larger central candle was not.

Holding her bouquet of spring tulips, Belle leaned to get a better view of the couple past Zoe's shoulder. She could hardly believe that Aurora had asked her to be one of the ladies to stand up with her, but it had filled her with great joy.

At the table, the parson and Aurora each took up one of the lit candles and, together, they held their individual flames to the remaining central pillar.

"Along with their rings, Preston and Aurora have chosen this lighting of a candle as a symbol of their individual lives joining together into one," the judge offered.

With the middle candle now lit, in unison and with their eyes fixed lovingly on each other, Preston and Aurora blew out the flames on their individual tapers.

A murmur of excitement filled the church as they returned their snuffed candles to the holders.

Once more standing before the judge, the couple took hands.

Belle memorized the scene. Perhaps she would paint this later and give it to them as a gift.

A glint of light sparked in Aurora's eyes, and Belle could almost imagine it was pure love bursting from inside her as she smiled at her groom. From this angle, Belle could only see part of the parson's face, but she noted a groove in his cheek that indicated he was smiling down at Aurora in return. The lace of Aurora's sleeves ended in a small point at the back of her slender hands, where they disappeared into the parson's larger, sturdier ones. The man shifted restlessly, and Belle had the impression that he simply wanted the trappings of this ceremony to be finished so he could sweep his bride off for some alone time.

She could already envision how she would paint the highlights of candles shimmering behind the couple. The way the daylight filtered through the church windows to surround them with a soft glow. The rolls of the judge's bearded jowls and rounded paunch would contrast with the chiseled sturdiness of the parson's jawline and physique. Aurora's beaming smile and beauty would practically add itself to the canvas. And the line of bridesmaids—Liora, Zoe, and her—and the three groomsmen lawmen, along with Tommy, who was all decked out in a fancy store-bought suit, all leaning forward to peer at the happy couple, would add humor to the piece.

As the parson and Aurora exchanged vows, Belle cast her eye across the congregation.

Aidan and the twins sat snuggled beside Ma and dear Mr. Harrow—now Belle's stepfather. They had married at Christmas, and much to everyone's surprise—except Belle's, as she'd already known—the man had revealed that he was quite well-to-do. He'd already arranged to buy their land back from Mr. Hines. And his clock shop, which he'd built next to the post office, was already doing a smart business.

Taulby Eklund sat in the pew behind her family, and Belle was not surprised to note that his focus lay more on her pretty redheaded sister than on the couple before the judge. For her part, Zoe didn't seem to notice. But Belle couldn't resist a smile. Wash Nolan might just have some competition on his hands for the heart of her fair sister.

Belle felt someone studying her, and her gaze connected with Kane Carver's. His brows pumped slightly and, after sweeping her with an appreciative look, he gave her a quick wink. Belle's face heated, and she dropped her focus to the bouquet of tulips in her hands, before turning purposefully to focus on the ceremony.

The judge's voice bellowed. "I now pronounce you man and wife! You may kiss your bride, Parson Clay."

The church rose in unison with a cheer as Preston stepped close to Aurora, touched her cheeks, and slanted his mouth across hers.

Belle clapped and hollered her congratulations along with everyone as the judge shouted above the tumult, "May I present to you Mr. and Mrs. Preston Clay!"

"We did it!" The parson thrust his and Aurora's clasped hands above their heads in triumph, and then with a laugh, the couple practically sprinted down the aisle to make their escape.

As the bridesmaids and groomsmen followed, and Belle fell into step behind them, she couldn't resist one more peek at Kane. The man still watched her with that glorious gleam in his eye that gave a girl such a dangerous hope.

Please Review!

If you enjoyed this story, would you take a few minutes to leave your thoughts in a review on your favorite retailer's website? It would mean so much to me, and helps spread the word about the series.

You can quickly link through from my website here: http://www.lynnettebonner.com/books/historical-fiction/the-wyldhaven-series/

Dear Reader,

I have to tell you that God is just amazing. There were so many things at the end of this book that He pulled together, and it leaves me in awe. With every book, I feel inadequate to take on this task of writing that He has given me. Every. Time. And yet inevitably, with much prayer and labor, He helps me pull the threads into a cohesive image. When I am weak, He is strong.

I had originally come up with the title for this book based on the story in Acts about Paul and Silas singing through the night. Yet at a key point in my writing, God focused my attention on Psalm 77, and that passage sort of took over as the theme of the story.

Again, at the end, when Aurora was captive in the cave, I went looking for a song for her to sing—one that would have been around back in her day. And, though I'd never before heard the beautiful hymn "How Can I Keep from Singing," I was blown away by how perfectly it fit into the scene with the ideal message for what Aurora needed in that moment. If you would like to listen to this hymn, you can find it here: https://www.youtube.com/watch?v=VLPP3XmYxXg.

All praise to the wonderful Creator, who uses this imperfect vessel to share His encouragement with all of you.

All the best and . . . keep singing.

Lynnette

Want a FREE Story?

If you enjoyed this book...

...sign up for Lynnette's Gazette below! Subscribers get exclusive deals, sneak peeks, and lots of other fun content.

(The gazette is only sent out about once a month or when there's a new release to announce, so you won't be getting a lot of spam messages, and your email is never shared with anyone else.)

Sign up link: https://www.lynnettebonner.com/newsletter/

ABOUT THE AUTHOR

Born and raised in Malawi, Africa. Lynnette Bonner spent the first years of her life reveling in warm equatorial sunshine and the late evening duets of cicadas and hyenas. The year she turned eight she was off to Rift Valley Academy, a boarding school in Kenya where she spent many joy-filled years, and graduated in 1990.

That fall, she traded to a new duet—one of traffic and rain—when she moved to Kirkland, Washington to attend Northwest University. It was there that she met her husband and a few years later they moved to the small town of Pierce, Idaho.

During the time they lived in Idaho, while studying the history of their little town, Lynnette was inspired to begin the Shepherd's Heart Series with Rocky Mountain Oasis.

Marty and Lynnette have four children, and currently live in Washington where Marty pastors a church.

58978434R00177